The Savage Professor

ALSO BY ROBERT ROPER

FICTION
Royo County Tales
On Spider Creek
Mexico Days
In Caverns of Blue Ice
The Trespassers
Cuervo Tales

NONFICTION
Nabokov in America

Now the Drum of War:
Walt Whitman and
His Brothers in the Civil War

Fatal Mountaineer:
The High-Altitude Life and Death of Willi Unsoeld

The Savage Professor

A NOVEL

ROBERT ROPER

ASAHINA & WALLACE

LOS ANGELES

2014

WWW.ASAHINAANDWALLACE.COM

Published in the United States by Asahina & Wallace, Inc.
www.asahinaandwallace.com

Library of Congress Control Number: 2014952701

ISBN: 978-1-940412-12-2

To Andrew

Part I

chapter 1

Landau moved to Berkeley from San Francisco in the early eighties. The choice was simple: more sun on the east side of the bay. A house he could afford (a bungalow on Cherry Street). But he really moved because of horror and fear, the fear attendant on running one of the first cohort studies of "the gay plague," which they didn't know yet was caused by a virus. Wise heads suspected that, and since the loathsome wasting was quite obviously passed from one gay fellow to another, why not to the eager docs and epidemiologists who worked at SF General? So each time he went to the ward where they housed the poor buggers, he thought of his chapel-going English mum with her bad teeth, how she would feel if he died young. How *disappointed* she would be.

Berkeley in the first Reagan kingship. All the left-wing realtors and professors with distinguished chairs were stunned, were turning their faces from the affronting vision of the bad right-wing movie actor taking over. Landau, half-Brit, didn't care about American politics so much. They were like a language learned from tapes, not to be depended on at points of stress. But he caught the mood of dire affront, heard the beneath-all-mention tone. All right, then *let* the country go to hell. Berkeley itself was doing very well, thank you. House prices were starting their spectacular rise. If you had enough to buy that first bungalow, in a few years you might trade up to something that would make you a millionaire. In '85 he sold Cherry Street and moved to a house off Cragmont in the hills. An "Italianate villa," as the realtorese had it, faced in cracking vanilla stucco and built in the twenties by an eccentric developer who put up only ten dwellings before going under. By luck it bordered one of the footpaths that enfilade the Berkeley Hills, connecting the curvy, contour-ploughed streets with steep walkways full of askew steps.

Berkeley had a world name. Landau discovered this odd fact on trips across the suffering globe, chasing the immunodeficiency virus and drug-resistant TB and other causes of statistically representable misery. In a windblown, godforsaken wetlands outpost in Botswana, where HIV had established itself to the tune of twenty-five percent, mention of Berkeley elicited a strong response. "Oh, ho," a village headman, a Sekgoma of the Bamangwato, said to him. "Oh, yes, Berkeley, Berkeley, indeed."

"What, you've heard of it, sir?"

"Yes. Yes."

"And what have you heard, sir?"

But the old man would only smile, shaking his head ruefully.

It was a name recognized as instantly as "New York," strangely enough. Colleagues in states of the former Soviet Union all knew it—they had been there as students, or a cousin had, or they'd hoped to go there as postdocs. Now they lived in decayed housing blocks and drank and worked in labs without Internet or refrigeration, but at the mere mention of *Berkeley* they grew animated. Once there had been a moment there, under those careless California skies. A shining outbreak of something.

The old hillside villa. Here he repaired after his days at UCSF running teams of homeless-monitoring, young-injector-studying public-health types. Here he limped after vexing sessions with his endlessly manipulative departmental antagonists, traversing the gray bay of San Francisco early and late in a series of vehicles for which he became locally noted, the white Lincoln, the turquoise Jag, the Porsche that needed a muffler, the Volvo longboat. When he cast his mind back ove. his semi-glorious, too-soon-terminated scientific career, the eras correlated in terms of autos driven and girlfriends struggled with, his different multiyear projects often conceived as he fell in love and celebrated with the purchase of another car, and concluded as his dire faults as a man became the subject of complaint.

The villa had been an anchor through it all. The house was almost too obviously an expression of his flawed personality—so said Deena, still a good friend and the denominating girlfriend from the convertible Lincoln period. There were cracks in the stucco, though he had paid over seventy grand for a structural retrofit, and the house was as solid now on its creeping California hillside as modern engineering could make it. Inside, a scouth of books, as the Scotsman said. Some that had been with him since the beginning, since before he went to St. Paul's, where he had

2

been a subsidy boy, a scholar on the foundation. Books bought as a lonely Bohemian maths grind at LSE, where he had gone instead of Cambridge, for "political" reasons. Plain paperbound books in French, bought at outdoor stands along the Seine, as they ought to have been. A solid selection of the approved high-lit product of the last forty years, books spoken of in the pages of the *Guardian*, the *Times Literary Supplement, Les Temps Modernes.* Mystery novels by the hundreds, by the thousands. Oodles of sci-fi, and pornography, an eclectic sampling, still consulted sometimes in the dead of night, with the left hand. Math texts read for brain tuning. The full epidemiological monty, of course, everything in any way relevant to his own lines of study plus all others, everything ever attempted by his busy generation, in special nine-foot-tall shelves of stained cherrywood.

The section of American novels unusually robust—these had been his way of trying to get to know his father, who had died young. Parts of his father's Yankee character had seemed to wink at him from the stories of Jack London, of Stephen Crane, of Hawthorne, Melville, Farrell, Hemingway, James Jones—the whole Y-chromosome-addled bunch. A renegade union organizer, driven out of the States in a prewar purge of Reds, dear old Dad had retreated to London, where an older relation, a man also named Landau, a Lithuanian Jew, had owned three cinemas. In the year of Landau's birth, '42 his dad had been dying of congestive heart failure while outwardly prospering for the first time in an errant life. All that remained now were six framed Kodak shots: in these Landau Sr. showed a face of great good cheer, a charming, not-unhandsome face that said to his never-to-be-met son, "We could have had great fun, you and I—I miss you and, you know, in a useless sort of way, I love you."

*   *   *

One cool night in late October 2006, a Wednesday, Landau took the N-Judah Muni Metro to Civic Center, took BART across the bay, and drove from the BART parking lot home to north Berkeley in his powerful black 525i, yet another flash car bought used and on the downside of its expected lifespan. Semi-retired now. Romantically unattached. Soon to be sixty-four, good God. Will you still feed me, will you IV me, etc. He was going home to be alone, not an unwelcome prospect, to eat a piece of wild salmon bought the day before and cooling in his refrigerator, on the second shelf down, with a fruity New Zealand sauvignon blanc also cooling in there somewhere. Useless now, professionally eunuched. Still going to his office two days a week to ride herd on his junior colleagues, who, doing what comes naturally, were tearing off great chunks of his research empire, figuring that he'd be gone in another year or two, why not.

He was in a mildly valedictory mood as he gunned up Cedar from the flats, comfortable in the worn black leather of his cushy Beemer seat, the two degenerative discs in his lower back giving him not much trouble—maybe it was all the lap-swimming he'd been undertaking recently, at the suggestion of his chiropractor friend, Georges Vienna. Once a sleek dolphin of a man, Landau was now more manatee—Deena said he looked like a Jewish Helmut Kohl. When he got in the pool at the Berkeley Y a sizable displacement of fluid ensued, yet he did not wallow, no, he struck out powerfully, and he did not soon tire. Others spoke of swimming as a chore, as the epitome of hamster-on-a-wheel-type exercise, but Landau looked forward to his sessions—alone with his thoughts, he often sang to himself, as the gray whales are said to do.

His housemaid, Elfridia Mattos, had been in to clean this day, and the house looked thirty percent more orderly. The terra-cotta floors had been mopped, the glass doors onto the west-facing deck had been washed, and there was a pleasant scent of citrus-zested cleanser. Elfridia, from Chiapas, four foot seven, late twenties, sometimes came to work with two cousins. All of them were pretty, short-necked women with tar-colored hair and hazel eyes. When negotiating over pay Elfridia seemed embarrassed to ask for anything, but Landau had heard her cracking rapid-fire jokes in her native idiom, and he had come to realize that she was a gifted raconteur, someone with a wicked tongue.

"Elfridia, as of next week, I will leave an extra sixty dollars in the envelope," he had told her recently.

"Hokay, if you wan' to, doc-tor."

"That way, when you bring the cousins, maybe it divides out a little better."

"Hokay."

Landau perceived that all was well with his house, everything spic 'n' span, even the cat-food bowl laid out on a fresh piece of newsprint on the floor, from the green sports section of the *San Francisco Chronicle*. He put down his leather satchel full of manuscripts and had a prolonged pee in the cramped downstairs bath, unable to wait the extra thirty seconds required to mount to the larger facility on the second floor. Such are the vagaries of the aging prostate in its eternal embrace of the diminishing male bladder. Had a slug of German mineral water while standing in front of his fridge, looking for his salmon fillet, and there it was, on the third shelf down not the second, Elfridia must have moved it. He went back out to the foyer. Here, on a glass-topped entry table that had never looked quite right— Deena said it was "designerish," "an idea not a table"—was the mail, all Sierra Club membership pitches and credit card offers. When had he last received a personal letter, a love letter, more to the point? In 1998. From Clarissa Plante, a French-Canadian epideme met in exotic Jo-burg, slender, athletic, smart, brunette. Fifty pounds lighter then, Landau had appealed to her as a romantic figure, as he had appealed in those days to a number of interesting women, most of them docs of some kind, world-saving globe-trotters, bio types. And where are they now, all my gal-pals? Yes, and why am I so alone now, boo-hoo, boo-hoo?

He opened a mailing from Nancy Pelosi, requesting his help defeating the evil Republicans in the upcoming elections. Nancy looked good in the photo. It showed her standing between Harry Reid and Charles Schumer, dressed in a tight blue skirt that barely reached her knees. Happen to know she's older than I am, but she's still a babe, look at her, any male of a certain age would give her a throw. If you were only here tonight, Nancy, I'd ply you with some of the fruity, put some sounds on the stereo (maybe *Steamin'*, Miles from back when he still felt the need to entertain), and history would be in the making, romantic history.

He heard a distant buzzing. So restful was the silence of his hillside villa, surrounded by trees—camphors, sycamores, redwoods, madrones, eucalypti—so thick the silence that customarily obtained in his remote neighborhood, with well-behaved liberal families on either side, that the distant barking of a dog, or the thin, eerie cry of a Steller's jay imitating a red-tailed hawk, came as a shock. Visitors who stayed awhile, foreign types especially, Londoners, Muscovites, always marveled at the silence, and sometimes it made them anxious. Tonight Landau could hear every creak and tick of his wood-and-stucco castle, not that there were all that many creaks but far, far away was a dim electric motor sound—maybe a slow-speed drill being used for home repair, or an alarm clock buzzing under some bedclothes.

It switched off. The thought of bedclothes recalled to him the book now resting on his bedside table, the new Andy Blunden bio of Wittgenstein, which he had been burrowing into for a couple of weeks, reading each night before falling asleep—surely it was a serious enough book not to be read that way, with logical passages merging into dreams, but he was angry with Wittgenstein for some reason, did not want to show him too much respect. The respect signaled by clearheaded morning reading.

Why not read him tonight, though, and take down the old *Tractatus Logico-Philosophicus* in support? Have them with dinner, on the metal bookstand, in a fair, openhanded light. Either that or the new Michael Connelly killer-thriller. He headed upstairs toward his bedroom, half thinking of changing out of his wrinkled office-going pants and shapeless tweed jacket, half of what to read tonight, the taste of what he might read almost as palpable as the anticipated salmon in the fridge. The Connelly then, just for fun. A thriller not a thinker. But no, no, the Blunden, and read it while you're still half-awake. You might learn something.

Landau's bedroom, a grand crow's nest, all tall windows and green views and shelves of books leaning this way and that, sat up high in the treetops. Year in and out there was a pleasant scent of leaves and living wood. What are you, a visiting friend from north London had once asked, a bloody chimp, Landau? At home in the forest canopy? Bed all disarranged, though—strange. Elfridia had forgotten to put it in order. Pillows strewn, covers all bunched. Standing on one leg as he pulled off his pants, he imagined a scene of Elfridia and her young cousins loafing the afternoon away, getting into his liquor cabinet, tuning in some *norteño* music on the stereo. Making fun of the professor's weird artwork and stressed furniture. *Híjole, ven aquí, Juanita!* as they found some book of choice porn and went off in squeals of laughter, imagining him having a bit of a stroke, sitting nude in the orthopedic recliner, his thick thighs splayed out.

One pant leg off, he balanced on the other foot. In olden times, he had swotted up Spanish and gone south like the other California Sandalistas, although in his case, under cover of a study being run out of Stanford on hep C. Got to see all those countries down there to some extent, liked Mexico the best, who would not? Mexicans were carnal, crazed, and vivid, their country violent and mysterious. By contrast the average Costa Rican was a plate of overcooked spinach, the average Nicaraguan a mud puddle. Gross stereotyping but there you were. Funny how that south-of-the-border era had ended, just suddenly over one day, on to other pastures. An epidemiologist of your kind is a tourist of pain, Deena had once said—all you need is a choice disease to study, a bit of funding, and you're happy as a clam.

He stumbled, threw himself toward his bed. Just barely managed to execute a half-twist that put his bottom on the mattress and not his head. The profound thump of his 240 pounds produced more of that electric buzzing sound, closer at hand now, half-sputtering. After a few seconds it stopped again. Landau looked right then left in the rumpled bedclothes, felt the covers to either side, found a foot, a leg. He made a sound he later described to the police as *Unnggrrhh!!* and propelled himself off the mattress onto the floor, onto his hands and knees. Wearing his boxers and his sport coat and his black nylon socks. Scrambled over to a bookcase, stood back against it, palms pressed backwards.

Good God—that was a *leg*, man. A human leg. Landau's down comforter was humped near the right-center of the king-sized bed. It was a $1,200 SeaCrest goose down comforter bought last winter, the sort of indulgence one tells no one about, for shame that it should have come to this—that one should look forward to going to bed each night because of the warmth of one's blankie, not because of the nearness of a lover. To sleep under it was to feel bundled within a sun-warmed cloud. He lurched bedward again and pulled the covers half-down. A woman with glossy gray-brown hair down to her white shoulders lay facedown in his sheets, immobile, nude to the tops of her buttocks. Apparently zonked.

"Excuse me. I say, hello there."

Something about that back. A line of tiny moles, across the smooth swale of lower back, awoke a memory. Like a map of the Aleutians, curving southwest. The hair, though going gray, was vital and thick, a rich fan of it. Who had hair like that? Who that he had known?

"Excuse me. I say—I'm going to touch you now."

Landau pressed two fingers to the near shoulder. It was warmer than room temperature, but not warm enough. He felt for the carotid pulse. Not there, and therefore: there is a dead woman in my bed. Not one of the Elfridianas, thank God, they were not so large nor so pale. Then Landau knew who it was. Oh God, oh God. Horror, shocked horror, manifested in his thumping heart for a long moment. Oh, why are *you* here? He turned away as if to shun the unmoving figure. Walked round to the other side of the bed, turned and bent to see the face better. No, obscured by hair.

When he had known this person, whose name was Samantha Bernstein Beevors, a scientist of large and intimidating reputation, formerly a colleague, once a lover, she had been vain of her wondrous hair. Not really brown—more classically chestnut, full of glinting red and gold. He knelt upon the bed and swept the hair from her face with a finger, revealing eyes frozen open and a mouth stuffed full of, good God, a pair of boxers. His own striped boxers. He scurried off the bed.

The buzzing began again. The sound was coming from down *there*, under the airy comforter. Vaguely aware that he should do no such thing, Landau gently pulled the covers down to her calves. Some odd object protruded from her shapely backside, tubular, flat-ended, pink. The buzzing halted again. Landau now recognized a device that for years had been secreted amongst the socks in his chest of drawers, a vibrator, in a word, a pink plastic vibrator. Not his own, technically. His racing mind sought to explain to some imaginary police investigator how he had come to possess it. Yes, but what *for*, Dr. Landau? If it's not yours, if you have no use for it, and you kept it where, in your sock drawer? For how many years?

The buzzing began again. The sputter-buzzing of batteries giving out. He recalled a scene from ten years ago, fifteen, involving a companion from the blue Jag period, someone who had introduced this comical version of a sex toy into the mix on an evening of now only half-remembered frivolity. Margo. Margo Hollinger, French historian. Professor at Stanford, writer of weighty books, and how did I ever meet her, can I remember? No. Such are the ungovernable vectorings of the mind under stress that Landau considered for an instant how to get in touch with Margo, persuade her to explain to the imaginary detective who it was who had paid $6.95 at most for the most ironic vibrator on sale at Harmonies, the feminist-flavored sex-aid emporium on San Pablo Avenue...Half a minute later, ashamed of himself for worrying about such a thing, he did the decent thing and twisted the plastic shaft to the "OFF" position, then gently settled the covers back over the naked woman in his bed.

No reading of Wittgenstein tonight. The first to arrive on Landau's woodsy block was an ambulance playing its siren, although he'd made it clear on the phone that the situation was postmortem, and they need not hurry. Then, Deena and Harold came. Deena lived now with Harold Blodgett, a Berkeley law professor, the Barbra Streisand Chair of Constitutional Law, nice enough guy. When Landau called her for moral support, he half hoped Harold would be home and would interest himself in the situation, since it couldn't hurt to have a lawyer present. Twenty minutes after the ambulance arrived, after Deena and Harold arrived, a Berkeley police cruiser slid silently into the now dark street, roof lights strobically flashing. Officer Thomas Ng—about thirty-five, five foot five, placid of demeanor—and Officer Frances Hashimoto—a little older, taller—entered Landau's house.

"I'm the one who called you. I'm Landau. A woman named Samantha Bernstein Beevors is dead upstairs. I can show her to you if you'd like."

"All right. Is she your wife, sir?" asked Officer Ng.

"No. I know her, though."

"Is she your significant other?"

"No, I wouldn't say that."

Officer Hashimoto, turning away, spoke some phrases into a walkie-talkie.

Ng: "But you know her, right, sir?"

"Yes. I knew her rather well once. For a period of time."

The officer waited for more.

"She was my colleague. A person I used to work with. In my professional life."

"Okay. And how long has she been staying with you now, sir?"

"Not staying here. I haven't seen her in years. This is a complete surprise, her being here. Having been brought here or having come in while I was gone. A complete surprise."

Again, the officer waited.

Landau also knew how to wait. He took a breath and tried to let go in his mind of the need to show innocence. No, you *are* innocent. Think of that.

"Has anyone been with the body, sir? Other than you, since you found it?"

Landau opened his hands, hoisted his shoulders two inches.

"You don't know?"

"I couldn't say."

"I have, Tom," piped up one of the young EMTs walking past at that moment, one of three who had arrived with the ambulance. "I wanted to be sure she was a forty-four. I went up there."

Officer Ng turned toward the young black man who spoke.

"And?"

The young man nodded.

"Okay. Thank you. Jamal, right?"

"Right."

"I know you. You're from El Cerrito."

Landau hadn't wanted to get the young fellow in trouble. But it was okay, apparently.

"Can we sit down somewhere, sir? I have to make a few notes," said Officer Ng.

"Let's go in the den."

Ng cleared the newspapers off the loveseat and sat down. "Could you spell your name for me, sir, slowly?"

"Yes, it's Landau. L-A-N-D-A-U."

"This is Cragmont Avenue, correct?"

"No, Hopwood Lane, actually. We're on the corner of Cragmont. My address is seven Hopwood Lane."

"The dispatcher said Cragmont."

"Yes, that's what you have to tell people so they can find it. But it's Hopwood Lane."

"Okay."

And so on, and so forth. Even I have seen the TV shows, Landau thought. He particularly liked the one where autopsies were shown, where bullets were modeled as they ripped through guts, maggots crawling through wounds. And where is our expert crime scene unit, may I ask? Is this guy even a detective, Officer Ng? Why doesn't everyone have on rubber gloves at this point, isn't that standard?

*   *   *

Fifteen minutes later, as Landau headed upstairs to his bedroom, followed by the two officers, other police personnel were arriving, in other vehicles. In the end maybe there *was* a CSI unit mucking around, it was hard to tell. He showed Ng and Hashimoto the body of Samantha Beevors. The officers became alert as they entered the room, scanning side to side, looking at the floor, the ceiling. Landau had the idea that his bedroom was being sized up as an infamous torture site, a Ted Bundy's basement type of place—maybe the plump professor had done in dozens here, grinding their bones, sniffing the dust.

Now Officer Ng, though not Officer Hashimoto, did put on gloves. He stood at the foot of Landau's bed looking thoughtful.

"Would you say that she suffered much, sir?"

"I wouldn't know that. I wasn't here."

"Yes, but what's your opinion? Did it take her long to die? Speaking as a doctor."

"Well, I'm not a doctor. I'm an epidemiologist. It's different. I don't know if she suffered or not. I sincerely hope not, of course."

"So, you heard nothing? No sounds of struggle or screams or anything?"

"No. It was all over before I arrived as far as I can tell."

The officer nodded. Took a half step forward.

"Except, the buzzing. You said."

"Right. There was still some buzzing."

"Which you could hear all the way downstairs. Despite these blankets. In the kitchen, you said."

"No, in the foyer, not the kitchen."

"The foyer. Okay. The front hall."

"Right."

When Officer Ng pulled back the down coverlet, Landau felt ashamed. This is not my work, he wanted to declare. I never hated her *this* much, though, true, I did come to hate her. Harridan, fanatic, evil witch. Yet— not to end up like this. He felt ashamed in front of the other woman, Officer Hashimoto, wanted to turn to her and say, "I know it's my bed, I know she's wrapped up in my expensive coverlet, head on my pillow, but I stand foursquare against this sort of thing, normally. Savagery toward women, I mean. You have to believe that. I have always deplored that."

Hashimoto whispered something into her walkie-talkie.

"One more question, then. How did you identify her, sir?" asked Officer Ng. "I mean, when you first came in and found her like this."

"Well, I just recognized her. I know her."

"With her face all pushed down like that?"

"You get a pretty good look from the other side. If you crouch down."

Ng went to the other side of the bed. He crouched. "Okay. But she's got something in her mouth, I can't really see. What is it, a gag of some kind?"

Landau decided not to respond. To argue the fine points of gags, how she had gotten a pair of his underpants in her mouth, could only prove unprofitable.

"Maybe you turned her over, Doctor? And had a better look? That's what I would've done. I mean, you're a doctor, so it's all right, right?"

"I didn't turn her over. I left her the way she is. The way you find her now."

"Or, looked around for some ID. Is her purse up here, did you find that?"

"No, I didn't look for a purse. Like I said, I knew her. I knew who she was."

"Okay. So she left it downstairs, the purse. Is that right?"

"I don't know."

It occurred to Landau that Officer Ng had been watching the same TV shows. Maybe that was what police training consisted of these days—an assignment to watch many shows. So you could catch criminals in their pathetic slipups. He, himself, was experiencing this mainly in terms of how it resembled TV episodes, movies seen, the three or four thousand police procedurals he'd read over the years, and the other guy had probably read quite a few, too. It was an over-literary-ified situation. Now just forget all that, he told himself. Pretend you've never seen or read anything and stick to your story. Don't go acting all smarty-pants on him. He won't like that.

"That's what I would've done, though," Officer Ng repeated. "Turned her over. You don't see that every day, do you, a naked dead woman. Dead and helpless."

Landau took another long breath. Wanted to say, just for fun: "Yes, all right, I turned her over. Had a really excellent look, poked around a bit, too. Okay, you got me there, Officer. She was quite a piece of talent in her day, this crazy mind-bending bitch, and she used that, oh God did she. And, to be completely frank, I had a nice suck at one of her titties, for old times' sake. Probably would've plunged in with the old ram but for some residual necro-aversion, a feeling of taboo. Can't say I've ever been into fucking dead women. Although, never say never."

Instead Landau said, "I did pull back her hair a little. For a better look."

Both Officer Ng and Officer Hashimoto became more alert—not that they hadn't been alert before.

"And how did that go for you, Doctor? When you touched her?"

"I don't know how it went. I just got up on the bed, on my knees I guess, and pulled back her hair from her face."

"Would you like to show us how you did that, sir?"

"Don't you need to dust for fingerprints, Officer?"

"That's okay. Not too worried about that now. Why don't you show us how you got up there on the bed with the body."

Landau didn't want to do that, though. Getting up must signify something—that you were so crazed, such a demented criminal sadist, that you'd even do it in front of the cops. Wallow around on the bed with the corpse, giggling, eyeballs rolling, salivating.

He pantomimed doing it instead, pulling a hank of hair from the side of her face. Using a single finger.

"Did you touch the body in any other way, sir?"

"No. I did not."

"You're sure?"

"I was horrified. I was kind of a little out of my normal mind, to be honest."

"Out of your mind?"

"I was shaken. Appalled. I mean, it seemed disrespectful to touch her. Gruesome."

"But you've handled lots of dead bodies, haven't you, Doctor? In your line of work?"

"I'm not a real doctor, like I said. But, yes, I've handled a few. I've been around people dying."

"And how did that go for you, sir?"

"It went well enough. How do you think it went?"

The interrogation petered out soon after. They went back downstairs, but the evening wasn't over yet, not nearly—police personnel continued to pour in, crew after crew of them, medical examiners, uniformed officers, officers out of uniform, forensics techs, first responders. He never got to eat the salmon and have the glass or three of wine he needed. Officer Ng disappeared at some point and Landau found himself answering more questions posed by an actual police detective, someone whose badge identified him as such, a chunky white man named Byrum Johnson. They sat in the kitchen drinking decaf. Deena also at table. Deena patted Landau on the back as he became fatigued. Harold was also in the kitchen, standing alone along the wall, saying nothing, not looking especially interested.

Samantha Beevors' body came down on a litter just past midnight. Landau felt more tired than anything as he watched its slow progress down his flagstoned front steps. Never got to say good-bye to you, Samantha, when everything blew up that time. When you tried to ruin me, when you went so savagely whacko, as you always did on everybody, every man who ever jostled you even slightly in the hierarchy. I'm sure you never thought you'd end up dying in my bed, of all places. Detective Johnson seems to think they killed you elsewhere, then brought you here. He'll know soon following tests. But why did they bring you to my place? Did you say with your last breath, "Go ahead, kill me if you have to, you bastards, but take my body over to Landau's, leave me in his leafy love-nest so he can get in some trouble. It's my last gift to him, my final gesture"?

"Dr. Landau, I'm gonna clear out now," Detective Johnson said mildly, turning away from the kitchen window. "You'll stay in town, right? Not planning any international trips soon, are you? All right, now I know this probably rings hollow, but I want to apologize for us tromping through here in such numbers, we don't get non-drug-related homicides very often in the hill neighborhoods, so the dispatcher probably told everybody to head up here. This is the whole Berkeley criminal investigative apparatus, down to the janitors. We'll be a little more restrained with the next crime, not that that's much consolation, but there it is."

"It's okay, Detective. Just as long as nobody ruined my new bidjar."

"Whatever a bidjar is."

"It's a kind of rug. So—you consider this a homicide, is that what I'm gathering?"

"Don't know. I shouldn't say anything, but it looks a little funny, don't you think? What're the chances that she broke in to your house and died of a heart attack in your bed? On her own?"

"I see what you're saying. The maids were here, too. It had to have happened after they left, at about three."

"Right. I want to find out what the maids saw."

Half an hour later, having chewed the evening over with Deena and Harold—Harold, despite his apparent uninterest, having noticed absolutely everything—Landau was once again alone. In his now violated house. Listening to the silence outdoors and in, silence returning like water seeping back into a dry riverbed. Freddy, his neutered tom, appeared out of deep hiding, to peer at his empty feed-bowl on the kitchen floor as if to say, "Well? A lot of excitement, okay, but where the hell's my dinner, man? Are you feeding me or what?"

"All right, all right, although it's a bad idea to eat in the middle of the night," Landau told his cat. "Where am I going to sleep tonight, Freddy? Somebody just died in my lovely bed. A madwoman, a scourge, at one time, a close friend. I'd rather not go upstairs by myself, silly as that sounds. Well, here's your can of food. Eat it all, and we'll talk things over in the morning."

chapter 2

Landau had never planned on becoming a disease-chaser, and the whole career, now mostly over, seemed an accident—a fundamental wrong turning. Should've been a lawyer, a journalist, a wordsmith of some kind. A neither-this-nor-that kind of thinker, amoeba-ing forward on the basis of style alone. A modest facility with mathematics had been his downfall. While he pursued the things that actually interested him, poetry and history, he racked up good results in his sciencey subjects, so that at the end of his education he found himself in an absurd position, as a graduate student in statistics. He had come to Berkeley to get out of England—California being the place to go, plus he had a cousin in San Francisco, dear dead old Dad's only living relation. Then, a pregnancy with the wrong person. Needing to get serious about earning a living, he ploughed on with statistics on the theory that it's best to dig the ditch you're in.

Liked some things about it, mathematical modeling, for one. Whole enterprise horribly bloodless, but diverting for that very reason. Stumbled into a modeling-of-diseases course, statistics plus suffering, that was a little better. The biosciences belonged to the English at that time. Not that the Yanks would ever admit it, but Francis Crick bestrode the sciences as a colossus, a maddeningly protean genius, not just for discovering the structure of DNA but for figuring out how the whole thing worked, protein synthesis, coding, all of it. Landau had seen him in action. A tutor at St. Paul's took some students to the Cavendish labs at Cambridge one day in October '56, to hear a talk on some scientific subject. A large, sandyhaired man had been speaking as they came in the conference room—he was not the featured speaker, just somebody in the audience. Yet he continually spoke out loudly, wittily cross-examining the man up front trying to give his paper, tying him in logical knots.

Protein crystallography, that's what the talk had been about. Meant nothing to Landau, whole thing quite boring really, except for the brilliant talkiness of the man in the audience. This is science? One fellow stuttering and hemming while another makes jokes, "setting the table rolling" over and over, jokes with a logical innuendo? And afterward, a lot of good-natured talk as the men gathered together in front of the blackboard, writing more nonsense upon it. Not a lab coat in sight.

It was years later that he figured out who the loudmouthed one had been. Crick was famously noisy, someone who liked to do the other guy's crossword puzzle for him, eat his lunch. Had this been an inspiration to Landau? Well, he always remembered it. And he was in a very, very small way Crick-like, in that he enjoyed swotting up areas of expertise that he had no right to, immunology, microbiology, Asian languages. He was that rare prominent epideme without a medical degree, one who had never even taken a class in organic. (Crick had been a physicist before plunging into biology.) Yes, Landau *taught* in a medical school, he was continually surrounded by MDs, and he often told his ferociously bright students, "I am not a doctor but I play one on TV," quoting the ad for cough syrup. This had turned out to be a big theme for him—not quite being what he should. Having to hide intellectual deficits, make them up on his own, do homework.

One of the reasons Samantha Beevors had appealed. Also not an MD, also largely self-created. Had she been born twenty years later she would have been a computer scientist, *tout court*, and indeed, her work in the last decade had all been high-end programming stuff, the elaboration of complex models for disease, for giant drug-treatment campaigns. Figuring out what happens if you give this rather than that to the benighted millions. His judgment of her significance and the value of what she had done colored by their falling out, inevitably, but his considered opinion was that she had lost her way scientifically, modeling the models that modeled models. She believed you could make human misery predictable. Model everything.

He believed that, too, sort of. But at the far edge of an evolving retroviral plague there was a spirit of mad fun, the killer microbe rejoicing in its profound resourcefulness, o'ertopping itself, reengineering creation. Samantha would have said, "I program for that, too, and nicely." But she had gone global, become a celebrity, begun to believe her own press. No longer called herself an epidemiologist, no, she was a *biomathematician* now, also an *evolutionary biologist*, and when the mood was on her, a *population geneticist*, too. Obsessed with the question of drug resistance, how did you devise an inoculation regime that minimized that, for which researches the mighty had vastly enriched her. Landau and a few others sniping from the sidelines. The idea of the centrality of resistance, that that was the only question, disturbed him. My God, just count the bodies piling up from good old non-drug-resistant TB, if you want some evidence. From endemic malaria.

He awoke at seven fifty. Cat Freddy on top of him, kneading his chest. Voices outdoors, several. Landau lying on the hard, artsy couch in the downstairs den, staring at the cracked ceiling.

My God—Samantha's dead, he realized. Samantha Beevors is dead. The thought hit him with a twist to the gut. Good God.

His doorbell was ringing. Oh, a bloody circus out there already, TV station vans, people scurrying about, someone speaking commentary into a microphone. They saw him at the window and rushed the front door. So, just get away from the window. Go put on your pants. Do something.

The telephone rang. Then his cell phone rang, and he hunted the gadget down inside his sleeping bag, found it just as it stopped. A UC Berkeley number, with no name attached. More mad doorbelling. And now door-knocking, too.

He called back the Berkeley number.

"Yes?" asked an impatient baritone.

"Harold, is that you?"

"Oh, Anthony. Yes. I have those numbers we talked about. Those lawyers we talked about last night, the ones I thought might do okay by you."

Landau tried to remember. "All right, go on. I guess I'm sufficiently awake."

Landau took down the numbers—the office numbers of two eminent criminal defense attorneys.

"Call them this morning, Anthony, as soon as you're able. I'll call ahead if you tell me which one you like better."

"Eeny meeny miney mo, Harold."

"In that case, I suggest Raboy. Cleveland Raboy. Slightly bigger office, and they never lose a case, never an important one."

"Am I important? But I'm not worried about losing, Harold. I have done nothing wrong. I want someone willing to take one for the team, though, to get out ahead."

"Meaning what?"

"Willing to deal with the press, for instance. There's a whole herd of them at my door right now. Trying to knock it down."

"Listen, Anthony—don't talk to anyone until you choose your lawyer. Don't let them get their hooks into you. I'll call ahead so he'll be ready for your call. Make it at nine thirty on the dot. Without fail."

"I'm feeling much poorer already, Harold."

"I know. It's what it is."

Not exactly a hand-holder. But steady, competent, thorough. Landau's male friends tended to be more ragged than Harold, less worthy, and he and Harold had never quite become intimate, although they'd tried. Harold might not want *him* for a friend, Harold being the Barbra Streisand Chair and all that. Or, perhaps it was only Deena that made him wary—that Landau had messed with Deena, too. That was surely part of the problem.

He moved in stately fashion down the hall of his villa, catching views out windows and through glass doors of people walking through his bushes. Trampling his native-plants garden. One man was waving at him through a kitchen window—Doctor, can I ask you just one question? Just one single question? Landau made some coffee. Get the *hell* away from my kitchen window, you fool, you chucklehead. Eventually, the man backed off, shaking his head regretfully—all right, it's your call, Professor, but I could have helped you. I could've put you on TV.

Already all over the web, good God. Death of Samantha Bernstein Beavers, as *facesofdisease.com* misspelled her last name. Focus so far on *her* death, *her* fame, no mention of him at all. Landau leaned against his expensive butcher-block island sipping the brew of Sumatra Mandheling, while exercising his slim new laptop. A CNN news report was just now being filed, 11:59 EST, "Samantha Bernstein Beevors, AIDS Pioneer, Dead at 57," with links to her vast CV and to a recent paper, "Forecasting the epidemiological aspects of antiretroviral allocation protocols in KwaZulu-Natal: Is there still time?" in *Nature Medicine*. He'd read it, could remember none of it. Uh-oh, here was his name on another story, and Landau quickly closed the lid of the trusty Mac and pushed it away from him. Must eat breakfast first. Give me another half hour.

Forty minutes later, as he eased out his back door on the way to the green plastic garbage container in his fenced backyard, there to deposit some compostable refuse as conscience and city ordinance required, the redwood-and-wrought-iron gate to the yard came cautiously open, and a slender young woman slipped through. Dressed in a silky pantsuit, her hair just so, her makeup refined. Microphone in hand. Raised her eyebrows at Landau, then bit her lower lip, as if to keep from laughing.

"Good for you," she said. "Really good."

"What?"

"Going right up there. Knocking on his door. Getting a foot in."

"Oh—yes, yes. But he threw me out. The bastard."

"You're Solly Gravenites, right? *Politico?*"

"And you are—wait—I know I've seen you before."

"I'm Katherine Emerald. Of KRON."

"Oh, of course. Katherine of KRON. Hello there, Katherine."

"So, what now, Solly?"

"Well, he's not saying anything. I guess we're stuck."

"Is that door unlocked?"

"Hmm, what, his back door? It might be. Yes."

Landau put his banana peels and orange rinds into the plastic dumpster. The woman looked hard at the back door.

"I guess I just don't have the balls," she said. "The raw chutzpah. He's a murder suspect, after all. Murder of a woman."

"No, don't be like that. They like talking to a pretty face. Go on."

"No, I don't think so, not today. I'll just wait back here with all the cowards."

"You're missing a big scoop. It could be your golden hour."

The young woman made some adjustments to her recording device.

Landau continued, "He's just a fat old professor. A bit depressed, is my lightning reading of him. Too much time alone. Got an old pussycat in there, mangy orange pussycat. Just waiting for you."

She looked at Landau more directly. Blinked twice.

"You're not Solly Gravenites, are you?"

"Probably not. Is that a problem?"

"Could I ask you one question?"

"No, I don't think so."

"Why didn't they arrest you yesterday?"

"Why didn't they? Well, you'd have to ask them. Because I didn't commit a crime? I did nothing wrong?"

Katherine Emerald nodded. She made as if to turn on her recording device.

"No, no, none of that, please. No electronics."

"Just so I get things straight. So I don't misquote you later."

"Very professional of you. But this is just between you and me, Katherine of KRON. What we say is just for us. For this special moment."

"So, what gives, Professor? What really happened?"

"You know. I came home. Found a woman in my bed. A former colleague. She was dead."

"Sarah Samantha Beevors, right? The professor, the Gettleman Distinguished Professor of Mathematical Biology and Something-something at Stanford, right?"

"Right. But more recently USC. They gave her a whole damned institute down there. Named it for her."

"Your former boss, correct? Your research director."

"Actually, I was hers. But we worked together. We were colleagues."

What am I doing? Landau asked himself. Really, what in the world? Stop talking now, right now. Enough of this little *divertissement*.

"She discovered the new cause of tuberculosis. Disease-resistant tuberculosis, is that right?"

"No, there is no disease-resistant tuberculosis. What would that mean? Tuberculosis *is* a disease."

She seemed perplexed. Then smiled at herself, a lovely smile. "I'm a complete scientific idiot, forgive me. I'm way out of my depth here."

"No, you aren't out of your depth, Katherine of KRON. I've seen you on the tube. You're very clever, when they let you be."

"Thank you. But the fact remains, I know nothing about what you do. Could you tell me about it?"

"You were clever enough to sneak in here and say I looked like Somebody Gravenites. You're rather quick, you are."

"You do look like someone else, some actor."

Landau was backing away now. Making little gestures, funny little expressions of regret.

"Professor, Professor—may I ask just one more question?"

"No."

"Are you an American citizen?"

"Am I what? I am a hardworking, taxes-paying half-American. Foreign national, to be technical about it. But why do you care about that?"

"I don't know."

Back safe in his kitchen, watching her exit the yard—glorious-looking young female, whatever else she was—Landau remonstrated with himself. Must not do that anymore. Must not stray off the reservation. But he had given nothing away—right? The whole incident was already a little like a memory of something experienced under a drug. The drug being the influence of her dewy young womanhood. Always has had a deranging effect upon me. Makes me want to show off.

After a phone conversation with his lawyer, Raboy, Landau took a bath. His home phone ringing every two and a half minutes as he calculated, his cell phone ringing a little less often. Deena called, and they agreed to have lunch if he could figure out how to get away from his house. He went to his bedroom. My God, they took my fancy comforter away—did they have to do that? Did they have the right? His chest of drawers was also different-looking inside, depleted of several pairs of boxers, all his striped boxers. The damp, heavy sumo-wrestler's bathrobe piled at his feet, Landau put on a pair of lavender-tinted briefs, and surely they must not be mine, must belong to someone else—to Jad, his slender son, for instance, or to some other svelte occasional visitor to his house. Good God, man, you start on a diet right now. Right this very hour. Look at those thighs. Why, you look like Rod Steiger in *The Loved One*. Mr. what's-his-name, Mr. Joyboy.

The bed spooked him, stripped bare as it was, violated. Beds in which people have died whom I've cared about: mercifully, it was a short list, the bed in which darling Mother died, a raise-and-lower hospital number, brought in for her last few wheezing weeks, and the bed in which Gramps died, Gramps not his real grandfather, rather old Isidore Landau, the movie theater owner, the family benefactor. Landau grappled at a memory now, the old gent dead in bed beside him one frosty winter's morning, their great pleasure, the two of them, old kindly grandpa-figure and squirmy ten-year-old boy, to sleep together on the old fellow's occasional visits to the flat where he kept Landau and his mother, off Stoke Newington Road, Hackney. Then, dead one morning, eyes open upon the ceiling, expression of dubiety. That why he hadn't been able to sleep up here last night? From a fright delivered to him fifty years ago, when he was but a tender lad, still wet behind the ears?

Early afternoon, just short of two. Here came Deena up the steps, bearing takeout bags. Landau had convinced her that he was besieged in his house and so she had taken his order for Cha-Am, his favorite Thai place on Shattuck Avenue, entrée number twenty three, chicken and fresh green beans, not too spicy, extra rice. As she swept up his front walk, some remnant press were coming after her, looking a little dispirited now, just going through the motions, not really hoping for anything.

"Deena. Deena, baby. So good to *see* you."

"Anthony, *you* are the big baby. The pretender."

"I know. I lied when I said I couldn't get out. I just didn't want to. Ooh—that smells so good."

"Please, don't maul me."

"Just trying to take the bags, sweetheart. Help you out."

They settled down in the kitchen. There was that correspondent in the side yard again, looking in at them, waving.

"No, leave the drapes open, who cares," Landau said.

"You want him filming you as you eat your peanut curry?"

"Peanut curry? Hey! I didn't order no stinking peanut curry!"

"I know, I know! Is only a joke, Anthony. You want too much your food."

"Food is all I have now, sweetheart. All that's left me."

Deena, on her own authority, pulled the curtains. She sat down and they began to eat.

When the drastic rush of first pleasure was over, Landau sat back in his chair, continuing to eat but at a more dignified pace. Deena had barely begun. *She* was the one eating peanut curry. Wearing her office clothes, a rumpled, forgettable skirt *mit* blouse. She was the departmental secretary for the East Asian Languages Institute, Berkeley, the daughter of two distinguished language scholars, Belgrade Serbs, lost everything getting out of Yugoslavia in the fifties, arrived complaining about America and never stopped, just the one daughter, exceedingly dutiful, subtly discouraged from following in the parental footsteps. Not smart enough, you know. Not true professor material. Another of Landau's self-starters, hot autodidacts. Went to Taiwan on a vacation at eighteen and came back speaking Min-nan, the southern Fujianese dialect, then picked up Guoyu, Taiwanese Mandarin, later from a boyfriend. Read novels in Japanese, emailed in nine languages. Landau's tutor in all things Asian-linguistic, the gentlest of task-mistresses, a connoisseur of imprecision and error, her own English, for example, stubbornly a little off, still accented after forty-five years in-country.

Acne-scarred shoulders. Some scars on her face. Gravy-brown hair, always a little greasy. All her life men had been discovering her, diamond-in-the-roughing her, thrilled to find someone whom surely no one else had noticed—why, you're quite attractive, you know. Come have a drink with me, I will condescend to want you. All the big empire-building professors wanted her in *their* office, please. Landau no less than the others. He had come into the Language Institute one afternoon in the eighties casting about for a translator, a toothsome Chinese girl grad student perhaps, and had been taken by this incarnation of Mitteleuropean longing. A hard, sexy face. Am I in the Slavic Languages Department, by mistake? Did I open the wrong door?

"Deena. I really stepped in it this time, I think."

"Why? It's okay, Landau. Forget it."

"No, it's all out there now. It's all over for me. I'll be ruined."

"It was over for you before." She shrugged and ate.

"Look at this," and he began to play with his laptop. But Deena refused to look.

"Come on. Just for a second."

"She is dead, Anthony. People will know what she was. *That* will come out."

He quoted from a blog, *ronniesvaleoftruth*, "'Professor Landau replied to the charges in a document sealed as part of the judgment rendered by the twelve member senior disciplinary panel,' etcetera, etcetera, 'Anthony Landau had a similar situation in 1992 when Doctor Afsaneh Khosaddi, of his San Francisco lab, filed a complaint alleging sexual harassment and misappropriation of research materials,' etcetera, etcetera, 'but the dispute with Doctor Beevors was much more serious and put in jeopardy a $6.7 million multiyear study financed by the International Fund for AIDS under WHO auspices and CDC supervision,' etcetera, etcetera, etcetera. Oy vey."

Deena tapped her plate with her takeout chopsticks.

"What, I'm wrong?"

"You must resist catastrophic thoughts. Struggle against self-pity, Landau. It's always the same with you. Time to grow up."

"Jesus, who made you such a toughie?"

"Remember, *she* is dead. You are still living. You know the truth. Now, you may have to tell it."

That evening, Katherine Emerald of KRON had a five-minute segment devoted to "the death of the beautiful AIDS doctor," as she described Samantha Beevors' passing. Someone had filmed them over the fence as they had their tête-à-tête. There he was, dressed in shlumpy khakis and turtleneck, Tweedledee-ish in aspect, what a gut now, bantering with the shy slip of a TV personality, who had bravely bearded him in his backyard. Something commanding in his posture, intimidating. An undeniably rakish way of looking at another person, at a younger female person. God, is that how I present? But I gaze upon male as well as female in that way, with the same cheeky intensity. However, must get rid of the beard. The suggestive Mephistophelian beard.

His phone rang when the segment ended.

"You have done irreparable damage to your cause. I'm calling to say that I'm reconsidering what I told you earlier today, that I would take your case. You owed it to me to mention that you had given this person an interview, good God, what were you thinking? How unbelievably stupid, stupid."

Landau paused. "I know. I'm very sorry, Cleveland. I told her absolutely nothing. I had no idea that someone would be filming us. Through the fence, I guess it was."

"You had no idea. Listen, that just doesn't cut it, all right? From now on assume you're being filmed wherever you go. We're going to have to figure out a more secure way of communicating, you and I, assuming that I see a way to go forward. Which I don't at the moment. I'm just appalled, I'm horrified, blecch, ugh."

"I'm sorry. Sorry."

"Listen—this is an international story. These few seconds of tape will be playing everywhere tonight, you've handed them a tremendous advantage, and I don't see how we overcome it, I simply don't."

"Look, I'm not even under suspicion of a crime. It'll blow over."

"You're not under suspicion? What, are you mad? And now they don't have to figure out how to characterize you, since you've already done that for them. Today it became twenty percent more likely that you'll be indicted, no thirty percent. My advice to you is, put your affairs in order. Plan on the worst. When we spoke this morning I would not have said that, I did not say anything like that, did I? Not as I recall."

All right, all right. *Now* I'm back on the reservation, Landau wanted to say. No need to scare me further.

"As I said, I'm sorry. It was a harmless bit of nothing. I hadn't spoken to you before I spoke to her, I'd never met her before. But I won't be fooled again."

Didn't like the lawyer-guy, he decided. Kind of over the top. Might just be his early-stage strategy, to whip Landau into shape. Even if you understood that, it was *pas gentil*.

Is that really what I look like, though? Is that the real me? Landau went upstairs and shaved off the villain's Van Dyke, saw his bare face for the first time in eighteen years. Ah, so there you are. Broad of cheek, fairly good jaw, no dewlaps yet. Something going on down below, some softening, but no triple chin yet. The face not that of a stranger, more that of a distant cousin forgotten for a generation who appears one night and reminds you of some essential family trait. Something louche, possibly morally weak. Well, there you are, for better or worse. After age sixty, a man gets the face he deserves, as someone once wisely said—as if "deserve" had anything to do with it. And what is a face? An evolving little bit of personal skin-frontage, both revealing and disguising of the nexus of intention/thought/sense-of-the-world that's knitted up behind the eyes. The part that, for want of something more solid, is proposed as your identity. Your this-not-that. The real, really-real you.

chapter 3

Landau's routine reasserted itself in the next few days. The press gave up trying to interview him. The lawyer stayed on the case and gave discreet public statements that began to shape a counter-story of hardworking major scientist harrowed by loss of close colleague, old friend, tragedy all around. Landau had not been detained because he'd had nothing to do with the regrettable death, of course, of course. Samantha Beevors, though her lab results were not all in yet, had likely died of natural causes. Heart disease, probably. Landau read on a blog that Beevors had collapsed at the 2003 International AIDS Conference in Durban, South Africa, which he had himself attended, though he couldn't remember seeing Samantha there and had heard no talk of collapses. Fainted at a public meeting, it was said. Half a dozen doctors had rushed to her aid—a good place to stage a fainting fit, if you had to. The blogger, UdoNarn, had been in the room, he claimed.

Landau sent his lawyer the post. Hopefully, the whole thing would now blow over, the whole legal thing. Four days after the discovery of Samantha in his house, he was back at UCSF meeting with his street-injector study administrators, two crackerjack lesbian women who had organized his investigations for years, managing logistics and training the field staff (referred to as "the field hands") and basically running the show. He had been tracking a population of teens living on the streets of the Haight as they entered their twenties, as they seroconverted, as they tested positive for hepatitis B and C, as they went from good-looking, smart-assed trick-turners to toothless street wraiths, most of them. A parody in the key of hopeless of normal human maturation. His fancy-Dan career of AIDS-drug testing and globetrotting and CDC consulting now pretty much had boiled down to this, this Lower Depths stuff, which was perfectly fine with him. His strong suit, really.

Georges Vienna, his chiropractor friend, came back from Indonesia where he had been on a long vacation. A trim-and-tanned fellow, Georges had been in Djakarta on the day of the recent Bali bombings, the second attack there in four years. Had spent the next two weeks volunteering on the storied Hindu isle, adjusting the sore-necked natives. Landau never discussed chiropractic with Georges and Georges never questioned the foundations of western science, in return. Instead, they swam together. Georges had a thing for Asian women but Landau's inspections of whorehouses in Vietnam and Thailand and the papers he had written about HIV rates and the sale of underage girls had amounted eventually to a powerful aversion therapy for amiable Georges, who, in his youth, had traveled often to Southeast Asia, seeking "experiences."

"I'm trying to remember who this Beevors person was—she wasn't Audrey, the one you went to Mexico with that time, I know. And she wasn't the neurosurgeon lady from Canada, the one with the long black hair."

"No and no," Landau said.

"Wait a minute. Wait."

Landau nodded. "Right. Now you've got it."

Georges looked at him commiseratingly. "Ooh, I'm sorry, Anthony. She got to you, I know she did. She was the big romance."

"No, not so big."

"You were in love with her. Seriously in love. She was the love of your life, you once told me."

"No, I never said anything of the kind. Does that sound like me? 'Love of my life'? Come on."

"That's what you told me. That's what you said."

Not going to argue about it, Landau decided. Have it your way.

"You were messed up over her for years. I remember it well."

"I don't. What is that concept, anyhow, 'the love of your life'? It makes no sense. It's incoherent."

"No it isn't."

"Life is movement, perpetual changement. Which life are we having the love of, can you tell me that? You have to solve that problem first."

Georges liked when Landau got this way: sententious about his own emotions. It fed into Georges' theory about the uptightness of all Britons, all half-Britons, too, for that matter.

"If you live a fairly busy life," Landau went on, "as I have, there's never just one love-of-your-life. There may be three or four. There may be half a dozen. The whole idea's confused."

"Oh, what a load of crap."

Landau decided to take a different tack. "There she was. Dead in my bed. I was shocked, deeply shocked, and then I was very sad. It has to do with the body, the actual physical body. How thoroughly it's been stilled. The loss of all that capacity. She was a vital person, Samantha, a large and fascinating person, and whatever else she was, she was immensely capable."

"Yes, that's all she was—capable."

"I didn't say that."

"Look, Anthony, I know what she meant to you. I was there. I held your hand. I took you to the desert when you were half out of your mind. I even tried to get you to go to Chiang Mai with me, for a little vacation. You were beside yourself. You were so fucking dark in those days, so fucking..."

"If I was dark, it was because she sabotaged me professionally. She brought that complaint against me, that spurious complaint, hoping it would ruin me. I would never do that to anybody, let alone a former lover. That's not cricket, you know. Not playing by the rules."

"You got to her, Anthony, and she had to get back at you."

"No, don't justify her, please. I did *nothing* to her, nothing. She went to war simply because it helped her professionally. That's despicable. It's beneath notice. And after me, it was down the black chasm of fame. She was never herself again. They had to stick her off in her own institute finally, with nothing but toadies around. She couldn't play with the other children, couldn't stop biting, scratching, destroying."

Here was the funny thing about Georges: the feeling-ful Californian, all impulse and intuition, a dissenter from Cartesian rigor if anyone was, was nevertheless a close reader of Landau's papers. The more dense and mathematical, the better he liked them. He aimed to have a whole collection of them.

"She claimed you'd taken her Monte Carlo numbers, misappropriated data sets, something like that. Am I right? Then buried her name on the paper. Didn't show it prominently, insulted her."

"I really don't remember what she claimed, Georges. She conjured up a whole stew of lies. She was deranged, completely deranged at the time."

"That was mid-nineties. Right?"

"Possibly. From a reputation-smashing point of view, it was convenient that I had been accused of something similar long before. You see, there was an earlier feminist harridan smashup, with another knife-wielding monster careerist. Someone who I should never have taken under my wing, but I was foolish, overconfident. I thought that generosity and fair dealing could tame her."

"Which one was that?"

"You don't know her. Afsaneh Khosaddi. Sometimes called herself Abigail. I took her on as a postdoc, and she filed a complaint saying that I had raped her. When that didn't wash, said I'd raped her psychologically, bad atmosphere, workplace talk of women's backsides, that kind of thing. Quoting chapter and verse out of the talk-show blather of the time. It was all about her tearing off a piece of my research territory. And the terrible accusations of soul-murder disappeared as soon as I let her get away with it."

"Okay."

"My point is, Samantha knew about that. We used to laugh about it together. Then one day she's put together a complaint of her own. Using the same terminology, the same type font practically. Makes me look like a serial abuser, you see, a predator. Again, when I ceded her a great chunk of research terrain it went away. She took control of the whole bloody grant for all intents and purposes. After that, she fell silent."

Georges asked Landau about the research he had done with the first woman, this Abigail person. Landau had to think hard.

"It was drug treatment stuff, about AZT and other early meds, because they had to be administered in sequence, and people doubted that junkies would stick with the program till it did them good. One of the first studies of that kind. High HIV-rate street injectors."

"I'd like to read that one."

"No you wouldn't, Georges. It's not like the brothel papers, not that they were so fascinating. Although, the central issue, maybe we got on to that before the others did. I suppose you could argue that if you wanted."

"No, I want to read it, I want a copy."

"Look it up on BioMed."

"Well, did you, Anthony? Did you have your way with her?"

"Did I what?"

"You know—did you screw her. Were you intimate."

"Now, that's private territory, Georges, even you know that. And a gentleman never tells."

"Come on. I won't think the worse of you if you did."

"Let me put it this way. She was a ravishing young woman, 'a type more Greek than Italian,' if you know what I mean. Endlessly seductive, a little unhinged. Family got out just before the revolution. Father close to the Shah, his personal urologist, actually, with SAVAK connections. Over here he couldn't get a license to practice medicine so he became a caretaker in an apartment house, became a real estate agent, put four kids through school, one to Stanford, one Princeton, one Berkeley, Afsaneh went to Swarthmore. Oh, America, give us your tired, your poor! I love these splendid immigrant stories. By the time she was on my projects she was an MD-PhD, but with a bad reputation, known for manipulation. I didn't care. I like dames with a screw loose. So, did I have my way with her? One never has one's way with such a person, Georges. One serves her purposes, then hopes to staunch the bleeding."

"Well?"

"No, I don't think I did. I don't recall that."

That led him, later that afternoon, to reflect upon his career. Not his science career, his romantic one. The realm that had opened up so promisingly to begin with, as an arena of pure fun. As a complete whale of an aging man now, a beluga whale, he was *hors de combat*, an inoffensive old duffer, sexless, useless, and the idea that he had had a romantic life would have shocked the other swimmers at the pool that afternoon. Georges two lanes over, briskly chopping through the lucent *eau*. Georges had had his many adventures, had been a prostitute-procurer, massage-parlor adept, before he got religion, and more power to him, if that was what he liked. Some men were able to be aroused by the purchase of favors, but Landau not. He froze up around prostitutes—he had interviewed hundreds in the old days, had studied tens of thousands, but as far as doing business, no, that was hopeless. If I am paying you for these intimate acts, then where is the interest for me? If you're pretending, nut-rolling or not even bothering to, well, I would rather read a book. Rather pare my nails.

That left women out in the world, collected in the wild, the ones that Fate gave you. Colleagues of one kind or another, quite often. Those who spoke his mumbo-jumbo were easier to chat up. You had to take care not to poach on inferiors, and he had been mostly honorable about that. Inferior-superior relations being no ingredient of his excitement. One might say that he had gone about looking for an equivalent of dear old Mum most of his life—solid person, decent enough person, intellectually his equal or better, caring but not too fussy, good legs. Was that asking too much? For the moon and stars? Okay, he had never found her, life had not delivered her, so, just push on. Swim harder.

A few laps farther along, he achieved the modest endorphin raise that made everything seem solvable. Life had not turned out for him? He was disappointed? Look—at least you're not dead. At sixty-four you have a few friends, you're still tottering about, you have a house and a bursting IRA, and you wrote some scientific papers that some people will remember for a brief period. You're lonely, you big baby, that's all, but so what. In your idiot heart you still thought you and Samantha would get together again. That there would be a third act, despite the lapse of a full ten years. Shows what a dry spell you've been living through, that you nursed that absurd fantasy. You never accepted the truth, the truth as someone sensible would see it: Deena, for instance. Deena's take on Samantha Beevors, based on a single encounter at a dinner party, had been that Landau was in trouble. She had maintained a diplomatic silence throughout the mad affair.

His son, Jad, had not called, kind of remarkable considering Landau's presence on the Web and in the papers. Smelling of chlorine and with that glow of full-chested well-being that follows a swim of sixty lengths or so, Landau dialed his son's work number, left a gruff message, then, back home, he was puzzled by something he saw in his library/den—a slim gap in a bookshelf. He realized that an item had gone missing. He thought first of Elfridia, of the fun-loving Chiapas maids who dusted and fussed in here. He knew what was where on his shelves, and this gap was in the modest pornography section, that part of it that included a bit of classic French filth sent him by an old London friend, Joseph Maxie, another academic-science worthy, a yeast geneticist, to be exact. Joe was a buddy from the deep diaper time, from St. Paul's and the whole musty-fusty British past. Friend with whom he had first explored Paris, had first teenagerishly smoked Gauloises, viewed the odd Jean-Pierre Melville film. They had bought dirty books together down on the quai, then smuggled them back across the Channel. Little devils that they were.

Joe had found an edition of the very kind of paperback that they had treasured back then, a book of smudged black-and-white offsets of women from the twenties or thirties, *poules* to judge from their workaday attire, shown pulling up their skirts while they enjoyed a glass of Calvados, or completely bare-assed but for a single garter, posed doggie-style. The book was hardcore in parts, the last pages offering women in leather masks, some tied up within an inch of their lives, breasts strangulated, throats encircled, fetishy, twisty stuff, of a kind that Landau had found deeply puzzling as a schoolboy. He had put it on the shelf right *here*, not knowing what else to do with it, since old friend Joe had bothered to send it.

No, the maids wouldn't have taken that. Probably, it was one of the policemen. There had been scads of them through here that night, touching everything, and maybe this would turn up somewhere down the road, as proof of his ominous psychopathology. Oh, well. If anyone ever asked him about it, he would try to explain Joe's facetious intent—"You see, we used to go to school together, and at fourteen we went to Paris on the boat-train for three days once, for a first taste of *vin rouge*. Joe studies yeast prions now. Prions are those things that cause mad cow disease. They occur in yeast cells as well as in human nerve cells. Isn't that fascinating?"

By gad, though—it was uncanny how everything seemed to point to this, to his lonely, unhealthy bachelorism. To that part which seemed to mark him out as not quite a solid citizen. Is that what I am, really, an unsolid citizen? The fact that I'm not married, that I have the remnants of an urge now and then, haven't been entirely a choirboy—is that what defines me? But surely this is the case with everyone, once prying eyes and fingers are allowed inside the boudoir. He decided not to worry about it. He experienced an exhilarating moment of panic, however, as he caught sight of himself in some mental mirror—recognized the Landau whom police investigators and crime reporters might take him for. The man as defined by his actions in the world, not according to some airy-fairy self-conception. By that crude standard, he *was* a bit funny. Even *he* thought he was funny.

chapter 4

Howe Street, Oakland. Kaiser Hospital. Grimmish stretch of functional California stucco structures, parking garage, patients swarming the sidewalks, black and brown folk, mainly. ER entrance over there. Landau on foot in the medical crowd, pigeon-toed, small stride for so large a man, something almost geisha-girl in his forward shuffle, moving just a little faster than everyone else. Looking, always looking. Up and down and all around. On the streets of Oakland in the eighties he had noticed small vials, two-inch-long glass ones as big around as a pencil, with black plastic screw-tops. Had begun to collect them, in a small way. When he showed them to friends, they were baffled—like him, they had been crunching them underfoot for months, but no one had bothered to pick one up. Crack vials, they were. Some of the very first.

Son Jad, short for Jared, ate lunch in a windowless room on the fifth floor of the Howe Street building. He had brought an extra sandwich for his father to munch on, plus carrots. Landau had to look up at his slender, balding son, a full six foot five, 195, marathoner, triathlete, stringently fit. Married now, hardworking Kaiser GP. Stethoscope, white coat, the works. "What the *fuck*, Dad?" asked Jad. "What the *fuck*?"

"I know."

"Samantha! Samantha!"

"I know. They can't tell us much yet. All they know is she died soon before I found her, maybe only a couple of hours."

"Just appeared in your bed, dead? After all these years? Did she still have a key?"

"I don't know that. They found nothing on her, no shoes, no clothes, no purse. It's as if she'd been transported there through the air."

Landau's son looked at him intently. Then his gaze went elsewhere, as if some new thought had occurred—these moments of lost focus, if that's what they were, were all that remained of a youth full of diagnoses of ADHD and other au courant deficits, when his teachers had argued for this or that psych drug, powerful brain-straighteners, paradoxical sedatives, antidepressants. The boy would enter a fugue state, and, true, he had been a mess in school, despite fleeting indications of intelligence. "I'm afraid we're losing him," the headmistress at a fancy alternative academy had said to Landau and his ex-wife, Margery, at one dark juncture, but Landau had refused to see the situation as hopeless—"I was just like that," he told them, "I was all messed up at age twelve or thirteen, always in a sort of dream—some new phrenological bump was forming, some new connections in the brain, and things worked out, eventually."

They put Jad on antidepressants. Did him no good whatsoever. Thereafter, Landau had decreed, he would have to experience adolescence cold turkey, or only under influence of such drugs as he could score himself. The fey fuguer had turned into a skateboarding snotnose, savagely at war with all adults, Landau included, Landau indeed preeminent. Father and son never really "bonded" afterward. And after the dark time had come the indifference. Jad chose to live with his mother, and Landau wanted to tell him, "I wish you all the best, son—I could never manage that myself." Something raffish about Landau, too powerful, bothered the straight-arrow college boy who emerged from all the skateboarding and video-gaming. He was going way over to the bad side, Landau suggested to Georges, would probably end up a churchgoer and a Republican.

"Dad, I have good memories of Samantha, very warm memories. We were good friends, though it sounds kind of funny to say that."

"I know. She was very fond of you."

"She was always joking, making things seem bearable. And she gave me cool presents."

"I remember that. You loved her for the presents."

"You had your thing with her, but I had a different thing. Maybe a better thing, almost."

"Absolutely, it was better. No contest."

"Karin made you a portobello mushroom sandwich, you want it?"

"Sure, that sounds good."

Karin, pronounced *car-inn*: six-foot-one-inch Stanford Law grad, ex–volleyball star, happily unemployed for several years now, glad to be Jad's wife and not much else. She would pick up her career somewhere down the road—there was no hurry. They lived in a steroidal mansion on Alvarado Street in the Oakland hills, built in the wake of the 1989 fire, which had wiped out hundreds of modest older houses in the neighborhood. The professors and tax attorneys and neurosurgeons who had lived in charming rustic cottages before had scored fat insurance settlements and had rebuilt out to the edges of their burnt-over lots, and it was in one of these white-walled palaces that looked vaguely like research facilities that Jad and Karin were having their life now, just the two of them—they were determined not to have children.

"Mmmm, this is delicious, Jad, really good."

"She can cook, my wife, that's for sure."

"Yes, she knows her way around a fancy mushroom. I always said that."

"Tell me about it, Dad. The accident."

"They don't know if it was an accident. You want the police angle, is that it?"

"Start with that."

Landau narrated the day, the evening, what had followed. The story he told had acquired fluency and polish and a certain degree of irreality, Landau having read all the news accounts, of course, and seen all the TV and other coverage. That nice Detective Johnson was feeding reporters solid information, Landau suspected—he wanted to discourage speculation about Landau as mad-dog murder suspect, as savage killer amongst us.

Jad, as usual, seemed to go away as you spoke with him. If I were a patient, Landau reflected, if I had come in here to report some worrisome pains down my left arm, I would say at this point, "Hey, Doc, am I boring you? You got something more important to do? I'm thinking I could use your full attention." But all reports on Jad were that he was an excellent doctor, perspicacious, sensitive. They liked him at Kaiser, had already offered him a bump up in status, fewer clinical hours plus administrative duties, the usual Faustian sign of favor.

"Dad, did you kill Samantha?"

"Did I kill her? Gosh, Jad, you come right out and say it, don't you? Cut right to the chase."

"Well, I know she got under your skin. She brought that suit and everything."

"Jad—am I the sort of person who would kill a helpless woman? A former girlfriend?"

"She was never helpless, but no, I wouldn't think so."

"You wouldn't think so?"

"No."

Hardly a ringing endorsement. An effusive show of filial support. But don't go getting all huffy on him, Landau advised himself, no, applaud him for wanting the truth. That's good.

"Jad, this is your father speaking. The only father you will ever have. Maybe you think I *am* that sort of person, because of all the bodies that kept showing up during your childhood. The ones down in my torture chamber, in the basement. All my guns and thumbscrews and whips."

"You did have a nice gun. A really nice little gun."

"I've never owned a firearm, Jad, I've never needed one."

"It said 'Heckler & Koch' on the handle. It was black. You let me play with it from time to time."

Landau puzzled this over. "Oh, the prop, you mean. The fake gun from Naomi's play. Okay, I remember that."

"It felt real. Felt dangerous in your hand. It was a perfect replica."

"Didn't I give that to you?"

"Then you took it away again. Because I was bad."

Ah, ah. Landau was recalling more fully now. The great hugger-mugger when Jad had showed up at school one day with the gun. This was pre-Columbine, but even so. We take this most seriously, Dr. Landau, the administrator had told him, even though we understand it's only a toy. And hadn't that been the beginning of the shrink-driven attempts at an intervention? Wasn't that the prelude to Landau allowing his son to be drugged for a time? Aged thirteen or so, when he was just starting to grow freakishly tall?

"You're the one who's been busted with a gun, Jad. The only one in *this* family."

"Yes, but it was *your* gun."

"Why is that important?"

"I don't know. It just was."

"Jad, my son. Some day we'll find a discount analyst and work all this out, but until then I advise you to take two glasses of red wine a day and sleep eight hours."

"Dad, how much do you weigh now, do you have you any idea?"

"I'm not a weighing sort of man, never have been."

"Care to step into my office?"

"No, I prefer not to."

Jad suddenly lost all expression. Half turned away. "Suit yourself. But just look at you. I mean, come on."

"I get weighed and measured every year. They give me an echocardiogram and probe and palpate and send me on my way. And remember, I swim like a fish."

"There's nothing magical about swimming. It has to be combined with not gorging."

The face with no expression suddenly looked displeased. Was swimming a sore topic? "Probably I swim five times as much as you do," Jad added. "And I swim *hard*. I cross-train. So, I have a good idea of the benefits of swimming."

"Good. Then that's settled."

Landau went shopping afterward, at one of the monster local health-food depots. Long crowded aisles, down which he bulkily wended his way, able to find exactly what he wanted, exactly, organic bulgur wheat, goat cheese from that nice little farm in Bolinas, the wood-cured balsamic vinegar di Modena with the antique label. Whatever else was going to hell in the sixth year of the George W. Bush presidency, food delivery and food obsession were continuing their explosive evolution, and one could fondle six varieties of imported avocado on offer in the month of November, four of them organic, thank God.

International capitalism was working out the details for everyone with some money: for health nuts and fair trade–organic partisans as for buyers of SUVs and consumers of cosmetic-surgery services. But why is my world, my chosen little corner of it, all about eating and drinking? Why that, and not some other fanaticism? Here, look at this fabulous wine section, occupying a full aisle of the store. Good God, the sophistication of it, the geographic reach, he thought. Eight new pinots from Oregon, a clutch of South African syrahs, six award-winning Argentinian malbecs. Raised at such-and-such a height above sea level, by fourth generation vintners in alluvial soil of large granulometry, six months in American oak, three in French. One good-looking bottle offered for $8.99. Why, that was basically nothing, basically pocket change. How did the world do it, year after year? Who was getting screwed, the pickers of the grapes? The middlemen?

Berkeley had once been about other hungers, sex, revolution, that kind of thing. Landau had been close to a group of aspiring revolutionaries for a while, back in the now-risible sixties, and he was that rare veteran of the storied era who believed that it had come close to doing something dreadful, catastrophic. The right wing and the center, and most of the left wing now as well, mocked much of what had happened then as the self-regarding inanity worked up by a generation of draft-avoiding suburban babies, but Landau had looked his fellow grad students in the eye while sitting around kitchen tables with them, calmly discussing blasting vectors, wiring algorithms, throw-weights. The thing about Americans is that they love abstract ideas, and given an abstract premise for hating each other they will grow demented in the exhilarating ensuing slaughter—why, just look at the American Civil War, and it's not over yet. The country is still divided down its heart. It's a violent country—it has a violent *destiny*.

In front of a cooler full of exotic yogurts, Landau felt someone's eyes upon him, and he turned to face a woman of about fifty, long gray hair, no cosmetics, yogini pants, earth shoes. Simply standing there staring.

"Sorry. I'll get out of your way."

But it wasn't the yogurts she was looking at. No, it was Landau himself. It amazed her that he was here, blandly, unapologetically here.

His first public sighting—that's what it was. His first celebrity unmasking. Now she wheeled away abruptly, somehow disdainfully—"Excuse me, madam," he wanted to call after her, "did you have something you wanted to say to me? You Birkenstock worthy, you? Yes, I'm here in public just like an ordinary citizen—they let us monsters out in the daylight hours. And after I finish here I'm going out on the street and eat a couple of babies. Juicy black ones."

Maybe she mistook me for someone she doesn't like—her ex-husband. Her brother-in-law. But no, no, it's me. In a way, it was remarkable that so *little* had been made of him, him and his curious case. It was Scott Peterson fatigue, perhaps. The wife-and-baby murdering California brute of the last few years had exhausted everyone, even the *San Francisco Chronicle*, and in comparison his own situation was barely tabloid worthy. The death of a scientist, a woman pushing sixty herself—come on, where was the thrill in that? No fetuses fished out of the bay, no armless torsos.

Five books had already been written about depraved, magnetic Scott, who resided these days on death row, San Quentin. Many women were said to be writing to him.

Landau found an email awaiting him at home. Elfridia, the maid, who cleaned at Deena's alternate Wednesdays, had failed to show up, Deena said. Elfridia's cell phone was now dead. Deena reminded Landau that the maids had once gone silent following a simple traffic stop—they lived in fear of the Immigration, and any attention from any police agency was likely to put them in deep cover. She'd hoped they'd show this week though, because she was having a party Saturday and the house was a mess. Was Landau free Saturday, by the way? And did he know what had happened to the maids?

chapter 5

H e didn't know, and then Detective Johnson reported the same thing, that Elfridia Tojolobal couldn't be found—her phone wasn't working, and she wasn't at the apartment on San Pablo Avenue whose address Landau himself had provided the police, where she'd been living with her cousins. Some men were there now, also from Chiapas. Detective Johnson spoke bad Spanish, he confessed, and probably he had said the one thing he shouldn't to the man who had come to the door: "With permission, *señor*, I'm looking for someone, and I'm with the Berkeley Police Department...."

"Right," Landau replied, "that would've put them off. She gave me that address over a year ago, anyway. Probably they just moved somewhere else."

"Maybe."

"What else can I help you with, Detective?"

"Well, if you hear from them, just to tell them that I would never report them. That's not how I behave. We want to know what they saw that day, that's all. And you want us to know that, too, of course."

"Of course."

"So, three of them, you say?"

"Three maids? Yes, sometimes. But mostly it was just Elfridia who came. She was the one I paid."

Landau was doing a wrong thing, he knew—meeting with a policeman without his lawyer present. But when the detective had called, reporting the missing maids, he'd mentioned that he'd seen Landau in Café Torino having a cappuccino, and Landau had replied that Torino was his favorite these days, of all of Berkeley's cafés, because you could usually get a window table. Somehow this had turned into a coffee date. Landau was often there on Thursday and Friday mornings, and the detective had observed that the problem wasn't getting a window table, it was getting one close to an electrical outlet, so you could plug in your computer.

"Plug away, Detective. There's a plug over there, and there's one behind the chair, too," Landau said.

"That one's dead. It's been out of whack for over a year."

"I like it here because I fit at the tables. I don't at every café."

"It's okay during the week, but Saturdays it's getting to be like the French Hotel, a big line, a crowd."

Kind of fun to be meeting a detective all casual-like. Berkeley cops probably hated Berkeley: think of all the sensitivity training they had to endure, the layers of political correctness inflicted on them. Generations of self-righteous left-wing city governments had made the force hyper-diverse, had fought to ban the bomb, free Huey Newton, free Leonard Peltier, shed no blood for oil. It would make for a certain amount of heavy ribbing when you went to conferences with your policemen colleagues from around the state: "I want you to meet my friend Byrum here," they'd say, "he works in *Berkeley*, the poor dumb bastard."

Detective Johnson didn't seem like a Berkeley-hater, though. He was dressed like any local on a casual Friday, in wrinkled pants, comfy shoes, a fleece top over a T-shirt, with a laptop squirting out of his arms. He even had a copy of the *Times*. Younger, better built than Landau remembered from that chaotic night at the house, only a week and a half ago, my God, it seems longer.

"Detective, don't you want one of those good cappuccinos?"

"At this point in the morning, Professor, I've already had about a quart of my own brew, so I think I'll pass."

"When do you get up usually?"

"Four thirty."

"Four thirty? Wow. Impressive."

"No, *you're* the impressive one, Doctor, *you* are."

"Why?"

"Because I've just read a bunch of your papers. The first one, from '71, was on rubella. Which I now know isn't the same thing as measles. You went to the Philippines with three pediatric specialists and studied an outbreak on Luzon island and the use of the new MMR vaccine that was coming in around then. You are one hell of a well-traveled distinguished scientist, sir. My hat is off to you."

"Thank you. But a lot of people travel for work. You don't necessarily get anywhere."

"When you look at the career as a whole, see the arc of it, that's impressive. I didn't know what an epidemiologist really does. What it all boils down to."

"And that is?"

"Kind of being on top of everything. Being where the worst things are happening, all the time. Getting to know the world the way the rest of us never do. Never have to."

"That's flattering, I guess. Are you buttering me up, Detective?"

"Look here." He fooled around with his clunky laptop for a while, couldn't get something to upload. "Show you later. Anyway, I figured out where you were year to year by logging your publications, and it looks like twenty-some trips to Africa in fifteen years. *Twenty separate trips.*"

"Couldn't be that many. More like a dozen. Only a couple meant anything, anyway."

"No, come on, and that's in between trips to Vietnam and Thailand and Cambodia. Going to Burma lots lately, I notice. Reporting for the UN special commission on the insurgency, the SLORC against everybody else, health consequences thereof. Major AIDS problem, Golden Triangle heroin-dealing, arms-dealing, child prostitution. You don't think of people in the jungle getting into prostitution and having an AIDS epidemic—that's more like a slum disease, right? But that's not true. Injector studies you did over there, strangely parallel to your San Francisco studies. Then, Latin America. Guatemala and Mexico mainly. I have you in Sinaloa last spring, after a couple of weeks in Mexico City. Sinaloa is the major Mexican poppy-growing state, I believe, that's where all the drug stuff starts."

"I guess. That's what people say, anyway."

"Maybe you were there on vacation. You've certainly earned a vacation."

The detective was shaking his head in amazement. But where are we going with this? Landau began to wonder. He could descry a portrait struggling to emerge, of a raffish "professor" figure who goes where the action is, to the cities of Asia to hobnob with prostitutes, to certain notorious drug regions, to the go-go zones. How stupid do they think I am, really? Is this not another TV show, *Columbo*, perhaps? With the fatuous perp trapped in his own superiority? Tripped up by flattery?

"And your point is, Detective?"

"Just that you're always taking on risk, always at the center of things. It must come from a deeply compassionate place, to want to encounter that much misery and do something about it. You show up where the world is at its most hopeless, at its sickest."

"For really, really hopeless, I would say, certain slums in Bangladesh. They beat everything, hands down."

"Okay. I'll remember that."

Landau waited. Then he said, "Seems to me you're working up a curious dossier on me, my friend. Is that necessary?"

"Oh, it's just the job. It's interesting to me, getting to know someone like you. Do you know who Glenn Seaborg was?"

"Seaborg? Hmm. Not sure."

"He was an atomic bomb guy. Manhattan Project. All that."

"Okay. Yes, I think I've heard of him."

"Another big thinker living quietly up here in the Berkeley Hills. Like having Einstein as your neighbor. They had a break-in at his place, and I was the cop sent up. He was eighty-six at that time. The most fascinating man I ever met, by far. Sharp as a tack although his body was failing, everything from the neck on down was useless, he said."

"Glenn Seaborg. Discoverer of uranium-235, if I'm not mistaken."

"No, not uranium—plutonium. God help him, he brought us plutonium."

"Oh, oh. That's a heavy burden. For him and for the rest of us."

"Right, I expect it was."

Detective Johnson then told a story about Darth Vader-ish Glenn Seaborg, how, that day when the policeman answered the burglary call, they'd had a sherry together. Seaborg could talk about a million subjects, but he'd turn everything back to arms control eventually—if you talked about golf, about your recent hemorrhoid surgery, somehow he'd bring it back to that.

"Did it in a making-fun way. 'Of course that's all I'd want to talk about, isn't it?' But absolutely determined to talk about that, really say the truth about that. Not be trivial, not at this late juncture. I was just some ignorant detective but he engaged me the way he engaged presidents, secretaries of defense, Eisenhower, Dulles, Churchill. Other brilliant scientists. Oppenheimer—another local guy, by the way. Berkeley Hills guy."

"Did you have a personal relationship with Robert Oppenheimer, too, Detective?"

"No, and I didn't have one with Seaborg, either. I just had sherry with him a few times. Oppenheimer, now, that would've been fun. He's my favorite from among those atomic bomb men. Teller's the only one I truly don't like. Doctor Strangelove in the movie. Unless you believe it was Kissinger who was the inspiration—have you read Christopher Hitchens on Kissinger, by the way? Now, that's a hell of a book."

What fun—just talking to my friend here, my new detective friend. Landau searched for a reason to cut this interview short, but the man's good face and forthright genial manner were disarming. No doubt he wants to get some angle on you, he's feeling you out, not so sure you're entirely innocent, but that's okay. You can ride with that. Just be your charming, becomingly modest self. He's a copper, but that doesn't mean he's the enemy. Even cops are sometimes what they seem to be.

"Byrum—did you get the autopsy results yet?"

"What? Oh, yeah. Some of them."

"And?"

"Well, it's funny. We almost didn't get to do one. The husband dug in his heels. Was strongly opposed."

"The husband? Bill Beevors?"

"Right. Also a big doctor-professor, as I understand. Said she would've been opposed to it, so he was opposed. Didn't want it."

"Samantha would've opposed it?"

"Right. Religious Jews don't like autopsies, see. But even the Orthodox come around, when we explain how sensitively it's done these days, how respectfully. Then, there's the public health angle. Jews are big on public health, usually."

"Samantha wasn't Jewish. She was born half-Jewish, but she never practiced a religion. No, she was a village atheist type, a scientific skeptic. Thought all religion was bunk, basically. Scoffed at it."

"Yeah? Well, the husband said different. Maybe she'd changed lately."

"I doubt that. Could she have changed that much?"

In any case, the autopsy had showed Samantha to be in good health for a woman her age, except for one fatal flaw. She had a minute problem with her AV node artery, what was called fibromuscular dysplasia of the AV coronary node. That had produced a stenosis—a blockage, in other terms—and she went out like a light, bing, bam, all she wrote.

"Could've happened at any time," the detective said. "Didn't have to be unusual stress, didn't have to be anything. But, probably stress was involved. The medical examiner thought so."

"Dysplasia, coronary dysplasia. That's exceedingly rare, I'm thinking. I've heard of renal arterial and spinal dysplasia, but never that."

"Yeah, well, but that's what it was. They're almost one hundred percent on that. And when it does happen it's fatal. Bottom line, her heart stopped, blood couldn't go, and she died."

It jibed with the blogger story, Landau reflected, about her fainting in front of an audience. So, Samantha had had a bad heart! All those years, just lying in wait for her—had she been aware of it somehow? Aware of her mortality? What was that novel with all the heart business—oh, right, *The Good Soldier*. By Ford Madox Ford. Ford Hermann *Hueffer*, to give him his proper name. A Hueffer and a puffer.

"The night she died—were there any medical examiners up at my house?" Landau inquired.

"Examiners? Probably. Sure, and they usually they beat us to the crime scene. They're very good in this county. Very professional."

"I wonder, because I didn't see anybody who was doing that kind of work."

"You don't necessarily see them, Professor, but they're there. They kind of hang back, until they get their body to play with."

And that was about that. The detective made another attempt to pull up something on his computer, succeeded this time, and showed it to Landau—it was the long list of the trips of the last two decades, correlated with his paper publications. Mad movements all about the globe, an unconscionable number of them. Suggested someone just unable to sit still, someone profoundly restless. Just think of all the frequent-flyer miles, had he only been smart about that. Then the detective had to rush off, to a meeting, and Landau was left by himself in the café, wondering if he had advanced his cause or done it grievous damage. Hard to tell.

When he left the café he found a parking ticket on his windscreen—not a citation, it turned out, just a note scribbled on the back of a blank form. "If you hear from the maids," Byrum wrote, "please get in touch with me immediately. I am making formal inquiries in Mexico and elsewhere but they could take some time. Things being what they are down there. Pleasure talking to you today, sir, it was a distinct honor. Byrum."

chapter 6

To market, to market, to buy a fat pig. Or am I the fat pig? So Landau reflected as he bought flowers down at Monterey and Hopkins that quiet Saturday morning, to bring to Deena's later. Didn't really need food but went into Monterey Market anyway, across the street from the flower shop, along with what felt like five hundred other Berkeleyans of roughly his vintage, finicky eaters and cookers all, wrinkled and gray-haired now, the rampart-rushers of '68 gone cranky, gone peculiar. In the narrow aisles of the grungy but bursting veg market, one had face-offs with angry Free Speech grandmas, all of them intent on getting their own stuff right now, *right now*. Sneaky old Asian ladies, too, with kampong-honed moves, with ballsy ways that put him in mind of Wangfujing Street, Beijing, the market there. Kept him on his toes.

Was he wrong, or was there a lift in the public mood? The Dems had just taken Congress. Nancy Pelosi, local gal, was to be the new Speaker of the House. Is that why the fight to get a shopping cart is more benign today than usual? Less grumpy-desperate? And look, that woman over there is actually smiling at me. No—she's looking my way, but she's not smiling, and now she's turning around. Another celebrity sighting? Have I been outed again? Once these people know me as the woman-scientist-murderer of Hopwood Lane, they will turn on me with a special savagery, because the oppression of women has not been forgotten hereabouts, not at all, and it's but one small step from snuffing an ex-lover to tossing acid on helpless schoolgirls in Pakistan. You may get away with that kind of thing in other places but not here in Berkeley, by God. And here came that woman, wheeling up out of the string bean and parsley aisle, almost running into him.

"Sorry to bother you. I'm Melody, from the pool? Arthur Fromm's wife? I think I know you."

"What? Oh—hi there. Melody. Yes, of course. Melody."

"I recognized you, although I'm more used to seeing you in a bathing suit."

"Dark vision, that."

She didn't seem to understand him at first. Then she smiled.

"No, not so bad. But I wanted to tell you, I was sorry to hear about your friend. I knew her slightly, from a long time ago. I used to be one of her students."

"You were Samantha Beevors' student?"

"Yes. I was in the school of public health in the mid-eighties, when she had an appointment. I'm not talking about here—I'm talking about the U of Illinois."

"So you're some kind of doctor?"

"No. I'm just a physical therapist."

"Ah, can you fix my bad back?"

"Probably. But not here. Not right now."

"My chiropractor wouldn't allow it, anyway. He's very jealous. Only he can touch my lumbars."

"Georges Vienna, right?"

"Yes, how do you know that?"

"Everybody knows Georges. And you and I talked about him once—at the pool."

Now, why don't I remember that? Landau wondered. I've been forgetting things lately, many important things. Can't remember ever looking closely at this woman before, the way she deserves to be looked at. The way I'm looking now.

"What's the physical therapy take on chiropractic? Have they got it all wrong?"

"Well, it's crackpot science," she replied. "But some of them have a gift, and they can bring enormous relief."

"Maybe that's true for all of us, don't you think? Doesn't matter what ideology we've got sluicing around our overheated brains, if someone's got the touch, really got it, then nothing else matters. Carries all before it."

"Yes, but I prefer that my doctor know something about real science. The same way I prefer that my accountant know the fundamentals of profit and loss. Let's not leave everything in the realm of the touch, the magic touch, please."

"I'm with you there."

She seemed about to hurry on. Landau wished that she would tarry a bit, but he couldn't think of anything to say.

"Your friend. Doctor Bernstein Beevors," she continued. "One of the reasons I didn't go on in public health is because I had her class in biostatistics, and I went to her office to talk to her once."

"Wicked hard grader, I bet."

"Not so bad. Having her for a professor was like having Socrates teach you basic arithmetic. Completely wasted on us innocent boobs. She said that she liked teaching first-year students because they were so wrong-headed. She was very kind, very sweet to me."

"Hmm. Not my memory of her, but no matter."

The woman paused for a second. "Well, we knew her in different capacities. I liked biostatistics, I saw the point of it. But sometimes I fell asleep in class. One day I fell asleep standing up in the back of the hall. Like a horse falling asleep in a pasture."

"Indicates what, drastic boredom?"

"I guess. She listened to what I had to say, and then she said that some people were cut out to be public-health administrators and others weren't. Some should go to med school. Deal with patients directly."

"Oh, so you *are* a doctor."

"No. But she was right, I wasn't happy till I was laying my hands on people. Going skin to skin. Roughing them up a bit."

"Okay, now I get it."

Funny little encounter. A bit of a charge, a man-and-a-woman sort of charge, almost below the level of detection. Am I fooling myself? Woman comes up to a human whale in a veg market, Landau reflected, smiles up into his face, says a few ordinary words and listens to what he says in return. About how she likes to touch people. Rough them up. Gee, I don't know, but it's sunnier in here all of a sudden. Look at these organic miniature beets, I want some. Garlic shoots, fragrant bunches of them, and little butter lettuces, raised organically at Long Lea Farms, Olema, California. Give me some of them, too.

The day passed happily enough, but with a background feeling of mild desolation. Often that was the quality of time spent in Berkeley, on the streets and under the blue, blue skies. And why? The place was rife with pleasure, agreeable sights often met the eye, and the weather was boringly splendid. In November you might walk about in a short-sleeve shirt, with leather sandals on your feet, sandals over socks. (Deena had reprehended him about this several times: do not wear white socks with sandals, Landau, please, not in public anymore. But he did it anyway, rejoicing in the dorkiness of it—his mother had dressed him that way as a boy, and it made him think of her.)

But the desolation, the mild anxiety. The perfect skies induced, by their very serenity, a feeling of failure; if you cannot succeed here, where nature is your pal, then there's not much that can be said for you. Imagine what a lazy washout you'd be in Cairo, say, or Vladivostok. Somewhere a bit challenging. Landau fell into a low-grade grumbling at himself; you almost achieved something, he complained, but you lacked endurance, and your life, as Chekhov once said of himself, has lacked a general idea. You've had fabulous advantages yet have ended up like this, asleep on your feet, out to pasture, indeed. Funny that the detective sees you as such a star, an exemplar—even if he's simply bullshitting you, telling you that to soft-soap you, you know the truth, and it's not that good.

*   *   *

That night, at Deena and Harold's house. Part-ay *on*. The occasion was Harold's winning of a prize from the International Association of Constitutional Law Societies. Harold was entirely prizeworthy, why just look at him. Absolutely the crème de la crème of academic Berkeley there, non-hard-science Berkeley. Landau knew these people socially, but he was unable to talk to them. Couldn't go up to one in front of the tabouli bowl and say, "I just saw the new Coen brothers movie, I liked it, what about you?" They'd sneer. In the first place, who the hell were you to speak to them? And in the second, their precious brain space was occupied with more recherché materials than *O Brother, Where Art Thou?* No, but they knew who he was, surely they knew. Knew he was some soft-money guy over there at UCSF, trailing a bit of a reputation but nothing world-shaking, and they'd met him a half a dozen times but couldn't remember his name, no, not quite.

They talked about their travels, about their brilliant children. They'd had a sabbatical last spring in Barcelona in a house designed by Luis

Barragán, had just flown in last night from Milan, after giving the Dessini Lectures in Bologna. Landau knew the brag-value of globetrot-ting, so he didn't derogate them too harshly for that, but it became old, the internationalism. Enough about what a jet-setter you are. And here was one of his favorite examples, a professor of French history, nominally an Englishman, who had written a famous book about masturbation. A stocky, nervous fellow with a thick face and a chesty laugh, whose almost-English accent waxed or waned as he drank or didn't, who had done grad work at Cambridge thirty years ago and still looked all tweedy. And here was another, a famous professor of Bible studies, probably the grandest panjandrum in the room, a short man with the face of a sleepy Bacchus, a winner of many prizes himself, recent retranslator of the five books of Moses. Landau had been seated beside him at a dinner a few years ago. It had been the impossibility of discussing anything not about the man or his work that had impressed Landau, who foolishly had broached an unrelated subject only to have the grandee fall into perfect silence, as one does when a child says something impossibly foolish.

"How's it going there, Professor Lex?" Landau asked now, looming above the head of white curls. "You remember me, don't you? Landau. Anthony Landau."

"Oh—hello."

"But enough about me. Let's get to something important. What are you doing these days? How brilliant are you being?"

The man's half-lidded gaze slid across Landau's face, then away. No wonder these people don't remember you year to year, Landau remon-strated with himself—you're always spoiling for a fight, always getting up into their faces. The eminent figure walked away, unperturbed. Some friends were waving to him from across the room, and he went over there, to be treated with the fawning subservience he deserved.

All around the elegant ecru room, as important people continued to arrive, heartiness was breaking out, human sociability of one kind or another. So you couldn't say these were academics in the dusty old style, half-dead, intimidated by rowdy life. No, they lived large in their own way. Owned expensive things and constantly traveled, and they had sex with each other in odd combinations sometimes, and they reproduced. What was the problem, then? What was hard for Landau to take was the unrelenting *importanza*, the conviction of immense self-worth, and he thought that American academics were just a little worse than any others, and California academics worse even than East Coasters. Was it his mildly radical heritage that turned him against such types? His notional inheritance from a left-wing father? Yes, possibly, but these people were all left-wing, too, savvy Euro-Marxists, as they described themselves. But yes, his dad would've found them amusing, Landau liked to think. Would've thumbed his nose.

All right, all right, calm down now. You're at a party, make nice. Look for people to *enjoy*, not to condemn, you prig. What's the matter with you, why so ornery, so unclubbable? No—just be a good fellow.

He went over to the drinks table. Started with a big glass of white. Harold was nearby, flanked by three men who must have been fellow law professors. "Anthony, thanks for coming," Harold said. "It's very good to see you."

"My pleasure. And all honors to you, sir," and Landau touched his forehead lightly with his wineglass.

"I'm thinking, the committee made a big mistake."

"No, I don't think so, Harold, not at all."

Harold wanted to introduce Landau to the other men. They were all somewhere in their forties, all professors at Boalt Hall, Berkeley's prestigious law school, as Harold was. A bulky Chinese man with a mild moon face spoke in a voice so gentle that Landau immediately felt protective of him, wondered how he survived the rhetorical slash and burn of law school discourse. His Mayan-like face and neatly combed hair made him appear to be a schoolboy grown up too fast. Another, a wiry white man with narrow spectacles, watched Harold no matter who else was speaking in their little group. His wondering expression bespoke earnest discipleship—can you believe it, it seemed to say, I'm here talking with *Harold Blodgett*. And he accepts me as an equal, almost an equal.

Half an hour later, headed for the bathroom, Landau saw Deena saying farewell to the Chinese professor at the door. The man was speaking classroom-learned Mandarin, while Deena replied in something infinitely more fluid, more full of flavor. Deena looked terribly sexy tonight, but what else was new? She was being herself, that was all, in a bottom-hugging skirt and sleeveless silvery top, from which a single bra strap showed. Her Chinese dialogue concluded, she turned to Landau and said tartly, "Come, follow me into my kitchen. I need you."

"All right, but I have to take a leak first."

"Be quick."

Harold was in the kitchen when Landau returned. Deena was arranging dolmas and picholine olives on a big Fiestaware platter, while Harold stood next to her, laughing as he told her something that Landau couldn't quite hear. They looked comfortable together—married. Landau had never seen Harold looking quite so ebullient, in fact. Big prizes did that for you.

"My young colleague, the torture-memo writer," Harold said now. "That's who *that* fellow was."

"What, the one who just left?"

"Yes. My law school friend."

"Oh. Oh."

"Took guts for him to come tonight. Not exactly his crowd, politically. Personally, I despise every tendency of his corrupted mind, but I also like him, for some reason."

"From Dick Cheney's lair to a kitchen on Keith Street, eh, Harold?"

"Yeah, that's about the way it goes."

Deena looked over her shoulder. "Anthony, carry this out to the music room, please. And don't spill it."

"Okay."

"How's Raboy doing by you, Anthony?"

"Oh, okay, I guess."

"Anything new?"

"You know, that's the funny thing, Harold. No big alarms going off. No small ones, either. I guess the emergency is over."

"Well, better that than the other."

Landau nodded.

"Anthony, I never actually told you how sorry I was that you lost your friend. I know she was more than just a friend to you, that you went way back. I'm sorry, and I wish it hadn't happened."

"Thank you, Harold. That's kind of you."

It sounded like something he had practiced saying. Had rehearsed last night in front of a mirror. But that was okay. We aren't all of us models of spontaneous graciousness.

"It was a terrible thing, and I hope they figure out what really happened."

"Yes, me too," Landau said.

As he carried the platter out, he found himself wondering why he hadn't been invited to this party weeks ago. Harold had won his prize way back in September. Either it was because Deena took it for granted that he was part of her ménage, hardly needed to be personally invited, or perhaps Harold and she had debated the wisdom of including him among these A-listers, given his cranky performances in the past. Oh, who *cares* how or why I was invited—just put the platter down, there, that's a good fellow. Have another drink.

"Anthony, old man. What up?"

It was Richard Flense, the faux Cambridge don, the eminent historian of sex.

"What up, yourself, Richard? I'm down with whatever up."

Flense barked his resonant laugh. It made Landau feel warm toward him, slightly.

"Been going to Myanmar or wherever it is you go? Looking into more whorehouses?"

"Yes, I have been going occasionally, but not for about half a year now."

"Wish I had work like that."

"No, it grows tedious, Richard. They need scientific cover while they stir up trouble for the generals, the NGOs do. I provide them that cover. They rent me out."

"Ah, very good."

Flense often chewed his tongue. He had a thick neck and an impressive horsey head, as impossible to misconstrue as was his laugh.

"What's with you, Richard, writing another dirty book?"

"Oh, I have been writing a book, but not about anything fun, like sex. No, writing my big dark book on death, the one I've been working on for almost thirty years now. It'll kill me in the end."

"Death, eh? There's a subject. Why didn't I think of that."

"How the idea of it has changed over the eons. And goes on changing."

"That must be tough, Richard. You're sort of writing against a moving target, aren't you? The culture shifts wildly in thirty years. Not to mention three hundred, or three thousand."

"Tell me about it. It's maddening."

"When I was but a wee lad, Richard, history was something solid. The Napoleonic Wars. The Corn Laws. Now you history fellows write about anything at all, about the idea of 'the gift,' about 'textuality,' about masturbation, God help us. Which I enjoyed very much, by the way. I enjoyed your book."

"Did you, really?"

54

"Yes, I thought it was quite bold. Think of the ridicule that would have befallen if you hadn't brought it off. You'd have been known ever after as the silly professor of wanking, the nutty don who took jacking off seriously."

"It was a book that I was able to write with one hand, so to speak."

"Yes. Indeed."

"They're making a big deal of it in France. I'm an American pretending to be English, which amuses them. They appreciate imposture, the French do. It's in their DNA."

Landau took a third glass of wine. It puzzled him why Flense was being so friendly: they hadn't spoken in years, beyond a casual hello-there. Landau by ungovernable impulse became ultra-English around Flense, affected a parody posh U-English, to tweak the silly fellow. But here was Flense saying right out that he was an impostor, a poseur. Extraordinary statement coming from him: exactly what was the case.

Landau ate eight dolmas without noticing. Flense had turned away for a moment, and now here was his big head again, invading Landau's space.

"What really happened, though, Anthony? With Samantha Beevors, I mean?"

"What, you heard about that?"

"*Heard* about it? Why, people are talking about nothing else. *Le tout* Berkeley is obsessed with it. You are the exclusive hot topic, Anthony. People can't get enough of it."

"Funny, nobody talks to me about it. You're one of the first to say a word."

"Surely the *New Yorker* is some kind of indication of general public interest, no?"

"The *New Yorker*?"

"Yes, yes, the *New Yorker*, their big writer, what's-his-name."

Flense perceived that Landau had no idea what he was talking about.

"You don't know? Really? He's been asking around about you. He's planning a big story, one gathers. Brenda Appel knows all about it. He wrote that series about satanic child abuse, the one that got turned into a book. He's a bit of a star, Marcus Somebody-or-other."

"I have no frigging idea what or whom you're talking about, Richard. I'm afraid you've lost your mind."

Where was Brenda Appel, Brenda Frigging Appel? Going to get to the bottom of this right now, Landau decided. An article in the *New Yorker*—why, how absurd.

"Where is Brenda, the estimable Brenda?"

"I don't know, haven't seen her tonight."

Brenda Appel was a fixture at parties such as this. She was the wife of a distinguished Berkeley chair, a kind of West Coast book-world eternal aspirant, Brenda was, served on various PEN committees, showed up at lit conferences. Always asked you who your agent was. But Brenda Appel was not here tonight—Landau determined this by rushing about for two minutes, a dolma between thumb and forefinger, Richard Flense trailing behind.

"Damn her, anyway. Where is she when you need her?"

"I'll speak to her tomorrow. She knows him from college, I think."

"I can't believe that the *New Yorker*, in its magnificence, would care a fig for me or Samantha. Who is Samantha Beevors to the *New Yorker*?"

"What, are you kidding? Samantha was big, she was Nobel Prize material. Would've won a MacArthur except she was a little old when she hit big. One of the ten most important women scientists of the twentieth century—I heard them say so on TV."

"Oh, God, that ten-best list. Her mother made that up, I think."

"Why was she staying at your house, Anthony? I thought you two were on the outs."

"She wasn't staying at my house, Richard. She was *found* at my house—there's a difference."

"My question stands."

"Eh, I have no fucking idea. That's where she put herself—or was put by someone else."

Flense stuck his tongue out between his teeth, moving his eyebrows waggishly.

"Don't give me that look, Richard. Cambridge men don't leer, don't insinuate—no, they only aver."

"She was hung up on you, I always heard. Had never quite gotten over you."

"Oh, what rot. She wasn't hung up on me, she was hung up on her gargantuan career. Her glittering top-ten career."

"Bill Beevors is desolated, they say. Has fallen into a black depression."

"Oh, I don't like to hear that. I'm sorry if that's true."

"Yes, I like Bill. He's a good fellow."

"Yes, he is."

Good fellow, sort of, Landau said to himself. Schnook, victim—guy with a "kick me" target pinned to his rear. Bill Beevors had married Samantha at a time when she thought it useful to have an esteemed Stanford Medical School husband. When she ruined things for herself at clubby Stanford, as was inevitable, Bill Beevors also had had to fold tents, after a good thirty years in Palo Alto. Had to follow her to USC, on lesser terms.

"Listen to me, Richard," Landau now declared. "You're way too interested in this—it reminds me that you're a notorious gossip. I'll have no more to say on this subject, upon advice of counsel."

"Have I offended, Anthony?"

"Yes, telling me about magazine stories, about *New Yorker* stories. Look at me, I'm all upset, I'm in a sweat."

"I'm sure they'll treat you very kindly. You're a distinguished figure in your own right. Myself, I'd love to be the subject of one of their profiles. When will they get around to me, I ask? To wonderful me?"

"Something else Cambridge men don't do, Richard—lust for press coverage. And you need to stutter."

When he returned home that night, Landau already had the headache that normally would have afflicted him the next morning, a tension-and-dehydration type of needling prefrontal headache. He stood in front of his opened refrigerator not knowing what to think or do, then drank deeply of the cold Gerolsteiner *Mineralwasser* that he stocked by the case, almost a whole liter of it. Banged around in his kitchen without turning on any lights—where was Freddy, where was his damned cat? Open a food can and he'll come. The familiar tin-pucker and moist suction sound occurred, but still the cat failed to materialize, and Landau thought it odd that he would be outdoors tonight, because it was getting late in the year already, it was November already, the cold damp coming on. The life of my cat in the hillside dark, in the spectral, living night—who could ever write that savage, bloody drama? The vet absolutely forbad Freddy's roaming at will, said he needed to be an indoor cat at his age, and the vet also recommended declawing, to cut down on his ability to hunt. But Landau regretted that other little surgical adjustment he had made to his pet, the one that had made of him a pretend-tomcat, and he wasn't inclined to rob him of his claws, too. And I like it that he captures the odd songbird or wood rat. The life of the land is consecrated in righteousness, they tell us, for cats as for us humans. Let nature be nature.

He sat in his darkened kitchen for a while. Noticed that his chest was rising and falling rapidly. I'm heaving, he thought, I'm all upset—I haven't been running, haven't been climbing steep stairs, yet I'm gasping like a landed fish. All right, get a hold of yourself, man. Is it *New Yorker* anxiety, fear that someone might actually write about all this? But what's to fear from that? It's the other thing that Flense said, "You are the exclusive hot topic, Anthony. *Le tout* Berkeley is talking about you." Now, why do I cringe to imagine others talking about me, finding me of sudden interest? It's in connection to something unfortunate, something sad, but even if it had been a different sort of occasion, I wouldn't have liked it—even if I were the big prizewinner, like Harold, raking in the laurels, being reckoned one of the immortals. I long for prizes, too, as any man does, but I also squirm. People having their own ideas of you, detailed peculiar ideas: why, how *dare* they.

His breathing grew a bit calmer after a while. Head still throbbed, though—come on, get up, get yourself some Advil. He aimed himself for the cabinet where the vitamins and nostrums were, scraped a chair, and when he did so he felt an answering thump beneath his feet, in what would have been the basement, had his house had one, rather than the standard California crawl space. The low chamber down there was one of Freddy's favorite domains, so maybe that was where he was, catching the odd mouse tonight. The house went on creaking and groaning for a while, but Landau was unalarmed—it was a living house, on a moving hillside. He lived in earthquake country.

Would he ever feel as he once had, as he had felt as recently as a couple of weeks ago, about his house? He still didn't much want to sleep upstairs, funny little namby-pamby nightmare boy that he was. Still spooked about it: please, Mother, may I sleep in your bed tonight? Yes, Anthony, all right, come along, and bring Teddy if you like. Was that what he feared other people would perceive, his fuzzy, squishy core? No, that was okay: that the boy still lived inside him, remnants of the boy, he felt all right about that. Fatherless boy, hard-trying earnest boy. Scholarship boy who never cried. And now, to his astonishment, he was weeping, the tears were sweeping down. Hot, salt-smelling tears, out of nowhere, and he went on blubbering for quite a while, over nothing. Made himself stop, stand up straighter—come on, stop this foolishness now, get your head above the blubber-waves. But then slipped beneath them again.

What was he crying for, for Samantha? Had he been denying the great, profound tragedy of her sudden death, at too young an age? Or was it that he still missed her—still, after nine years? Yes, a little of that. The wound had healed, after a fashion, and he had moved on, yet he had found no one to replace her, and probably he never would. All right, stop crying in any case. But the blubbering went on, moist simpery blubbering. Crying for all of it, for the whole thing—for the *Appointment in Samarra* aspect of it, too, the way death lies in wait for us all, even the most invulnerable. In her charismatic egoism Samantha had seemed immune to death, and if some physician had dared speak to her of a coronary anomaly he'd found on the odd EKG, why, she'd have made him feel a fool. Would have stared him into the ground. Coronary dysplasia, indeed.

After a while the crying stopped. He stretched his neck and slumped down in a chair, exhausted. Was that a bit of the genuine "grief work" there? What they talked about on TV all the time, the deep-down working through, the "grief process," the Kübler-Ross–approved process? Whatever it was it had felt like something his body needed to do—an organic transaction even more than a psychological one. And now I feel a bit better. Think I'll go upstairs now, dare to sleep in my own bed tonight, like a big boy. For I am a big boy, indeed—yes, and I am master of my own domain.

chapter 7

Landau did nothing the next day, stayed home reading the *Times*. Did the Sunday crossword puzzle in ink and felt proud of himself. Fed and petted the cat, who first put in an appearance around 1:00 p.m., when Landau himself arose. A remnant headache, some sensitivity to light, nothing much. He called Deena to discuss the soiree of the night before. But she couldn't talk just then and promised to call him later. Spoke to Georges and planned a swim for tomorrow, at the Claremont, the high-tariff local swim and tennis club to which Georges belonged. Landau himself belonged to the Berkeley Y, a lesser facility in every respect, but institutionally more attractive, more his kind of place. Speaking of Berkeley, it was all there at the Y, in the over-chlorinated water, all the brown and black and yellow folk as well as the lefty whites. Landau had had it up to here with diversity talk, but the rubbing of elbows, the races all jumbled together in water, that seemed to him on balance a good idea.

Sundown so early now, barely 5:00 p.m. Had aimed for a walk up through the eucalyptus stands above his house, up along Grizzly Peak Boulevard for a mile or two, but dusk was already here, wintry foreboding dusk. Freddy had stayed by Landau's feet all afternoon. Sometimes he could convince himself that his cat knew him, felt for him—it was the odd sign of fealty now and then, unconnected to the feed bowl. He watched the sun decline, auburn and rose beneath a high-domed heaven. Walked onto the deck outside his kitchen windows to have a sniff of things, heard a scrabbling down below that drew his gaze that way—shocked to see a fat raccoon waddling off into the bushes, followed by a second, then a third. Why, the cheeky, overfed devils. They had colonized his house's under-parts in previous years, requiring him to spend hundreds coon-proofing the crawl space, but it had never worked for long, and they came back when they wanted. The thumping of the night before, here was the real reason. So, I have roommates again. Four-footed ones.

October 1989, during the World Series of that year, he had come upon an entire family of raccoons in the middle of his quiet woodsy street, placidly at rest. Parents, three cute kits, all of them simply posing on the pavement in the autumn afternoon. Not two hours later, there had come the greatest earthquake that Landau had yet lived through, the Loma Prieta, which had been heralded all over the region by wild animals behaving strangely. Said to be in response to premonitory tremors in the earth. So, batten down the hatches, mates, here comes another big one. That what it meant? Seeing raccoons in the gloaming? Raccoons owned the deep of night, if you came wheeling home at 3:00 a.m. you often saw them munching your garbage with impeccable sangfroid, but it was odd to see them like this, before the sun was truly down. So, better go down there and see. Show the flag, come on, do the hard thing.

Armed with a flashlight and a coat hanger, he ventured along the flag-stoned path that ran beneath his deck. There was an apron of hard-packed earth down here, adobe, protected from the elements by the overhang. Kind of a dead zone, saw no sunlight and grew nothing, not a single weed. Gad, it smelled, smelled like a den already, raccoony. How long has this been going on? Not clear how they were getting in and out, the latch on the crawl space door was still intact, but yes, disturbances to the earth beneath the bottom of the door, digging signs. Landau thought of a raccoon's paw at that moment, so anthropomorphic, with its clickety-clackety claws, digging in the cement-like earth. And over there was, indeed, an upturned hand, protruding beneath the crawl space door. A small hand, thin and bony. He straightened up and hit his head hard on a deck timber, a mental flash coinciding with the smash against his skull, and a spasm of fear and disgust raced through him. The blow to his head brought him down onto his knees, down upon the hard-packed earth.

Flashlight gone, dropped it somewhere, oh shit. Oh, oh, find it, here it is, oh God, oh God. A hand, a pale small hand. Not a raccoon's, no, a person's. Extending under the under-dug door as if begging to get out. A female-looking hand, it was. Landau grabbed the latch of the crawl space door to free her, and the smell that a pull on the door released was darkly vast, intensified by the enclosure, a smell out of Africa, of all places, East

Africa, if he didn't miss his bet. Uganda-Congo border, the Uganda side, and then he could see a pit under a turbulent sky, sixty or seventy bodies all tumbled together, a burnt-out church nearby, a lot of red earth. On one of his jaggy Africa trips, one of the last. But this that was before him was but a single arm, a severed arm, with sleeve material still attached. Fifteen feet within, nestled against the crawl space wall, was a human form, the face angled away, one thin knee upbent. Landau shone his light in that direction and looked and did not allow himself to look away. All right, you can breathe now. But get out of here, go settle yourself. Just get the hell out right now.

Standing up too quickly beneath the deck, gagging, gasping, he hit his head again against a timber. Something not quite right, oh, there it was, the arm, the beseeching needful arm. It had followed him out, had been kicked or dragged as he hurried through the passage. Not torn off at the shoulder, no, very evidently gnawed off. The palm and curled fingers full of personality still, oh, help me, please, they seemed to say, I beg of you. Don't leave me here, please save me. Using his hanger, with which he had planned to beat off raccoons, he hooked the arm back up the slope, back inside and out of view. The Poe-ish nature of the situation came upon him suddenly, causing a weird despairing grin to break out across his face. He clicked his flashlight off, then clicked it on again. Forced himself to go back under.

A young girl, in a shredded housedress. The right leg devoured above the knee, bent up because the bones had locked that way. Oh God, oh God. Hollowed out like a canoe she was, innards all gone, chest cavity all the way down to the back ribs, which were stained and yellowed. Everything else black, black. The brain half devoured, through the mouth it appeared, the jawbone hanging free. Make yourself look, Landau, go on. Then, don't ever look again.

Back outside again, gagging. He headed back up his flagstoned path. He could remember when he had put in this path, an Irish fellow and his crew, a team of energetic Guatemalans, had done it for him, the Irishman named Ian Something, Ian Pardee. Good workers, meticulous, cheerful. They had done such an excellent job that he'd had them build a retaining wall in the downslope corner of his backyard, and afterward he'd wished he had more work to give them, they'd been so much fun to have around. Pardee in the country on some questionable visa, those were the days when you often ran into stray Irishmen in the U.S., most of them back east but some trickling west, as their ancestors had done. There was a story he'd read in the papers, of a trio of brothers from County Down who had made it out to Mill Valley, of all places, who'd worked installing household appliances among the wealthy leisurely folk of Marin County, got in trouble with married women there, all three of them, women they'd met installing fridges. "It's the lingo," one of them had explained, "they can't get enough of it, hey? 'Say it in Irish,' they tell you, and the next thing you know, it's over the moon."

Glad I can remember that silly story, Landau thought. Made a big impression on me, obviously. Freud said there is never anything in behavior that's pure happenstance, and by the same token no thought ever appears in the mind for no reason, although to plot its etiology may be hard. But why am I thinking of Irishmen and their intoxicating, to American ears intoxicating, way of speaking the English? No idea. Here's my back deck, my expensive redwood deck, and here's what we call the side-deck entrance to the house. I will now pass through as I have passed through numberless times. Foolishly left the door wide open—a family of raccoons might have entered in my absence, might even now be making itself comfortable in the den, father raccoon taking a book down off the shelf, something in natural history perhaps, mother raccoon curling up on the couch with the kits, getting ready to read them a story, something by William Steig, maybe. All full-fed on gore. And here's why I'm remembering those Irishmen: because she also spoke a language that I have always found intoxicating, a language that's music to my ears, indigenous Mexican Spanish. And now not one word more from her in that language nor any other. Never one more.

*   *   *

There was the problem of whom to call. All right, call the lawyer first, be smart. But it was Sunday night, and the lawyer wasn't answering his phones. Landau left messages on two of them, suggesting that Cleve Raboy call back to discuss something that had just come up. By ten o'clock he had gotten no calls, so he left another message, sounding rather calm, he thought.

Deena called. "What's the matter, Anthony?" she asked after a few seconds, "You don't sound right."

"Oh, it's nothing, Deena, I'm fine."

"What is it? Where are you now?"

"I'm in my den. No—let me call it my reading room."

"I hear television is going."

"Yes, so?"

"By this time, the television is always on but the sound off, and you're reading a book. On Sunday night you are always reading."

"Oh, you know me so well, Deena. Maybe I just wanted a soundtrack tonight. I felt a little lonely."

She fell silent. Landau turned off the TV, thinking it might be bothering her. He couldn't remember having turned it on.

"Please, Anthony. What is the matter?"

"It's nothing. Last night I saw Arthur Fromm at your party, but I didn't see Melody Fromm, his attractive wife. What gives?"

"I don't know. Why, you are interested?"

"Not especially, just for informational purposes."

"He had a lover. Then, she had a lover. That's what I hear. Something like that."

"Arthur Fromm had a lover?"

Landau praised the refreshments served last night: Deena prepared her own food, and he asked if she had made the dolmas, too. She had. He had intended to ask if she'd heard anything about a writer for the *New Yorker*, but he didn't care about that now, really he didn't care.

"When my mother had faculty parties," Deena said, "in the fifties-sixties, a man who lived in the house behind us would come, and he would play the piano. And his name was something interesting—Albert Einstein."

"Einstein, you say? Why, that's funny—I was just talking to someone who mentioned Einstein. Said the Berkeley Hills were full of Einsteins in the old days, full of geniuses. But he wasn't really here, was he? He was at Princeton—Institute for Advanced Study."

"No, this was the son, Hans Albert. Kind of minor physicist. A woman from Keeler Street played cello, and they made music together. Schubert, Massenet, I remember those."

"Sounds very civilized."

"Yes, it was. The professors stopped their drinking and talking and thinking about themselves. So respectful for high culture they were, in a house where the hosts spoke good German. My parents thought that was funny, that they wanted only to hear Chopin, to talk about Schiller, but that's how they were back then."

"*Hochkultur und Geschichtswissenschaft*, it's better than *Kinder, Küche, Kirche*, no?"

"Yes, you're right, Anthony. *Hochkultur* is what it was."

He got off the phone, wondering why he was so sure it wasn't a good idea to tell Deena. Am I protecting her? Sparing her involvement in this mess? But it's more that I don't know how to say it. Deena—I just found a body under my porch, Deena. A half-eaten woman's body. It's that Mexican maid we both liked so much, Elfridia, I'm almost sure it is. That's why she couldn't clean at your house on Friday, because she was dead, Elfridia. She'd been eaten by raccoons.

No, tell her later, Landau decided, there'll be a better time later. First, notify the police, after the lawyer gives you the go-ahead. Do it in proper fashion, in proper order.

Here was something that he could do right now. More eating was going to go on unless he blocked up the hole beneath the crawl space door, stuck a piece of wood in there or something. But the idea of that appalled him— the idea of going down beneath his deck again, seeing the chewed off arm. Oh, whither your famous tough-mindedness, Landau, your legendary disease-hound's unflappability? You took twenty trips to Africa, sir, you larked about during Rwanda, during the Congo dustup. And now you can't protect one soul, one small body?

He thought of the burial pits, of the tales he used to tell of them, his tight-lipped renditions. But he'd been younger then, more in tune with the horrorful side of things. Now he was but a softheaded old granddad-type, querulous, labile. Why, last night I was blubbering all over my kitchen, sir. You should've seen me, a rank blubberer.

Call the nice policeman, then, make a clean breast of things. But you don't have to clean-breast anything, Landau, it's not your doing. You didn't commit a crime, you didn't commit anything. God—look at me, I'm Raskolnikov-ing. I'm already blaming myself. Where's the whisky—I need a shot of whisky.

Somewhere past midnight, Landau found himself beneath his house, a third-full bottle of pear brandy at his feet. He had arranged a kerchief over his mouth and nose, making him look like an Old West bandit. The smell was simply unendurable. Had it smelled this way all week? My God.

He pounded a piece of thick particleboard in place, to keep the varmints out. Poor Elfridia—Elfridia Tojolobal Somebody-or-other, to remember her name in full, which he couldn't, quite. But say what you remember of it, go on, pronounce it correctly: Elfridia Tojolobal. My God, is it really you here, Elfridia? Has this happened to you, pleasant, slyly funny person that you were? How do I begin to apologize for this fateful turning, this bizzarity whereby you find yourself not alive tonight, not sleeping at home in one bed with your girl cousins, but here beneath my porch? Your young life at an end, an absolute end?

He picked up the bottle and had a deep swallow. Down at the bottom of his block a car backed out of a driveway and began motoring slowly toward him, its headlights pushing a zone of illumination before them. The area beneath his deck was briefly illumined as the car passed, and Landau held out the bottle of pear brandy as if to offer it a drink. Yes, it's me, he wanted to call out, it's Landau, the masked marauder. I'm down here under my house doing nefarious work. Got another dead woman here, my second in as many weeks. Who knows how many will be dead by the end of this? Now, where are you going at this hour of the night, neighbor? Let me see your license and registration, please. Come on, come on, hand 'em over. The whole world has become suspicious.

Part II

chapter 8

Landau arrived at SFO in the wee hours, having caught a connecting flight in San Antonio. No problems with immigration—he was nothing to them, raised no flags. Back ravaged from thirteen hours in the air, no upgrades possible, just sitting back in coach with the rest of the hoi polloi, in a midget seat. Took a taxi over the Bay Bridge. Samir, his driver, came from Lahore, he announced, had a wife and kids still back in the Punjab—kept ranting against the Pakistani intelligence service, which had been persecuting his family, beating up cousins and uncles. Hey, Samir, it's four twenty-two in the morning! Landau wanted to rant back at him. My capacity for outrage is exhausted, along with the rest of me. Get me home in one piece and I'll give you a nice fat tip. But keep one eye on the road, please. Stop turning around to face me.

Feeling kind of loopy, mentally sprained. Had spent the last twenty-three days in Buenos Aires—Buenos Aires, of all places. What, I'm not allowed to leave the country, sir? But I *am* allowed, I'm a free man, traveling on a valid passport. I am not under any indictments, as far as I'm aware. I needed some time to think, that's all.

He had promised to return, and now he had. Toward dawn the taxi zigzagged up into the Berkeley Hills, and Landau's spirits began to lift. A remembered place—good, that's good. Tree-smothered narrow lanes, oddball houses, looked pretty cold out there, must be mid-thirties. Rounding the corner onto Hopwood Lane he looked for his own house, and there it was, where it belonged, the vanilla villa, standing faithfully forth. Junk around the front door, unpicked-up garbage, police tape over the door itself. Police tape? Uh-oh: back in the TV show.

The house smelled cold, smelled forlorn. Shamefully he had abandoned his cat with only the briefest of notes to the Shteyngarts, his neighbors to the south, who sometimes left kibble on their porch. Had not allowed himself to worry about Freddy-care and canceling the *Times* in his rush to get gone, to get himself out of the country, and for what—a sentimental journey? A final forlorn getaway? But B-A had always been *their* town, his and Samantha's, and he had needed to see it again. It was where the whole foolishness had started.

Fell asleep on the downstairs couch. At 8:00 a.m. a pounding at the front door—three Berkeley cops, one of them Officer Hashimoto, from the bedroom inspection. They wanted a word, please.

"Sir, if you would come with us, we'd like to ask you a few questions, sir."

"Come with you where?"

"To the station, sir."

"No, I don't think so. I'd rather not."

"Sir, Detective Johnson asked if you would please come down as a courtesy."

"Well, Officer Raintree," Landau said, peering at the man's nameplate, "I'm not feeling very courteous this morning. I just got back from a long trip. How about this afternoon, say around four?"

"It would be better if you came in now, sir."

"Am I under arrest?"

"No."

"In that case, it wouldn't be better. I'm not going anywhere."

Somehow, he fobbed them off. Got them to wander away, grumbling. They were so well-behaved, the sensitized Berkeley lot of them! God bless them.

I've lost weight, Landau realized: twenty-five, thirty pounds. In the bathroom mirror he looked markedly reduced. It was all that mournful walking, crisscrossing Buenos Aires following painful memories. On the other hand, it might be a tapeworm, or stomach cancer. When a man of sixty-four drops thirty pounds overnight, well, it can't be good, can it?

Even so, he felt well. Had a long, hot shower, in the Roman-style bathing chamber installed in '02, at great expense. He recalled studying tile samples with Mindy or Windy, some name like that, a hardworking renovation specialist—they'd agreed on sea-green travertine fused with "Mustique" glass, in a special organic process. The shower was as big as a small bedroom now, with exotic shpritz features. It did indeed make him feel like one of the lesser Romans—Commodus, perhaps, son of Cisternus.

Slept five hours. Ate canned soup for lunch. The phone rang and he took it on the machine, "This is Mark Wormser, of the *New Yorker*. I wonder if you've read the stuff I sent over. I'm—"

Landau picked up. "Yes?"

"Oh. Hello there."

"Yes?"

"Professor Landau, Mark Wormser here. I left you some messages."

"What can I do for you, Wormser?"

"Well, I wondered if we could talk sometime. About Samantha Beevors."

"What about her?"

"Well, I'm interested in her work. I've talked with Doctor Humphreys, with Doctor Moscowitz, with Ariel Anenberg at the Health Institute, with Bill Beevors of course. Wladislas Slem, of your own department. My editors and I are trying to decide if this is the right moment to put her in perspective—to begin to try to put her in perspective."

"How interesting."

"You're familiar with the magazine? With the *New Yorker*?"

"The *New Yorker*? No—never heard of it."

Brief pause.

"The *New Yorker* is—"

"I know what it is, bloody hell. You can't get away from it, the bloody *New Yorker*."

Slight chuckle.

"Well, her recent Africa projections, Doctor Beevors', I wanted to get into that with you. Do we read these as summary projections, or are they more of—"

"What's your point, Wormser?"

"My point?"

"Come to the point, please. Say it in English."

Silence. Then the man began again: "I have been following you for years, sir. I guess I just wanted to say that. From way before I got onto Doctor Beevors. You're central to it all, aren't you? You're the person without whom the whole era is inconceivable, intellectually. It goes back to your first treatises, to the first modeling treatises, I guess."

Wait a minute there, Landau thought. I know you, Mark Wormser. I know who you are.

"Wait a minute. You're the science fraud guy, Wormser, isn't that right? The one who's always showing scientists going too far, being Promethean. Getting caught with their knickers down. You also wrote that abused babies series, kind of off the mark for you, tabloidish, got you useful attention, though, a lot of it. That whole period when we were salivating over three-year-olds' penises, saying that every uncle in his cardigan was into diaper sex. We never got to the bottom of all that, did we, we Americans? No—we just moved on."

"I did write on ritual Satanic abuse, that's correct. Exaggerated accusations thereof."

"Okay. So I know you, Wormser. But where you really hit your stride is on these science stories. The one about the neurologist—the one who got it all out of a textbook. Would go into the operating room in the morning with his drill and his scalpels and skull clamps and just take out masses of tissue, scramble all the eggs, invent. Had no degree, had never been to med school. Had comparable results to the actual surgical neurologists, God help us. Some woman was on to him, some former colleague, and he killed her. If not for that, he'd still be scrambling people's brains."

"Guilty as charged, sir. I did write that, yes, I did."

"Good on you, Wormser. And let me take a daring leap now: I'm the next monster to be exposed. The next one succumbing to his own self-intoxication. Destroyed Samantha Beevors, didn't throttle her in his own bed perhaps, but bullied her to death, drove her mad, made life impossible. Stole from her, literally stole from her. There's a swell piece here, male chauvinism, science hierarchism, twenty-first-century plagues, it's all there. Juicy sidebars on the math, on drug-resistance cul-de-sacs. Kind of thing your average *New Yorker* reader likes to keep up on."

Another slight chuckle.

"Actually, I don't see you as the villain of the piece, Professor—not at all."

"No?"

"No. You're a hero to me. Probably why I got into science writing in the first place. 'Best 630 words of speculative prose written in the last half century'—that's what my biostatistics professor, Dingell, said about your first treatise. He began his whole course with that, with your first."

"Good for him. Smart man, Dingell, whoever he is."

"What can we compare it to? 'On Computable Numbers, with an

Application to the *Entscheidungsproblem*'? Turing's first? For me it was that transformative. That revelatory."

"Baloney."

"I want to show the social-intellectual nexus out of which Beevors emerged. That whole generation of epidemiologists and biostatisticians and infectious-disease crusaders unthinkable without you—those who emerged from you as Athena from the head of Zeus. I've been wanting to write this story for years, and now, with the Beevors angle, there's some journalistic mojo on it. But that's not what I care about—that's just the door opening onto it."

Oh, this one is good, Landau told himself. Watch out for this one.

"So, Wormser—you'll do my bidding? In all things? Prominently feature all I've done for the poor pitiful AIDS sufferers? The drug-resistant TB victims? I kind of see myself up on Mount Rushmore. Take Teddy Roosevelt down, put me up there, instead."

"I didn't know that about you. That you were funny."

"Am I? I don't intend it. I'm entirely in earnest."

Called Deena after but she wasn't picking up. Wanted to call Georges, too, but Georges saw patients all day Tuesday, so he called Raboy, his lawyer, instead. Raboy wasn't in the office, and are you really back in the States now, Dr. Landau? asked the receptionist. So glad to have you back.

Did a big load of laundry. Listened to phone messages. While the laundry was drying he ventured belowdecks, toward the region of his house that had become a nightmare corner in his mind—he was breathing quickly as he followed the garden path and stuck his head up beneath the joists, took an anxious look. Forest of yellow tape, jungle of it. So the police had been excavating down here, the police and others. Looked like one of those archeological sites where they map every square inch of ground, go over it with toothbrushes. The planking had been removed, so one had an unobstructed view into the crawl space, the foul burrow back there, where she had been deposited, Elfridia. Landau had been afraid he'd find her still present—that the police and coroner would not have come up to collect her remains, would have overlooked her somehow. Right knee still upbent, remnant housedress on, right arm missing. But no, she was gone. Still a bit of a gamy smell. Perhaps the raccoons were back, remembered the good munching they'd had here. The forest of tape no impediment to them—raccoons admitted of no impediment.

I don't know, thought Landau, I just don't know. Hardboiled crime investigators see victims all the time, and it rolls right off them, makes no nevermind. Myself, I'm genuinely cast down. It's that this thing has happened at my house. A madman has been playing up under the skirts of my house, ranging up into my own bedroom, even. It has to be a man who did this—only men do such loathsome things.

The battery was dead on his car, so he roll-started the heavyweight BMW down the incline of Hopwood Lane. At 4:00 p.m. he walked into the Ron Tsukamoto Public Safety Building, a location he had visited formerly only to pay parking fines. The guardian officer buzzed Detective Johnson. Holiday decorations out, Kwanzaa this, Hanukkah that, the moon and star of our Muslim brothers. The Christmas elements were oddly few—as if, feeling itself the dominant culture, Christianity had elected to keep a low profile, for fear of hurting feelings. Those bloodthirsty Berkeley Christians, about time they stepped back, after all these overweening years. Especially the Unitarians.

Detective Johnson, when he appeared, was wearing a sport coat and tie and looked relaxed. Something different about him—new haircut. They went upstairs. His office was about as big as Landau's shower, with desk, phone, three metal chairs, file cabinets in bureaucratic gray. Just what to expect in the way of an office for a detective fitting the outmoded idea of an honorable public servant, someone who did the world's work.

Yes, he had received Landau's emails, the detective said. Had received no responses to his replies, though, and why was that?

"Because I was using a computer in a public facility. I didn't wait around for responses. I'm sorry."

"Okay. So, Buenos Aires. Why Buenos Aires, Professor?"

"We had an Argentine chapter, Doctor Beevors and I. We met at a conference there to begin with. Had so much fun we went back in '90, '91, '93, '94. Couple other times. One time we rented an apartment, and thereafter we always returned to that address."

"You went back for conferences?"

"Yes. After a while we had some minor studies going, and we pretended to tend them. It's different in B-A. It's like Paris with barbecued meat. You should go some time."

"*Lechón a la parrilla*. I know about it, it's an Argentine dish."

"Right. You know something about a lot of things, don't you?"

"A little, very little."

Samantha had had her own Argentine past, Landau explained. She had worked there with Ettore d'Iulio, one of the preeminent South American epidemes, man now in his eighties. One of her protectors, her institutional allies. She'd gotten in a few hassles down there, insulted some colleagues, but d'Iulio had been behind her, so it hadn't mattered.

"How do you spell that, Dee-ooly-oh?"

"Little dee apostrophe, eye you el eye oh."

The detective opened his laptop.

"Okay, that explains why *she* would go. Now tell me why you did this stupid thing, and I'm sure your lawyer is very, very angry with you."

"I explained that in my letter."

The detective searched his emails. "Where you say you have to talk to 'some people'? Heitor Burgos-Pereira, Juan Jorge Soldana, Emilio Chertok, people who knew her, is that who they are?"

"Yes."

"And did you talk to those people?"

"No. D'Iulio was around, but the others either weren't in Buenos Aires anymore or were on vacation—it's Christmas there, same as up here."

"What did he say, Dee-ooly-oh?"

"He said he knew about the coronary dysplasia. I think he thinks I killed her. He remembers when our affair came to grief, that I acted a little funny, I said some mean, crazy things. We were never very friendly, d'Iulio and I. We were rivals for her affection."

"Did you kill her, Professor?"

"Oh, I like how you slip that in. No, I didn't. But what do you think, yourself?"

"I don't think so either. But you know me—I have to do my job."

"I know."

Detective Johnson fooled around on his computer some more. "Wow! This Dee-ooly-oh guy, impressive. This is some important scientist, down there on the Argentine pampas."

He slewed his laptop around. It was the University of B-A Web site, and the list of d'Iulio's publications was near endless. "He must have an out of sight *h*-index," Detective Johnson said, hurrying to check d'Iulio on the Web site that records the number of citations of a scientist's papers. "My God, he's off the charts, would you look at that. Shall we take a look at yours now, Professor?"

"No, why bother? It's nothing like that."

"It is, actually. It's very robust. I've already checked."

"Means nothing, mere citation porn. But how do you know about the *h*-index, Detective? That's very smart of you. Very *au courant*."

"I live in a town full of scientists, and I need to concern myself with that. Anybody would do the same."

"No, not anybody."

"Ettore d'Iulio. They have a lot of Italian names down there, people in Argentina. He's a major twentieth-century health guy, health sciences guy. Thank you for bringing him to my attention. Another one of these great brains intersecting my humble life-path. It gives me a special feeling—gives me a thrill."

*   *   *

Free as a bird. You can go now, Professor—and thanks for coming in. When Landau walked out of the police station onto Martin Luther King Jr. Way, he had an attack of disorientation—weren't there supposed to be harsh consequences, punishments for what he'd done? He had *emailed* the news about a second dead woman to the police. Had sent it in from another continent, most casually. Surely they thought he'd taken French leave, and if truth were told, Landau had flirted briefly with the idea of going long walkabout, cashing in his CDs, liquidating the bursting pension, becoming an international man of mystery. You saw it in movies all the time, people disappearing, as if that were a great thing—oh, just what I've always wanted to do, go live my few remaining years in some squalid city in Ecuador, say, pretending to be a Canadian geologist. Dr. Fred LaPlante, the tall fat guy with no friends. Lives above the *tienda* over there.

Why had he run away, for twenty-three days? Had the detective pressed him on it, Landau might have said, "It seriously got to me, seeing that poor girl's gnawed-off arm. I'm grieving for her, it may not look like I am but that's what's happening. Grieving for both of them, in my useless sort of way."

His phone rang. The lawyer's office: someone higher up than the receptionist was asking if it was true he was back, and if so, he needed to come in soon, tomorrow. They could arrange his surrender then.

"My surrender? What are you talking about? I don't have to surrender."

"Sorry, I misspoke. We need to speak with the police, that's all, because we owe them that much. You've put us in a terrible position vis-à-vis the police."

"I've just spoken with them. Everything's fine. I'm walking out of the station right this instant."

Silence. Apparently, he had made another boneheaded move, speaking to the police, without a lawyer present.

"No, everything isn't 'fine,' Doctor. It's not fine at all."

"Look here, Marsha—"

"Masha."

"Masha, Marsha, stop nannying me, please. Short-roping me. I can't make it in tomorrow, the day after is better. Around noon."

"Wait right there. I'll call back in thirty seconds after I speak to someone about how we need to proceed."

Waited thirty seconds. Then five minutes more. Got in his car and started driving, slowly. It was that time of day when the streetlamps begin coming on, when the more cautious California drivers begin turning on their lights, although they aren't needed yet—the time of day when all good men are thinking of turning homeward. Landau drove toward the bay, rather than toward the hills, conceiving as he did an idea that made this appear sensible, the need to buy some bottles of wine at an overpriced foodie boutique that he hadn't patronized in a year, down around Fourth Street.

What is that out there, in the cold, shadowy world? What calls to me? The world itself calls to me, he decided, because it has spawned a perplexing murder or two, this mundane geography has—off these familiar streets has come a maniac who likes to stage his killings at Anthony Landau's house, of all places. And here came more of the fruitless mental labor of the last twenty-three days, poring over his life, fossicking among the personal and professional elements, in search of someone with an anti-Landau grudge, a grad student disrespected, a colleague seething for imponderable reasons, something left untended, some loose end.

His phone rang. It was Raboy, the high counselor himself.

"Be at my office at ten sharp. We'll tell you what your options are at that point."

"Oh, okay. Wait, I'm pulling over now, Cleve. Don't want a ticket for driving while talking. I'm in trouble enough, I think we can both agree."

A few seconds later he said, "There. Parked now. And how are you, Cleveland? Keeping well?"

"Fuck you, Landau."

"Fuck me?"

"Yes, fuck you. Be there. Ten o'clock."

He had pulled over in front of a church. Small wooden church with a short steeple, needed a paint job. Along one shrubby side he made out a straggle of men, Mexican-looking men—well, you saw them often in west Berkeley these days, waiting on corners for someone to give them a day's work. Could be a soup kitchen, therefore, or a homeless shelter, the church. I wonder what's on for tonight, macaroni and cheese? Brown rice casserole?

For no particular reason he got out of his car. Joined the line. Mexican men have a stoic acceptingness, he had often thought—the way they ignore you is somehow philosophical, we're-all-in-this-together-like. The men waiting near him had rounded shoulders; would look up at you, from under a pulled-down baseball cap, then look away. Several were wearing Red Wing brand work boots—perhaps there had been a sale on Red Wing locally, or maybe they meant something stylistic in Mexico.

Landau caught a mood of mild despair. If this is a soup kitchen, these guys aren't doing that well; if they had the scratch they'd be renting their own apartments, cooking beans in their own little kitchen, playing *bachata* music on the radio. The whole point of being in the bloody soulless U.S. is to make money, send some of it home, and if you're not doing that, well, what's the point? Does life have a point anymore?

The line began to move. Landau found himself in a classic church base- ment, with smells of stewed chicken, an old upright piano against one wall, an underlying smell of Pine-Sol. The Mexican men sat at the various mismatched tables, waiting. Three women up front, busy young women writing on clipboards, smiling at this or that visitor—everyone seemed familiar with the drill, seemed to know what was going on. I've stumbled into a cohort study, Landau realized with a start—I recognize the mood, the clipboards, everything. A study on STDs, on prostitute visitation among undocumented workers, something like that. Good God, one of the young women up front was actually someone he knew: Dolores Huerta, cheerful, competent Dolores, one of his street-injector monitors from San Francisco. Hey, what's going on here, Dolores? Are you moonlighting on me now? I thought we had you under contract, but no, you're working for some competitor. Then he recalled that Dolores lived in the East Bay now, had a new wife and a house in Rockridge. I went to their housewarming party, and she works for Vladdy Slem now, good old prove-the-obvious Vladdy. Dolores Huerta—sort of a friend of mine.

"Dolores, is that you?" he whispered as she walked by his table.

The young woman pulled up short. Blinked.

"Dolores, it's me," Landau went on whispering. "It's Anthony, Anthony Landau. Hello there."

Sharp intake of breath. "Oh, my God! Oh gosh."

"Yes, I've gone undercover. I didn't mean to startle you."

Dolores was dressed in skinny black jeans, Converse All-Stars in sexpot red, hair cut à la Audrey Hepburn in *Roman Holiday*.

"I—" Her face fell. She suddenly turned and hurried away.

A few moments later she came back.

"You'll have to get out. Go on, or I'll call the police."

"The police? What are you talking about?"

"Yes, the police, get out. Go on, get out now."

She had paled, Dolores; her jaw was working, nostrils dilating.

"Dolores, what is it? It's me, don't you understand? Hel*lo* there. You know me."

"I told you, get up. Get up and get out."

All right, Landau thought. He stood. No longer a hero to lesbian women, it appeared.

Out in the mystic night again, the cool, shadow-spreading night. What was that that just happened? Good God, did I do something to her, too?

At a loss, he phoned Georges.

"Hello?"

"Georges, is that you? Look, I'm on my way to Enoteca, you want anything? Some prosecco, maybe?"

"Anthony? Jesus, where the hell have you been? Get your ass over here, right now."

"All right, all right. I'll be there in a few."

chapter 9

Georges had once been George—Landau had always admired the economy of the change, the single added "s" making him seem European, an old school *flâneur*, perhaps, not just some chiropractor from Englewood Cliffs, New Jersey. Georges was subtle in other ways, too— each year before your birthday you could count on a call from him, to talk about a swimming class you should take together, or a movie you should both see, never anything directly about birthdays or another year slipping past, no, that would be too crude. Georges had no brothers or sisters, Landau either. Both had learned how to make friends out in the world, and both were still learning. Deena said that they would end up in a rest home together, not in the same room probably but on the same floor. Playing inept chess. Helping each other count blood-pressure pills.

Georges had a new girlfriend, whom Landau had not yet met. He sang her praises in an ironic way—she was called Heather Ming, and she was another lovely young Asian person, no doubt, drawn to Georges by a mysterious magnetism he had, which he professed not to understand.

"Another waitress, Georges?"

"No, she's a geophysicist. She's an expert on shale fracturing—fracking, whatever they call it—which I'm learning about."

"Oh, yes, that gas thing."

"Right. You can talk Mandarin with her. You'll like her."

Georges said nothing about the bodies of dead women turning up at Landau's house. But Landau was not about to let himself be patronized in this regard, and he brought up the subject himself, that and the recent run-off to Argentina. Georges said there had been a lot of TV talk the last couple of weeks. Heads were soon to roll in the county prosecutor's office, it was said, because they should have brought Landau in on a forty-eight-hour hold, which was a provision that permitted the gathering of evidence from a crime scene, without the necessity of formally arresting a suspect. Several years ago there had been another eccentric white-collar criminal in Berkeley, who had slipped away because he'd been such a solid citizen that the police hadn't thought he'd bolt. He'd gone to Brazil and was still there as far as anyone knew.

"Are you calling me an eccentric white-collar criminal, Georges?"

"No, I'm not. I don't know that."

"You think I might have murdered the maid, is that right?"

"Well, it's an interesting question, you have to admit. I don't know you well enough to say for sure, one hundred percent for sure."

"What, you don't know me?"

"I know you. But no man knows another in his full roundabout. His full psychosexual roundabout."

"Oh, Jesus. What's your best guess, given that no man knows another?"

"That you wouldn't have, because you wouldn't leave her under your house. You're too protective of your fancy pretty house. But sometimes things run away with a person—you might have lacked options. What do you know about cutting up a body? Putting caustic chemicals on flesh, making it disappear? It might be smarter to do something so wrong that it tends to exonerate you. Bury her under your deck—that's clever, in a way."

"Oh, come on."

"You must figure they have a GPS on you, that they're following you, so how would you get her out on the bay, say, to drop her in deep water? You couldn't."

Here we are, once more in the TV show. Following a script full of hoary conventions, a script written by others. I guess that's what the Frenchman meant when he said, *Il n'y a pas de hors-texte.*

"Georges, I never once thought of that. That they might be following me. It never once entered my mind."

"With two dead women, they have to have someone following, they have to have a whole detail. Yet you slipped away. Right out from under them."

"They still trusted me then, the fools. Hah. Hah."

The assumption seems to be, Landau reflected, that even if I am a murderer Georges will remain loyal. We are both men of the world, after all, and nobody's perfect. Not in the full psychosexual roundabout he isn't.

"Just for the record, I didn't kill anyone. I'm too finicky to kill. And why would I kill Samantha, after so many years? And the Mexican girl was a sweetheart, a sketch. You never met her, did you?"

"No, I don't think so."

"You still have a key to my house, right?"

"Probably. It's here somewhere."

Heather Ming came over early. Landau knew it was early because Georges met her at the door saying, "Heather! You're early! But come in! So good to see you!"

Landau had conjured an image of a slinky, third-generation Asian femme fatale—Georges had consorted with people like that before. But here was a different modern stock figure, a severely uncosmeticized young woman with a strong, broad face, not very smartly dressed for a date, nervously handing over a bottle of cheap wine. A science nerd, that's what she was. Here in Georges' bachelor pad she was out of her depth, looked disoriented, a little frightened. The lights were low; there was DeBussy playing somewhere. He was a champion smoothie, old Georges, and maybe that was more than she'd bargained for.

As soon as she began to speak, however, Landau stopped fearing for her. Dead-on California girl accent, seemed to regard Georges with amusement—he was this older guy, cute in a way, obviously with a bad case of yellow fever. It suited her purposes to be here, that was all. Maybe she'd had nothing better to do on a night a few days before Christmas.

Landau made a quick exit, promising to call tomorrow. Christmas, Christmas, what's on for Christmas? Nominal invite from son and daughter-in-law. Christmas Eve in the vast, clean modern house, with other successful young couples, all childless, of course. Oh, joy to the world. Landau had a self-pitying passage, during which he acknowledged his own loverless condition, the likelihood that he would remain so till the end of time, since women now considered him monstrous. Only bleakness before me, and only a couple months ago I was fairly okay, I did have friends, I was grumpily managing retirement, the phone rang now and again. Damn those two dead women, anyway. Screwing things up for me.

Worse: the TV vans were at his house again, the ones with giant antennas on the roof. Now how does word get out, do the police tell the news outlets that the "suspect" is back in town? Landau motored past the turn onto Hopwood Lane, sinking low in his seat. No stomach for bravura turns in front of the cameras this evening—"Dr. Landau, welcome back, how are you? Kill any more women today, sir?" ("Hey, get your ass off my lawn, you press vulture. Or I think I might kill *you*.")

Rolled downhill, aimlessly down. Stopped at the Berkeley Rose Garden, no reason, there it was. Promontory amphitheatrical garden, tennis courts, view down the hill to the lights of the drowsing college town. He parked his car furtively, then hurried toward the rose-viewing area, scent as of dilute rosewater in the air, as if some elderly ladies were lying out, perfuming the night. Nature called, and he relieved himself in a mulched flowerbed, taking what seemed like fifteen minutes to empty, flick off, empty some more. Terrific shock when he turned around, and a woman was above him on the path, watching him. He made some expostulation, *grmph, freckk*, and she turned away, sorry about that, so sorry.

"Can I help you madam!"

"I'm sorry! Please excuse me!"

Completely in shadow, she was. Slender young woman-shape, dressed in a pantsuit. Medium heels.

She made a downward pushing gesture, as if to say, no harm intended, I mean you no harm, let's forget about it.

"I know you, don't I?"

"No, I don't think so."

"Come on. Out with it."

"Okay. I'm Katherine Emerald. You called me Katherine of KRON."

"Oh, Jesus. *You* again." It was the one who had betrayed him, filmed him over the back fence.

"I saw your car, that's all. I was driving home, so I pulled over."

"Aren't you afraid, Katherine of KRON? I'm a slavering madman. You're out here with me unprotected. I could kill you, eat your liver, and no one would ever know."

"Can I ask you one question, Professor? Why did you come back when you had already gotten away?"

Landau moved past her up the path. Not talking to you, not anymore I'm not.

"Professor? Do you have a theory about what happened to Elfridiana Mattos? The dead maid?"

"Not 'Elfridiana,' please. Her name was Elfridia. Get that right at least."

"Okay, Elfridia, sorry. Because, they're saying now she was tortured.

Surgically altered before the animals got to her. Have you got a comment on that? On her extensive genital injuries?"

Just keep on, he told himself. Keep on going.

At the top of the path, he suddenly whirled. "Press harpy, I'm asking you to leave me alone. I don't want to talk to you, now or ever."

"I know, but she was carved up, Professor. With scalpels, razors, something very sharp. Maybe a box cutter. Possibly she was the target after all. Her and not your former wife."

"Not my 'former' wife, not my any kind of wife."

"Okay, but what about it? Can you make any sense of that?"

Cameras must be whirring somewhere. Landau could almost hear them, a whole host of them in the trees.

"Who told you that, about sexual mutilation?"

"I don't know. It's what they're putting out now."

"Who, the medical examiners? That nice police officer, Detective Johnson?"

"I don't remember."

At least she protects her sources, he reflected. What passes for honor among these parasites.

"Look here, Katherine of KRON. I don't know anything about torture, God help us. What I do know is that you've been blogging—I've read you myself, in my weaker moments. You media scrummers, you put our heads out on pikes, arrange for the crows to pick our eyes, yet somehow you think we owe you something for it. I feel sorry for Brad Pitt now—my brother, Brad Pitt. Fellow celebrity sufferer."

"But what about it, Professor? Someone smart like you, with a deep understanding of abnormal psychology, you must have some insight. That whole classic cathexis, bondage, burial, savagery toward a woman's genitals, that must ring a bell, no? It's textbook. Completely textbook."

"Wait a minute—did I just hear you use the word 'cathexis'? Oooh. Oooh."

Hurried to his car. The Beemer had parked itself drunkenly, one wheel on the curb, and fifty feet ahead of it was parked an exemplary young Prius, in a girly pastel, clearly the vehicle in which the young newswoman had arrived.

"Professor, I can help you," she was saying, panting uphill after him. "You're being put out on a pike, but that's just because you're not shaping the story yourself. I can help you with that. I'm good at that. Let's work together, you and me, to tell the truth. You and me together."

"Okay, I'll think about it. I'll get back to you."

*   *   *

After a night in his car—sledgehammer sleep, hardly any dreams, despite the cramped position—he found himself in a café on University Avenue, ordering a bran muffin. The students all gone, it was the holidays, so Berkeley was a third less crowded. Kind of a rusty-dusty café, homeless guys at a few tables. Hey, I'm a homeless guy myself, Landau reflected. I smell ripe, haven't shaved in three days, and I can't go home, my home has been taken away from me. Boo-hoo.

Maybe I'll catch up on my presence in the yakosphere. But he had left his laptop behind, therefore he bought a copy of the *Chronicle*, the pathetically diminished local newssheet, with a six-page front section, lots of articles about cooking. Here he was on page four—he was old hat already, it appeared, sucked dry as a news topic. Accompanying photo showed him with the devilish beard, two years ago. Landau could remember that day it was taken: someone had written an article for the *Scripps Wellness Letter*, and he had been called to the UCSF press office to comment. He looked cold in the photo, disapproving. Was brooding over the cathexis even then.

The article was kind of solid, surprisingly. Bradley Limon, *Chronicle* staff writer, had talked to many of his epidemiology colleagues, including Vladdy Slem. Limon sketched in his whole career, and was there not a shadow of the *New Yorker* guy's efforts, of his intellectually dutiful approach? Somehow Landau could tell that Limon had talked to Mark Wormser, knew of Mark Wormser, anyway. Wow, the *New Yorker* is preparing a piece! What excitement, what a prod to local efforts! Let's see if we can scoop them!

Landau read the full front section. There was an editorial contra the Iraq war—how daring of the editorialists, at this late date, to take a stance against the war. More threadbare analysis, more liberal chest-beating: the tone was that of a drunk at a party who pokes you with a finger, brooks no disagreement.

Two things happened at once. Landau's cell phone rang, and a workman entered wearing a builder's tool belt, an Oakland A's hat, and Red Wing boots. Call was Deena. He wanted to take it, very much so, and yet he also didn't. The Red Wing man looked familiar, somehow. Had the bent shoulders of the men from the church basement, although in his case, this did not suggest defeat, discouragement; he was well-formed, moved decisively, looked as if he could really wield that hammer.

"Deena. Can't talk long, sweetheart, have to go to a meeting."

"Where are you?"

"I'm back, I'm downtown. Did you hear about me from Georges?"

"All right, call when you can. I need to speak with you."

They had been out of touch for almost a month. An unconscionable length of time. Still he had that instinct to keep her away from all this, because if anything should happen to Deena, he would never forgive himself or the world—and she was the only one about whom he might say that, the only woman or man. All right, maybe his son, too. Maybe. The man with work boots sat at a table on the other side of the café, and now he pulled a white MacBook out of a plastic bag and was soon tapping away. Not an indigent, apparently. Landau heard him order a latte. His face was hidden, but not his blue-black abundant hair, all interesting waves and shevels—Mexican heartthrob hair.

Ten to ten. All right, get on with it then. He wished that he had a tool belt to wear, with tape measure, hammer, dangling phallic wrenches attached. The lawyers wouldn't feel free to bully him if he came in dressed like that, but I must go as I am, Landau told himself, and a few minutes later, he gained admission to the severe conference room, on the third floor of a building three blocks south of University. Shook hands with Masha Dimitriopoulous, whom he had not yet met in the flesh. Now they came in from four different doors, the Landau defense team, no smiles, no endearing chitchat. There were eight plastic water bottles around the oval table. And the big dog himself? He slipped in last, pulling his door firmly shut.

"Doctor Landau, we are not the enemy," Raboy announced.

"I know that, Cleveland. I know."

"Just so that's settled."

He sat down across and three people down from Landau. Some complex message in that: this is not you vs. me, a battle of wills, this is democratic Berkeley, after all. We are all equals.

"How you feeling now, you okay?"

"Physically feeling? I'm all right, thank you."

"You gained some perspective in, where was it, Buenos Aires?"

"Yes, Buenos Aires. Yes."

Pause.

"Whatever the reason, no more traveling, okay? From here on in we need to know where you are at all times, and we need to be on the same page, always."

"Okay."

Two taking notes. The rest of them all watching—looking him over searchingly.

"Let me just mention one consequence. When it comes time for setting bail, the prosecution will say you're a flight risk, you have a habit of whimsically getting on airplanes, and for that matter, you've taken three hundred international flights in the last seven years alone," and Raboy nodded at one of the note-takers, who nodded as he went on noting. "We will argue, unsuccessfully, that though you went off you came back, like a good citizen. The point is, bail will be higher. You have many contacts overseas, you could easily skip to London, Johannesburg, Ho Chi Minh City, the list goes on and on. You see what I'm saying."

"Okay. High bail not good. Low bail better. I get you."

"It won't be low, in any case. But there are degrees of high. Since we're talking money, the retainer has changed. I explained that in two electronic messages. You never responded to them. Maybe you were busy, dancing the tango—otherwise engaged."

Landau nodded. "I'm not happy about it, counselor, but if you're determined to squeeze me, okay. But there are limits, ol' buddy."

"We are so far okay with our research budget, but that could enlarge significantly, remember."

"We had an outside total figure. I stand by that, as I stand by the Constitution."

Silence around the table.

Raboy cleared his throat. "If nothing else comes along, probably we'll be all right with that. But be prepared for the unexpected."

"Look, I'm not made of money. I can mortgage the house, but it's not that complicated a case, frankly. And I didn't do it."

Silence again.

Landau met everyone around the table now. Names, functions, hello there. Two were investigators. They were dressed as nicely as the lawyers, but with subtle distinguishing marks—one had a scraggly ponytail, for instance. That same one had had bad acne in his youth, and it gave him the aspect of a noble ruin. Three women, four men. The junior lawyers were younger than the investigators.

Raboy had a long face, long teeth, long forehead. Landau didn't like him. You can see the boy or girl in the faces of middle-aged wrecks sometimes, and you just know. You would never have been friends at school.

"Masha, why don't you tell us about the online angle."

"Okay, Cleve," said Masha Dimitriopoulous. "There were two thousand posts to one of the *Chronicle* stories in less than an hour—a truly spectacular rate of response. We've been nudging the discussion in a useful direction, and it's amazing how much of the chatter is procedural now, very different from the Scott Peterson case, to compare it with that, which was what, three years ago. That also happened around Christmastime, the wife went missing Christmas Eve, Laci Peterson. There's something about murders around the holidays that gets people very upset, but in a way, having Doctor Landau out of the country let some of the steam out, until Elfridiana Mattos turned up. But, again, a flare of outrage and deep upset has been followed by a surprising calm, because Doctor Landau wasn't here and wasn't speaking, wasn't inciting a response, and not much more came out about the case at that point. Now it's got a different tone, intellectual almost. What will be the approach in court, etcetera. Again, Scott Peterson was three years ago, ancient days in terms of Web habits. It's been fascinating to track."

What was she, frustrated cultural studies major? Media "scholar"? Kept comparing him to Scott, Scott Peterson the paradigm, and that one had played out badly, the wife in her eighth month, fetus in the bay, massage-therapist mistress, all of that. Scott had told Amber Frey two weeks before Christmas that he was going to be "sad" this year, going to be missing his wife come Christmas, and that's when he did away with her. The case had been poorly handled by the defense team, everyone seemed to agree—rueful looks around the table—a nightmare from the defense point of view, with Amber talking her fool head off, CourtTV.com turning up other affairs, a total horndog the guy was, Peterson. And we have a potential image challenge ourselves, Masha concluded, and it's fundamental that Doctor Landau not speak for himself, no, let us do that, please. Just comport himself with all the dignity of his distinguished eminence etc., etc.

Another young lawyer gave another report now—they had been canvassing for people who would do well in court, if called on to testify about his character, about his whereabouts on this or that day. Was Landau aware that Samantha Beevors had had a close friendship with Jared Samuels, his son? And what was the nature of that relationship?

"Close relationship, you say? Well, it was close, I guess, in a way."

"Was it intimate or not?" put in one of the investigators, not the one with the ponytail.

"Not *that* kind of intimate. Good God—she was as old as his mother."

They kept looking at him, all of them. You think boys don't sleep with older women? Even with their mothers sometimes?

"He took his mother's name, right?" asked the second young female attorney, not Masha, but another one.

"Sorry?"

"She's Margery Samuels. Normally his name would be Jared Landau, not Jared Samuels. Jared *Landau*."

Landau opened his bottle of plastic water. He took a small sip.

"Yes, that's true, I suppose. Look, there was a period. We were estranged, my son and I. He went to live with his mother for a while. I think she was more pro-skateboard at the time—something important like that."

They kept looking at him. Encouraging him to babble on.

"He took her name. It was some kind of jab at me, possibly. I don't think it's all that important, to be frank. Was just one of those things."

"No, come on," said Raboy with some intensity. "Come on, work with us here."

"I don't know what more to tell you, Cleveland. Teenagers do funny things. Some are even angry."

"There were expensive gifts. She took him to Hawaii. The friendship lasted from when he was a schoolboy till just a couple of months ago, am I right?" and Raboy looked to one of the note-takers for confirmation.

"How do you know that?"

"We've been looking into a lot of things. But the question is, what does this mean for what we're trying to do for you, Doctor? Does this hurt us or help us."

"Doctor Landau," Masha piped up. "Just so I have this straight—they kept their intimacy from you?"

"I don't think they 'kept' anything from me. But why shouldn't they be seeing each other now and again? She was like his favorite aunt. A zany aunt who gave him funny presents. They liked each other. She never had any kids of her own, you know, and she missed that."

"That's not quite true. She had a child she gave up for adoption, a girl I believe."

Landau took another sip of water. "What?"

"She had a daughter. Now about twelve years old. Ten, I'm sorry. She would be about ten now," said Masha, "eleven next fall."

Landau fell silent. The others, too. After a while, he waved an airy hand.

"She would've been forty-six then. That's late in the game, no? She was always traveling here and there, in front of audiences every other week. I don't know. I never noticed anything, certainly, personally I didn't."

"Were you still her lover then, Doctor? Still engaged in intimate relations?"

"I can't be sure. We were engaging up to a point, then beyond that we weren't engaging at all. I never saw her after about 1996."

The session went on. Trying to maintain his sangfroid, Landau was, projecting a certain indifference, at least attempting to. But this is just great, he thought. My son was in bed with my mistress, and she and I had a child together. Or she had it with the boy. A whole other kind of TV show—a whole other kind.

No further revelations, nor did he quite understand the defense strategy that they were shaping—what about his idea, discussed briefly with Raboy on the phone once, that someone was out to ruin him, to commit crimes of which he could be accused, someone who knew him? Was that so obvious an idea that nobody needed to comment on it? Who would that be, though? He had wracked his brain.

Wake up, wake up, he told himself: he was falling asleep as another of the junior associates, Carl by name, reported on developments in the county attorney's office, their decision to indict or not. And though she feels as if she's in a play, she is anyway—come on, man, it gets no realer than this, this is your own life, don't you care? Carl was reporting that the prosecutors had backed themselves into a corner, would probably have to indict, even if they didn't think they had a good case. The public expected an indictment. What was that movie about a law case, with that great scene with the defense team planning strategy—oh, right, *The Verdict*, with Paul Newman. James Mason playing an evil corporate defense attorney, commanding his eager-beaver minions, and it all came down to a stolen phone bill. But wait—why are you thinking about movies now? This is really happening, sir! Really!

Forced himself to focus on young Masha Dimitriopoulous' sweater, a lime-green sweater. Four pearl buttons ran up the throat of it, three of them primly fastened—they communicated probity, somehow, a quality one hoped to find in one's lawyer. Forced himself to look at Raboy next, to concentrate on his mouth, his teeth. Wasn't it Shakespeare who coined the phrase "long in the tooth," meaning that our teeth seem to lengthen as we age, because our gums are receding? Shakespeare, you mighty genius! Dentistry yet another of your areas of expertise, along with heraldry, falconry, canon law, glove-making. Shakespeare, I give you Shakespeare, gentlemen! William Shakespeare!

"Doctor Landau. Can I get you something to drink, some coffee maybe?"

It was the other female attorney, whose name was Taylor.

"No, I think I'll pass, Taylor. On second thought—maybe a nice cup of tea. I'm feeling drowsy."

"It often happens. Clients try to think so hard, so hard. They exhaust themselves, they knock themselves out."

Stumbled out onto the street past three thirty. Feeling befuddled, in a waking dream. All right, you recognize this boulevard, calm down, you're in Berkeley. You've just seen your lawyer, and they've filled you in on some matters. That's good, things are moving along. Take one step down the sidewalk. Now take another.

chapter 10

How many postdocs had he had? How many grad students in various capacities in a forty-year career? By rough calculation Landau arrived at the figure of 235, which was on the high side, but not too far. Among this phalanx, this regiment of sturdy health-soldiers, all of them ambitious, thinking people, had been one bad apple, or not. It might as likely have been a senior colleague, but no, for the moment consider the youngsters. Look into their fresh faces. What do you see?

I see hope and lust, lust to succeed, Landau thought. I see annoying goodness for the most part. Not a one ever came at me with a weapon. Callow, nerdy, needy, but no women-slashers, no rapists among them. What did I know of their private lives, of course—relatively little. In a few cases, more than I wanted. I tried to rule that out of discussion, telling them, you come to my lab to work, to learn, so spare me tales of what a piece of work your mother was. We have all had mothers.

No, no, think harder. And Landau came up with someone, with a man named Emory Forbush Musselwhite, born Normal, Oklahoma, stout sandy-haired young fellow who had hung around for three years, whose dissertation Landau had supervised. Appallingly written, though showing command of numerical concepts, and then at his orals he had been nearly speechless, tongue-tied with over-brightness, over-preparation. Landau had somehow gotten him through. Thereafter, embarrassingly grateful, worshipful. Emory had begged not to be banished from Landau's lab, sent forth into the cold, discomforting world, but Landau had insisted. A letter, arriving two years later more or less, had made demented threats. Landau had ruined his life, etc. Was somehow a Judas, a betrayer.

Searched for the letter but could not find it. He had never gotten an academic job, tightly wound Emory, but look, here on the Web site of Bluware Systems, of Pearland, Texas, Emory F. Musselwhite had lately been profiled as the new Senior Manager in Distributed Engineering, whatever that was. The photo showed a perfectly aged version of the former student, sandy hair thinning, neck fatter, eyes now behind heavy specs. A welcoming smile on the placid face.

This a mad slasher? No. No. You only had to look at him.

Christmas Eve. He celebrated at the palace, son Jad's enormous sterile house—it evoked for him spreads in architectural magazines, mansions in Marina del Rey owned by Kuwaiti princes, that sort of thing. Bone-white walls, furniture that encouraged one to laze, to peel a grape. Statuary here and there, also oversized oil paintings. Canvasses of primordial forms, painted by Karin, the talented daughter-in-law—she had been a studio arts major, then a psych major, before turning to the law. Threatful shapes that loomed up out of lurid chaos. Whatever else they were they were not over-controlled, throttled by a search for technical perfection—and who had painted like that, Landau asked himself, some brilliant amateur of the past had. Oh, right—D.H. Lawrence. Paint just rudely glopped on.

Not a bad party, after all. Bunch of yuppies, but the mood was warm, there were even kids running about. One other older person, a woman from Karin's church group, an attractive, pale widow who was all in a lather about Israel. Landau's half-Jewishness awoke only in encounters with ardent anti-Zionists; he didn't like the settlements, either, he was not a big fan of Bibi's, but why are you so hung up on the Jews, my dear? All right, all right, you're not hung up, you tell me. Sorry—my mistake.

Earlier in the day, he'd gone for a swim with Georges. Georges had remarked on his svelte new form—what is it, Anthony, are you on a diet? Have you got dysentery, leukemia?

"No, but I walked a lot down there. Twelve hours some days. And I sometimes forgot to eat. I've been off my feed ever since I found that poor hollowed-out girl under my deck."

"That doesn't sound like you, not hungry."

"No, it's unnatural."

Taking more care with his appearance now. On the day after his marathon meeting with the lawyers, he'd gotten a friendly email from Masha, which went:

Dr. Landau, you are an impressive-looking man. I just wanted to say that right out. Please shave regularly and buy yourself some new shirts. You are on a public stage now, for better or worse. I will be happy to help you shop if you want. I buy my father's clothes and he looks great. Everybody says so!

I don't need to tell you this, but a well-put-together look is important in many ways. You need to stay well rested and go to the barber before any court dates. We have a professional cosmetologist who works with us, if you don't have your own person. Turtleneck shirts are okay, but the look of an ironed broadcloth shirt with a clean tie can't be beat. While you're at it, why not buy yourself a couple of new suits. If I am impinging on your personal prerogative please forgive me! I just want things to work out for you.

Signed with emoticons.

Son Jad, now here was a topic. Landau observed him throughout the evening, wondering if he wasn't seeming melancholic. The towering son was a no-big-deal sort of host, friendly but offhand—oh, thirty-five people are coming for dinner, dear, is that what you said? Fine, although I'd rather watch TV by myself. His son's ADD hangover or Asperger's or whatever it was looked to Landau like nothing more than a case of torturing awkwardness sometimes, and he sympathized. His peers seemed to enjoy him nevertheless and to listen to him with close attention—maybe what Landau saw as a social deficit was a generational marker, something that the children of PlayStation, Ritalin, and the hard drive all recognized. No, I will never understand him, not entirely, but the reason for that may be that he was screwing my girlfriend, his putative stepmother. No wonder things got strange between us.

Do I believe that, though? No, no, I don't. Too bizarre. Although my life has at times flirted with the truly strange, never has it crossed over into genuine weirdness. It has remained within hailing distance of the normal, or so I've always felt.

"Jad. We should talk sometime, Son."

"All right, Dad. Lunch this week? The hospital?"

"Fine. Tell me what your workdays are."

Jad told him, and they made a date.

"Jad, when was the last time you saw Samantha?"

"Samantha Beevors? Hmm…2003? Somewhere in there I think."

"Not very recently, then."

"No."

A fire was burning in the hearth. It was Christmas Eve, after all. A tall tree stood in the giant living room, curiously without ornament—not a shred of tinsel, no candy canes, nothing. Lots of presents on the rugs, but the tree was empty.

"Why do you ask?"

"Eh, no reason. She gave you lots of presents, didn't she? There was a Sony Walkman the year when that was all the rage. And one year a saxophone, I believe."

"No, a drum set. A junior set. You put up with that for a while, then when I came home from school one day you had taken it to Goodwill."

"Are you terribly-terribly angry about that, Jad?"

"Yes. Some wounds, you don't get over."

Landau looked closely at his son.

"You look a little sad, Jad. Just a little bit sad."

"Actually, I feel fine. The look on my face—I've never been able to help that. It's just there."

"Okay, so you're not sad. Good."

"Things are going well. Job is good, life with wife is good. There was a corkscrew-shaped hole in society and I found it. It took some wiggling to fit in but I did."

"You were always going to be all right—it was just a matter of time."

"That sounds oddly positive, Dad. You were always more tart than that. But what's with you, man? You're the main object of concern these days. What the hell's going on?"

"Oh, legal nightmare, what else. Don't worry—it'll turn out okay."

Here came some small children. Karin and another woman were leading them, holding in their arms baskets full of Christmas tree ornaments. Now some other young mothers came forward, also some fathers, also the anti-Israel lady. They were having a formal hanging.

Japanese people, Peruvians. Black fathers, Jewish mothers, someone who looked Turkish to Landau—Levantish, in any case. A man who might have been an Inuit. You couldn't throw a stone in Berkeley-North Oakland these days without summoning the whole UN, it was extraordinary. The children about half white and half mixed, whatever those terms meant anymore. Beautiful, healthful, excited kids. Kids were fun to watch, especially at a Christmas party.

Landau sat down on a white couch. The anti-Israel lady sat down near him.

"I really want some grandchildren," she whispered behind her hand, smiling. "No, I *really* want some. I *lust* for them, from the deep-deep well of my being."

"I know. I'm desperate, too, in a quiet sort of way."

"I'll *kidnap* some if I have to."

They laughed about it, and Landau liked her better. He was watching Karin now. Was this a performance, or did Christmas tree ornaments awaken something lovable in her? He couldn't quite remember why he had never warmed to her; if he thought about it, probably he could come up with the usual soggy list of reasons, but forget all that, just look what she'd done for him tonight. Invited him, in the first place. Despite the ongoing madness. Then, tried to fix him up with her church friend. Phoned him over a month ago, to urge him personally to come, because it wouldn't be a party without him, you know. He hadn't thought of it at the time but maybe she'd been registering solidarity—her husband's father was in trouble, and she wasn't turning away from him, no, she was standing fast. Her father-in-law, with whom it had never been easy.

His greatest fear about her was that she wanted Jad too much—that there was something off about that, it was too intense, her *Kirche und Kinder* drive to settle down and share him with nobody else, not even any *Kinder*. But how rational was that? Better that a daughter-in-law loves your son madly, is besotted with him, than that she sort of loves him, maybe, sometimes.

He took pleasure in the unaccustomed stream of Hallmark thoughts. All I need is for her to ask me to put a star on the top of the tree—but no, she had Jad for that, all six feet five of him. Jad with a coffee-and-cream-colored little girl in his arms, a very delicious little girl, tried to do the honors. The child couldn't quite manage it, though, so Jad handed her carefully to her father and arranged the final star himself. Applause.

"Karin, I enjoyed myself so much," Landau said half an hour later. "Thanks so much for asking me."

"Dad, you can't go yet! The serious eating hasn't even started!"

"I know, but I have some wrapping to do. I'm going to drop off a toaster oven for you two crazy kids tomorrow."

"Dad"—that was two Dads already, possibly a record—"did you get your own presents?"

"No, but seriously, I'm coming by tomorrow, and not with a toaster oven, either. I'll get them then, okay?"

"Okay, if you promise."

Big, big hug. She wanted him to kiss her, and so he did, on both cheeks. "I'm so glad you came. What about Teresa? Yes, no, maybe?"

"She's a very attractive woman. I need someone a little dinged round the edges. But I'm on an improving trend, look, new shirt, new Italian pants. Soon I might almost be presentable."

"Why do you even talk that way? Of course you're presentable."

"Okay. If you say so."

"You're very self-effacing. I don't know why you're like that. You're one of the least puffed-up spectacularly accomplished people I've ever met. You could be much more full of yourself."

"Okay, I'll remember that."

Out on Alvarado again. The street the palace was on. What was it, eight thirty, nine? A sliver of pearlescent moon lay low to the horizon, clouds scudding in front of it, hustling along. When the moon emerged from the clouds it seemed to leap forward, before seeming to slow down again. Landau watched this for a while.

Alvarado Road hugged the side of a canyon, and although it had the appearance of a normal California rich-persons' enclave, the neighborhood had been half-incinerated seventeen years ago. After that fire, the Great Oakland Fire of '89, the many burnt-down homes had been rebuilt, the scorched shrubbery all replanted, life had gone on. In another generation there would be another fire—it was guaranteed.

The point was that you didn't know when it would come, how big it would be. And you built out of fire-retardant materials, and you planted no shrubbery close to your house, so that the fire, when it came, would pass over, as the Angel of Death had passed over the ancient Hebrews. That was the hope that helped you move forward.

Lots of Jews in them thar hills, as a matter of fact. Only two houses on the block had Christmas lights up, Landau noticed, and a street nearby, Gravalt Drive, was locally known as Gevalt Drive, as in oy gevalt. Landau had known a mathematician who lived there, a prominent Berkeley maths prof, who had been working at home on the day of the big fire, noticing a faint smell of woodsmoke in the air, a misty cast to the sky, when a policeman knocked at his door and told him to evacuate now. No flames in the sky yet, no signs of an approaching holocaust, and the policeman had been quite relaxed, offhand. Probably a false alarm, he'd said, but head downhill to the community center just to be safe. I'll give you thirty minutes.

The mathematician took a shower. Took something out of the freezer to defrost for dinner. Locked up the house behind him, then on a whim went back in and got the manuscript of the paper he was working on, on the Cartier isomorphism. Thought about taking the cats but they'd be too much trouble, he told Landau later. Didn't take any family photos, didn't take his wife's fifty years of journals going back to preschool, didn't take his daughter's framed crayon drawings, the family insurance policies, the bankbooks, the tax records. The Matisse litho over the mantel that was worth something. Thought about taking all of it, had time to gather everything up, and more, but didn't.

Landau ran into the man a few years after. His house had burned to the ground, his wife had left him. That he'd had time, yet had done nothing— that had driven his wife wild, that was so typical of him. His daughter, now a teen, was in drug rehab. His mother-in-law had been out shopping on the day, and she'd declined rapidly after the fire—had some kind of dementia now. He was still working on his paper. Some days he had it almost nailed, he thought, but other days he felt it slipping away.

Landau got in his car and drifted downhill. What is the Cartier isomorphism, did I ever know? It has to do with algebraic geometry, I think, but I'm not sure beyond that, and I can't even remember the Berkeley maths guy's name. I would know him if I saw him again, though.

Rolled up the windows of his car. Getting cold and raw out there, rain coming, the air had a blustery storm smell, a smell of brine from the nearby sea. On a steep curve Landau's right foot made a sticking sound and the heel of his new Italian shoe caught and then slipped, as if the floor were covered with slick glue, and he reached down and, yes, it was wet down there, it was tacky-sticky. Some glue, then? Some spilled house paint, maybe? Oh, but I know that smell, I know it. What is it?

Under a streetlamp, hand brake on, the car idling. Landau felt the floor again and the well around his feet on the driver's side was all moist, Jesus, good God, and he suddenly threw open the door and bolted out of his car. Ran part way up the block, ran fast. Slicky-tacky sounds as he walked in tight circles on the road surface, beneath the streetlamp, leaving footprints. No, it's not paint, it's not salad oil, and he returned to his car and opened the left rear door with such force that the hinges partly buckled. Someone huddling there on the floor, between the back of the front seat and the bench rear seat, a dark-haired man or boy, a slender fellow, and

Landau took hold of the jacket material and pulled, to get him out of there. Pulled and then let go, in horror. The torso and head had subsided onto the street, the body was half lying out now, and he had seen the shoes, the saucy cheeky shoes. Red Converse high-tops, they were. Oh God. Mary Mother of God.

Rotating police lights. Six police cruisers, a whole team of them this time, Oakland police this time. Landau sat on the curb, feeling faint, as the burly young officer asked him to tell the story in his own words.

Ambulance approaching, two ambulances. One made the standard siren sound, increasing in pitch and frequency as it neared, the other emitting some freakish whoops and bleats. The Oakland police were walking around and talking into their handsets, giving an impression of professionalism. Okay, just hang your head between your knees, Landau told himself, wait till it's better. Take deep breaths.

"I was coming downhill from my son's house," he began. "I felt stickiness on the floor of my car that was getting onto my shoes, and it turned out to be blood. So I stopped."

"You pulled over here, is that right?"

"Yes, and I called 911."

"But then how did she get on the street like that, sir?"

"I told you, I pulled her out. Half pulled her out."

Hard to get him to understand. It was not an accident with the door flying open and someone in the backseat half falling out, dragged fifty yards on the street, and therefore covered with blood. That wasn't how it had happened.

"Mr. Landers, are you okay, sir? You warm enough? You look pale."

"Yes, I'm fine."

"Want this umbrella?"

Landau recognized that it was raining. It had been coming down for a while now. "Okay. I guess so."

"Why don't you just put him in the prowler," one officer said to the other.

Not long after the ambulances arrived, the two ambulances, one of Landau's lawyers, Carl, arrived. By then the police knew who he was, that he was Landau not Landers, and they knew that the woman in the back of his car had had her throat slit, and they had discovered that she had been disemboweled. And they knew who she was, too, because Landau had told them her name. He was standing in the rain in handcuffs now, a line of cars coming slowly down Alvarado, swinging slightly left to avoid the ambulances and the police cars, and as a Land Rover passed with two handsome young people up front looking out through the windshield, he recognized them from Jad's party—they were some of the wholesome guests, going home now.

"Officer, I'm this man's attorney," Carl said. "Is this man under arrest?"

"Hey, get out of the way, who the fuck are you, buddy?"

"I'm Glebefelder. I'm his attorney. Carl Glebefelder."

"Well stay the fuck out of the way, Glebegelder, or I'll cuff you, too."

Not your namby-pamby Berkeley police—no, these were crack-your-head Oakland police. They had a salty reputation.

The cuffs, the swooping siren, the swerving ride to the station. It was all just like on *Homicide*, only you were in it. The backseat upholstered in clear plastic, no door handles to play with. Serious grillwork between you and the policemen up front. No worrying about whether he was cold now, was he maybe feeling faint. No more nice nanny-policing.

Almost a relief to be treated like a common criminal—almost. It was Christmas Eve, and they were short on staff, so they took him directly to the detention facility on Sixth Street in Oakland. His lawyer nowhere in sight now. Maybe Carl was pulling strings behind the scenes, ameliorating, but you couldn't tell, because you couldn't see him, and that was worrying. Landau sat cuffed to a table in a room that might have been a reception area. He heard noise outside the door. Just from the sound of it he thought that the press had been informed, and one or two voices out there sounded angry, while others sounded amused, lighthearted. A sturdy black man who looked like a police commissioner from *The Wire* stuck his head in and took a long, baleful look at Landau—you degraded piece of human garbage, you—then they brought him a paper cup with tap water, which he was unable to lift to his lips because of the cuffs. Then two white officers entered, and they walked him out of the room, and Raboy was around, putting a reassuring hand on Landau's shoulder, "Okay, just let me do the talking, Anthony, how are you, you okay? Any problems?"

"Any problems? Are you kidding?"

"Officer, take these chains off, please. This man is not under arrest."

"Prrhmpff."

"Would you take these chains off, please? Officer? Are you listening?"

"They ain't chains," someone said from somewhere. "They's handcuffs."

"Lieutenant? I'm talking to you."

The upshot was two nights in the slammer. Only two nights, and not a classic jail cell, more of a minimalist dorm room. The famous legal hold, whereby they kept you without arresting you, and took away your clothes, including your nice new Italian slacks, bloodied at the cuff now, and submitted everything you wore to forensic analysis, while impounding your car—all of that happened. The BMW, as a matter of fact, went away and never came back to him—it was torn apart, the fine Beemer leather violated rudely, and he could have had it repaired but he was disgusted by it, he didn't want it anymore. He was being a big baby but the thought of driving around in Dolores' blood, getting a whiff of the odor every now and then—no, that wasn't for him.

But before that, before he sold the car for salvage, on the second day of his technical non-incarceration, Landau experienced a police interview. They took him from the detention center to the Police Administration Building, at Seventh and Broadway, and Raboy was with him, but Landau found a way to speak, he pretty much said what he wanted. About last week—about encountering Ms. Huerta five days ago in the church basement. They already knew that there had been an altercation, because people had witnessed that—"Not an altercation, more of a misunderstanding, a slight misunderstanding," Landau explained. "She had a little bit of a hotheaded gut response to seeing me there. Because of all this coverage and all this speculation about me. It would've passed if we could've talked for a minute. She wasn't really like that, Dolores."

"Wasn't like what?"

"Well, she was a rational person, normally. But she's seeing all this craziness in the papers, how I'm Jack the Ripper, and the police can't get me off the streets, for some reason. People hear that and then if they actually see you in a store, say, they have a big fear response. Some people do."

The investigator nodded, yes, that sounds about right, please continue.

"Fortunately, you-know-who was in the basement that night. Six or seven men got in line behind me, and one of them was following me, I'm fairly sure of it. Maybe there's a surveillance camera down there. They were signing forms, so you might even have a name. Take a look at the tape, that's got your murderer on it, I bet."

Rayboy touched him on the shoulder, and Landau inclined his head that way. But the lawyer said nothing—probably, he just wanted to be in touch.

"Professor, why did Dolores Huerta leave your employ?"

"Well, she was living in Rockridge, not over in the Mission anymore. It was a question of the commute, I think."

"Nothing personal that made it uncomfortable for her to be in your lab anymore, in your presence?"

"You know, we're not going to speculate about that," Raboy put in. "That's kind of beside the point."

"No," Landau said. "Nothing personal."

"How would you characterize your relationship with her? What was it like, basically?"

"Basically, it was professional, as well as friendly. She'd been with me a number of years, and we knew each other."

"To what degree friendly?"

"Well, they invited me to their housewarming. Dorothea, that's her wife, her spouse—I knew her, too. I saw them a couple of times over the last couple of years. They came to my Boxing Day parties—all of my staff get invited, though not all of them come."

Big mistake, Landau saw immediately. "Boxing Day party"—what the heck was that?

"So you're not American, is that right, Doctor?"

"Technically, yes. I'm English, although I feel more American."

"Why don't you take out citizenship then?"

"I haven't gotten round to it."

"Lieutenant, please, what's going on? We agreed to talk about the night and the crime, not the professor's citizenship status," said Raboy.

"You been here how long, Doctor, fifty years?"

"Forty-two come next September, as a matter of fact."

"How many Boxing Day parties have you thrown?"

"Boxing Day parties? Well, at least twenty. Today is Boxing Day, by the way. Funny coincidence. If this was an ordinary year I'd be out shopping now, and there'd be people trooping over in the afternoon. You could come, too, Inspector. You'd enjoy yourself."

The African-American policeman did not look interested. But then his affect changed, "Oh, *Boxing* Day," he said snidely, "*Boxing* Day. That's when the Earl of Bridgewater gives a shiny new dime to the loyal butler. A quarter to the gal who cleans the toilet. Gets cozy with the little people, for about a day."

"Yes, that's how it started, some people say. It's a Christmas-present-giving day, that's all, a day for presents."

His idea about the church basement and the man who might have been there—the actual killer—getting lost in all this. He fielded further questions about whether he had a "lab" at UCSF or an office, about whether Dolores Huerta had been a statistical analyst or "actually a pretty wised-up gal, knew a lot about life on these hard streets," as the police inspector theorized. Slowly it became clear what they were thinking, the narrative they were developing: that he was a cracked British lord dangerous to women on all levels, who made them uncomfortable in his "lab," who assaulted and raped on occasion, who stole research results, who of late had been getting into murder. Even his Boxing Day parties were part of it, coded expressions of a poisonous condescension, his monstrous sexual response triggered by women subordinate to him. Oh-ho, we've got a live one here, he could practically hear them thinking—this is the new Jeffrey Dahmer, a major freak. There'll be books and movies, and maybe the inspector would write one himself, *Unspeakable Evil: The Story of the Century's Most Degenerate Sex Maniac, Dr. Anthony Landau, As Told by the Oakland Homicide Detective Who Caught Him.*

"I think we're about done here," Raboy said, standing up abruptly.

"Doctor Landau—Doctor, the dead gal, Dolores, what about the lesbian thing? That got anything to do with it, you think?"

"Lesbian? Hmm, well, I wouldn't know. You think that's relevant, Inspector?"

"Did it maybe get somebody viciously angry?"

"Well— "

"All right, okay, okay," said Raboy, and he gripped Landau's shoulder, urging him to arise.

"Some men, they go kind of overboard with that. We're hearing that Doris, that she was assaulted somewhere else. Attacked *elsewhere* and then put in the car, maybe through a rear window. Cut up bad, deep incisions to the throat, the abdomen, near-expert incisions. They let her bleed out real slow, and she was only partially disemboweled, you see. More or less was holding herself together, holding her own guts in, possibly for as long as an hour. Too weak to move, and her voice box had been damaged. Then you come out of the party around eight thirty. If you'd come out twenty minutes earlier maybe you get to her in time, get her to a hospital, maybe there's a different ending to this. Who knows."

Landau sat still for a long moment. Looking at his lap.

"That's very distressing to hear, Inspector. I wonder how you know that, though."

"Body temperature. Pattern of wounds. Some blood was drier than the other, so that kind of puts a timer on it. Someone could've waited with her, listening to her, checking her pulse every now and then. She's groaning, pleading. Then when the groaning's done, he drives on down the hill."

Raboy tugged hard at Landau's sleeve. Come on, we're out of here, let's go.

"Look at the tape, Detective. He's on the tape. The killer is."

"Oh, right, the tape. Right, we're on that."

chapter 11

As it happened, there wasn't a basement tape. There had been a surveillance camera operating but it was installed outdoors, where the men lined up. When Landau saw the footage, it was frustrating, because the men as they trooped into the church mostly didn't show their faces—it was that infernal Mexican workingman's stance, shoulders slightly hunched, eyes humbly cast down, that ruined everything. Only one visitor to the cohort-study free dinner that night had seemed to want to show his face, and that was Landau himself, who, the moment he reached the side door, looked up—and this image of him, of a vaguely smiling, semi-plump Englishman, obscurely pleased with himself, bland of long forehead, found its way onto the Web, as did the whole forty-five-second video sequence (http://www.youtube.com/watch?v=4p4-RWBCEFRo&feature=related).

Eleven men had arrived behind him that night, and you got a clear look at a few faces. Nine of the eleven were wearing baseball caps, Oakland A's, Giants, San Jose State Spartans, Monterrey, Nuevo Leon, Sultanes, and one had on what Landau thought of as a fisherman's hat, with a soft brim turned down. He watched the video again and again.

One of these men had killed Dolores Huerta. One of these was the one. That was what he told himself, although, of course, he had no proof. Odds were that no one had been following him, that it had nothing to do with him, no—it was all chance.

No one seemed to be thinking the way he was, anyhow. The ponytail and the other staff investigator were moving heaven and earth, he was told, but they weren't running down the names the men had put on the study forms (a killer would not have signed his real name, of course, but you wanted to see those sign-ins anyway). Fairly soon it dawned on Landau that the theory that his own team was working on was that he had done it. Had killed two women, maybe three. He was a sly one, no ordinary monster—it would take real cleverness to prove anything against him, but oh, yes, he'd done it. Therefore, the defense would not be about denying or disproving but about diminished capacity, how a diseased brain fails to know right from wrong. Think Hannibal Lecter. Think Anthony Hopkins playing Hannibal Lecter—and Landau did bear the British star a resemblance, they both had big bluff heads, overly-intent gazes, and when Hopkins, a Welshman, tried to sound English, as he did sometimes, he seemed to come from Landau's North London neighborhood.

They'd get around to the videotape, to the sign-ins, Carl Glebefelder assured him, but first things first. Here was what was fascinating to the defense: hints that the DA would be presenting to a grand jury rather than to a preliminary hearing. Very smart, those DAs. By using the grand jury they moved more secretively, cut the defense out of certain information flows, thus gaining an advantage. Already it was a deep chess game.

On his twentieth-fifth or thirtieth viewing of the tape, Landau saw things differently—one of the blurry heads seemed to remind him of someone. On the fortieth viewing he was still half-convinced, but after that he didn't know. One of the Oakland A's hat-wearers, one who had moved through after Landau—well, you could see his left ear plainly, also a wedge of wavy hair. Could that be Mr. White MacBook? The man who had ordered a latte, who had sat down with a certain decisiveness?

One of those glorious early January days. Spring coming early, the rainy season already over, it seemed, hillsides going green. Landau rode his old bike to Tilden Park. Stashed it in the bushes then hurried down a wooded path. Let's see if they're following me here, too—but no, he couldn't see anyone, he was alone.

There was a lake below. To approach it one negotiated an oak forest, wending through hedgerows of poison oak, to end up beside a body of calm water, Lake Anza. Now the poison oak was stripped to bare branches, everything dankly dripping, but the day was fresh, paradisiacal in its way—the California winter so unbitter, so unchallenging! No wonder our brains go all to mush—O California, you hot tub of the soul! You winning girl who gives it all away!

Trying to make himself think like a cunning criminal. His route down through the woods provided him with good views—and there his contact was, or rather, his car. The point was to see without being seen, to conduct oneself like a sneak-thief. Had he packed his automatic? No, he owned no automatic.

He descended farther, and now he saw the whimsical detective, standing beneath a lakeside tree. Detective Johnson had an odd stick in his hand—it looked like one of those spring-loaded walking staffs, the fancy kind. Maybe we'll be taking a nice hike afterwards, a nature hike.

"Detective, you ever swim here?"

"Oh, there you are. No, I haven't, Professor. I've arrested some people here, but no, I've never gone in."

"It's plenty cold, but in September in the hot spells it's okay. It's pretty much bearable."

The detective planted his staff. "So. What can I do you for, sir?"

"Well, I have a feeling I'm about to be arrested. That the good times are about over. I wonder if you've been thinking about my case. Wondering if maybe I didn't do it. Didn't kill them all, drink their blood."

"I told you before, I didn't think so. But things have changed now."

"Yes, I know."

"Did you have something you wanted to show me, Professor?"

Landau had filled several yellow legal sheets with notes. He held these forth.

"Whatever you show me, I tell the DA about. You know that, right?"

"Yes, I know that."

"All right."

Landau relinquished the pages. They were not a confession—more an anti-confession. To the police they would read like a ploy, red herrings tossed clumsily across the path. But what can you do.

"I didn't bring my reading glasses, wasn't that stupid."

"Here, let me read them to you," said Landau.

He read aloud. There was a nemesis—an insider-enemy. Someone was committing crimes in Landau's shadow: that was the thesis of the notes. He had some institutional antagonists, people he had butted heads with over the years; here were their names, for what that was worth.

"So these people don't like you, is that it?"

"I can't even say that for sure. Some of them are almost fond of me, personally. But they tend to go apoplectic in my professional presence. I've stepped on them, and they've stepped on me, too."

"Let me ask you a simple question. If someone dislikes you enough to kill and try to blame it on you, why not do something more direct? Kill you, for example."

"That is a good question. I don't know."

They began to walk. The detective had injured his hip, he said; he played in a Frisbee league, Ultimate Frisbee league, and had taken an awkward fall. Hence the cane.

"Are you having me on, Detective?"

"No, why?"

"You really play Ultimate Frisbee?"

"Yes, and Officer Ng does, too. A few other police. Some firemen."

"Oh, I like that very much. I don't know why."

They *were* taking a nature walk, a nice limping nature walk. They circled the somber lake, the policeman lost in thought.

"Makes no sense to me, Professor, to be honest."

"I know. On the face of it, it's somewhat fanciful."

"Occam's razor. Why not believe that *you* committed the crimes, instead of some antagonist. Some mysterious shadow figure who's all involved in your business."

"The only reason is because I didn't commit them."

"I know. So you say."

They descended into a dark canyon. The path became uneven, and the detective slowed down further; he reached for Landau's elbow at one point.

"You okay?"

"Yeah, but maybe we should sit down."

"Okay," said Landau.

They sat upon a rock that looked like a squashed toad. The detective took out the notes again; he held them at arm's length and made them out a bit.

"What about these other killings, then? You say there are other killings."

"Right. Raboy's investigators have found them. They happened in the mid-nineties, mid to late nineties. San Diego area. Bodies cut up. Knives and swords and razors used. Then, they stopped."

"Did you ever live in San Diego, Professor?"

"You know, that's the thing. I sort of did. Not lived there but visited many times. I had a friend who taught in the med school, a statistical physiologist. I was a reader on his doctoral students' dissertations some-times—an outside reader, you know."

"Right. Okay."

The detective was lost in thought again.

"Professor. Did Mr. Raboy urge you to pass this information on to me, or suggest that you pass it on?"

"No, not at all. He'll kill me, actually, if he finds out. He'll skin me alive."

"Why are you talking to me then, Professor?"

"Well, I suppose it's because I believe in intercourse. Intercourse of all kinds. The free flow of thought. You have a plausible demeanor, Detective, and an honest face. I feel that secrecy will not serve us, in the long run will not serve us, not you and me. That we might be able to cooperate."

"Secrecy will not serve us—okay."

"Right."

"And so, you want me to know about these San Diego killings. Is that it? That maybe you were around for. That you could've done."

"That someone *knew* I was around for. Knew that I was in the vicinity, roughly at the right time. A number of people knew that."

All too clearly, Landau could hear the echo of this. At some conceiv-able criminal justice procedure in the foreseeable future, he could hear it being said, "Ladies and gentlemen, please note that the defendant, on his own, brought to the attention of law enforcement other savage crimes—crimes he was eager should not be overlooked. This is behavior typical of certain serial killers—they are immensely *proud* of what they do, enthusiastic about it, and their greatest fear is that their crimes should go unnoticed—unappreciated, as it were."

"Also, Detective, I want something from you. I want you to look at that video again. The seventh man in line behind me is the one, I think, the killer. He's wearing an Oakland A's cap. He's got kind of blue-black hair. Wavy hair that sticks out under the cap. There's just something about him."

"Wavy hair, you say?"

"Yes, wavy hair. I think he sat with me in the café that morning, the morning before Dolores Huerta got killed. He got my attention but didn't quite show himself. Didn't turn his face my way."

"Okay. I get it."

No, of course he didn't get it, Landau thought, how could he possibly get it? What he gets is that I'm an idiot—that I have some absurd theory, that I'm willing to accuse a complete stranger on the basis of his hair.

"What about Samantha Beevors, then? You're leaving her out of this, Professor."

"Yes, well, I thought we'd both agreed on that. That she should be left out. That she suffered a coronary event, a thrombosis, due to an AV node dysplasia. That was the whole story."

"No, I'm not so sure. Doesn't explain why was she at your house that day."

"Is that important? She was kind of a practical joker, Samantha. In certain moods. It could be she wanted to surprise me, that she had an old key, and she was just stopping in to say hello."

Here was the scenario that had been plaguing him—had been disturbing his sleep for some days now. Say that Jad and Samantha, say that there was something there. Some unimaginable wrong relation, awkward and bizarre. Maybe they'd liked to come up to his house in secret. Rendezvous there, have their wrong relation in his bed. Stranger things have been known to happen in this world. Maybe the electric toy was even a favorite—Samantha had always had a madcap side, and Jad, as a boy, used to poke around in Landau's sock drawers, looking for cuff links, loose change, condoms, other treasures.

No, no, correction. Karin, very jealous Karin, finds out about the wrong affair. Doesn't go for Jad, goes for Samantha, brings her to Landau's house, possibly at gunpoint, to shame her. Precipitates the coronary event. The nudity in bed, the vibrator—these were postmortem humiliations, conceived in the tormented spirit of the moment. Karin had done it—Karin in a jealous rage.

"So, that's it, Professor? That's what you wanted to share with me?"

"Yes, well, that's about it. I hope it wasn't a waste of your time."

At the top of the path up from the lake, Landau opened his phone: "Deena. I want so badly to see you, Deena. But I can't. I'm afraid, I'm terribly afraid."

She picked up. "Where are you? What are you doing?"

"Oh, I'm in the park, Deena. Amongst the trees and the breezes."

"Why don't you come over? I want to see you too."

"I better not. Just talk to me, Deena. Let me hear your voice. Are you in the living room? Are you going shopping later?"

"No, I'm not home, I'm at work. Maybe later. Shopping later."

"Okay."

He pictured her office. She had a nice one, smack in the middle of the Berkeley campus, in a cube of a building made of white marble. Lots of other good buildings around, interesting buildings, all with tall windows, old-style casements.

"What else is happening, Deena, hey, what's going on?"

"Nothing. You are on the news a lot. There is a conference coming, Singapore dialects, Hokkienese. I need to take my skirts to the cleaners. I will take Harold's velour jacket in, also. You want me to take your stuff in?"

"No, I'm okay with that. But thank you. Thanks for asking."

They had an excellent cleaner in common—Landau had discovered him.

"What are you wearing, sweetheart, can you tell me? It's so warm, probably you just threw on some pretty summer frock."

"Anthony, we don't talk about my clothes anymore. Is off limits."

"I know, but just this once. I like that floral-printed one with the square neck. It shows off your pretty throat, your collarbones."

They talked about this and that, Landau cheekily asking if she were wearing pantyhose, as usual. He had used to take an interest in her apparel, maybe an excessive interest, which survived their remarkably brief tenure as actual lovers. Now she belonged to another, and so he must not ask.

"But why can't I talk about such things, really—isn't it that I'm an accused sex-torturer now? Isn't that why I can't ask about your undergarments?"

"What are you wearing today, Landau, a truss?"

He laughed. "Yes. And a jockstrap."

After a moment he continued, "No, let me ask you something else. Do you think I did it?"

"Do I? No, of course not."

"Not even just a little? Georges thinks so. It's possible, he says—because he doesn't know me in the full roundabout."

"Georges doesn't think that, he would never think that."

"And sometimes, you know, I don't know myself, Deena. Isn't that funny? I wake up and I'm not *quite* in touch with the reality of it all. What if I *did* do it? What if I'm losing my grip, slipping mental gears? It happens."

"Don't talk that way. You have enough problems."

She asked what he was so afraid of. So terribly, terribly afraid.

"Oh, just that things have befallen. Happened to people I like. I need to stay away from some people for a while. But that makes me lonely.

I've been reading about other great personages in my situation—other suspected malefactors of the day. The one who sent the anthrax spores, for instance. They staked out his house for a year, named him a person of interest, without bothering to indict him. Wanting to screw up the pressure till he finally burst. The feeling is one of total separation from the human family, which is a family I've never been sure I actually wanted to belong to, you know?"

"What about your cat, Anthony? If they arrest you, who will take care of Freddy? I will do it, but you have to tell me."

"Oh, poor Freddy, he'll have to come visit me in lockup. Speak to me through the plastic window, the little phone thing they have. He has little enough to say to me in any case."

Landau found his bike, and on the breezy ride down Euclid Avenue, the hems of his sport coat planing out to either side, he was free for a moment, with his hair blowing straight back. He passed two police cars headed uphill. Such was his mood of persecution that he assumed they were looking for him—suspect spotted speeding downhill, he could hear the police scanner say, looks like Tweedledum in a herringbone jacket, bring him in. Some animal high spirits returned with this image—it was the feeling that he cut an absurd figure, combined with the feeling of going too fast, flirting with loss of control. He was but a human body enmatrixed in mortal reality, just like everybody else in the world. He might have a spill, bust his fool head open. Then it would all be over.

As he turned up Hopwood Lane the tiresome spectacle unfolded itself ahead of him. Several press vans again, strangers milling before his house, sandwich wrappers blowing across the yard. Don't they ever tire of this, the press folks? I know they're on salary, but how many hours of nothing will their editors underwrite, in this age of the collapse of journalism? There was the civilian crowd, too—my groupies, as Landau had begun to think of some of them. Yes, I recognize faces now, I have my own cohort of *tricoteuses*, the women who knitted in front of the guillotine. You'd think that in Berkeley they'd be organizing an anti-GMO march or something, but I'm more captivating than that, the sheer angrifying awfulness of me provokes them. Wait a minute, here was an actual placard: "PREDATOR FREE ZONE." Isn't that wrong, isn't there a confusion of messages? Shouldn't it read, "*NOT* PREDATOR FREE ZONE"?

Got off his bike. The usual hubbub of insults and questions, bodies giving way grudgingly as he pushed on, head down, toward the front steps. Out of the shoal of newsfolk and good citizens bearing witness, everyone moving sideways across his flagstoned walk, some of them jogging, others walking slowly backwards, Landau with his game face on, a small woman appeared, was suddenly right there, screaming at him in bad Spanish, spitting at him or splashing him with holy water, because he could feel his cheek all wet. Then other people were taking hold of her, pulling back on her, and there was a mad writhing there in front of him, on the ground.

"My God! Jesus!"

"He's hurt! He's hurt!"

Busty little white woman. Youngish. He knew her—it was Dorothea, Dolores' girlfriend, lover, wife, widow. Landau put his hand to his face; of course she would want to spit on him, heartbroken person that she was, and why should he deny her that satisfaction? But wait, his hand came away full of blood. No one came near for an instant. Then several people were taking hold, had appeared out of the crowd, carrying him up toward his house, his feet just skimming the path. I say, unhand me. But they did not unhand him, they hurried him swiftly on. No pain but a feeling of wet weight at his cheek. Someone fell down before him, another shrieker, and they carried him over her, then Officer Ng was at his side, Frisbee-playing Officer Ng, and a wail of distress was rising on all sides, filling the peaceful glen of Hopwood Lane right up to the treetops.

Landau's hands were both bloody now, so one of the carriers fished his house keys out of his pocket. He found the right one, and once inside the house, they slammed and bolted the door.

"You'll be all right, sir. Is there a bathroom on this floor?"

"Yes, at the end of the hall."

"Okay. Very good."

Hustling him along, urgently hustling. "Keep the pressure on, sir, there, that's good. You're going to be all right. You're going to be fine."

chapter 12

What had she said, and why screaming it in Spanish? She was from Bend, Oregon, not Mexico or Argentina or anywhere like that, a Methodist who worked for a title company. She didn't speak Spanish, or maybe she spoke a little, that was their language of love, the lingo Dolores had taught her. The one they used in private, in the boudoir. If he could have understood her he might have prevented this bloody insanity, might have fobbed her off with a condolence or two, but now he was past all that, in that velvet space conjured by expert sedation, just this side of full-on anesthesia, just an inch or two this side. Feeling no pain, in other words. Feeling marvelous.

One hundred ninety-four stitches, tiny plastic surgery stitches. And afterward they were all in a good mood, the docs and nurses, slapping themselves on the back—with a wound like that, well, you don't fool around, do you? You get the best people for the job, not some ER cowboy who stitches you up with fishing line, leaves you looking like a soccer ball. Now don't get it wet for forty-eight hours, and read these pages on wound care. Read them carefully.

Caught a ride home with a Berkeley policewoman. I like the police, Landau decided, male or female—they aren't the enemy, no, I was wrong about that. They've been watching out for me, waiting on the edges of the crowd, to intervene if necessary. Is Byrum Johnson behind that? Organizing my protection? Hard to tell.

Empty house, blissfully. He expected some maniac to emerge from a closet but no one did. They got tired after a while, even the maniacs—went home for supper.

Feeling a bit woozy now. Percocet for the pain, four capsules, washed down with white wine. Landau looked at himself in his bathroom mirror—a four-inch scar, someone had said, cheekbone to corner of mouth. It might even be attractive, like a dueling scar.

No, not so quick there. Don't be gratified to have been cut, carved up like one of the dead girls. No one deserves a public slashing, and she almost took out your eye, the stupid idiot. If you were Dr. One-Eye now, you wouldn't be so philosophical.

Goddamn her, then. Her and her box cutter. The fellow in the café had had a box cutter on his belt, and what was the meaning of that, if any? All weapons have a subtext they tell us, and a bullet to the brain is different from a cleaver to the side of the neck. Landau threw up suddenly in the bathroom sink. Big brisk unloading, hadn't felt it coming at all. Sickened by the violence to his person, the remembered feel of the knife. Took two more Percocet, to be on the safe side. Box cutters made him think of Lorena Bobbitt, but Lorena had used a common kitchen knife, it was said. His own story would include such details when properly told; it would take its place among the tabloid sagas of the past thirty years, many of which it resembled. And will I be a real American then? Will I finally be a citizen?

His kitchen, one of his favorite rooms in the world, now lopsided, disturbed. No one would maid for him, so he had to wield the mop himself. Mail piled up on all the counters, yards of it. You became a world celebrity yet still got credit card offerings, ACLU donation requests, home mortgage statements. Here was a kindly note from Citibank, to which he still owed a vast sum. Would he like to borrow more? The sky was the limit.

With a powerful swelling of his heart he recognized a tentative *tchh-tchh* sound at the door to his deck. The cat, the famous cat! Okay, be cool now, don't go all effusive on him. He's come to feed, that's all, and you're his undependable provider. Freddy entered trotting most businesslike toward a feed bowl across the floor, where a chunk of some meaty stuff had dried to a brownish curd. Sniffed it, tail held out straight, then flopped on his haunch and began licking his former balls. Insouciant fellow, free spirit! Landau cleaned the bowl for him and opened another can of food, then went the extra mile, laid down a fresh sheet of newsprint. All right, ready to go.

Two pieces of real mail. A note from Melody, the physical therapist person. She was opening an office on Gilman Street, in partnership with an acupuncturist and a sports medicine physician, calling it the Westbrae

Integrative Bodywork Center, hmm, not so catchy a handle. There was to be a *feng shui* ceremony cum reception, but the date was already past. She had written something else on the back of the card:

I don't know if you'll remember, but you mentioned your lumbar spine to me, that it's been bothering you. Why don't you bring it in to my new office? I saw Georges at the pool but forgot to ask his permission to work on you…I can only imagine what you're going through, but if I can be of any help, please get in touch. Times of stress express themselves in the body. I know, I'm required to say something like that, but it might even be true.

She had a nice hand, shapely, feminine. And here was her phone number, her private number, in fetching lavender ink. Well, well.

Feeling truly Percocetish now, cotton-wadded in the brain. Fell to petting the cat, good way to get himself scratched, since Freddy was still feeding. Another letter had a handwritten address, but upon closer inspection it was just ink-jetted on:

deer killer doctor I ben drinking the blood of little girls for 300 years when I get hungry is when the moon is out their will be seventeen ded girls on a plate when the moon is out look for a pretty one under your feet look for a fat one under the bed look for a dirty one what was it like to fuck the dead girl I saw you saw you under your house

Hmm. Hmm. It was a piece of thin cardboard, cut from a cereal box, apparently. The advert side showed the words "Honey Roaste—" against a yellow-brown background. Wait, a signature: "El Chueco," it said.

Chueco. Chueca. That was the name of a district in Madrid, full of gay bars, good restaurants, narrow twisty streets. He knew it fairly well.

Chueco had another meaning, too, and the fickle memory bird almost swooped down, to touch his addled brain. In the end he ambled off to his den, where his dictionaries were kept. An adjective meaning "twisted," the dictionary said. Oh, too clever, that. That was a fanboy's name, a piggybacker's, if he didn't miss his guess. Why did people think that serial killers couldn't spell? That they wrote in naïve stream of consciousness? If he had been a serial killer, he would have written in perfect declarative lines, radioactive with threat. The Unabomber, now, there was a real killer-writer for you. Wrote a good sentence, whatever else you might say of him.

A surging sort of calm now filled his being. Maybe back off on the pills, no, just one more. His pornography section like a mouth of missing teeth.

The police had been through at least three times already, on the night of Samantha, during the Buenos Aires weeks, after Dolores. Remarkable that anything remained. Out on his side deck, for a breath of air, he thought about the raccoon alcove just below his feet, wasn't bothered by that now, the pills took care of that. From his deck could be seen five dwellings, three cozily lit among the brooding trees. The Shteyngarts the closest, but it was unthinkable that they or either of their two perfect daughters could have ever written "what was it like to fuck the dead girl." Farther down the block, a family named Bamberg that he knew little. They had a teenaged son, gawky, big Adam's apple, Tony Perkins-like. Wouldn't look you in the eye.

He took off down Hopwood Lane. As he mounted the Bambergs' porch, littered with broken lawn furniture, a dog began to bark inside the house. He heard scurrying and then an abrupt end, as if someone had grabbed the animal's muzzle.

He knocked at the door. Someone opened it a bit. "Yes?"

"Hello, I'm Anthony Landau. I'm your neighbor," he said. "I live in that tall house up there."

"I know," said the woman at the door.

She was slight, middle-aged. Flat hair. Had opened her door but two inches, stood holding a cell phone to her ear, a forefinger poised above the keypad.

"Is this a bad time?"

"Yes, well, we're all tucked in for the night."

"Sorry. Just wanted to ask you something. Wondered if your son, I forget his name, if he housesits. Would he possibly agree to feed a cat. Put out a can of food once a day, in the morning, sometimes a bowl of water, that's all."

"My son?"

"Yes. Would he feed my cat."

An old black dog poked its nose out the door. A slight side-to-side movement of its nose suggested a tail wagging out of view.

"I may be going away soon. I would pay him seven dollars a day, and take no trouble with the litter box—Freddy is trained for the outdoors."

Drowning eyes. That was what the woman had, the drowning eyes spoken of in novels. Was he going to kill her, cut her throat right here on her porch? Why then had she opened the door? Was it some dictate of conscience, the immemorial injunction against denying the neighbor?

"I mean you no harm, ma'am," he asserted, unable to suppress a Percocet-flavored smirk. "All this talk of me as a savage killer is sheer nonsense. I would like to talk to your son, that's all. See if we could reach an arrangement."

"He's not home now. He doesn't housesit, anyway. He's not very dependable."

"Oh, I see."

Impasse. The old dog wormed its way out the front door, stuck its nose into Landau's crotch. Rooted there a bit.

"I'll ask him, though. He likes cats pretty much."

"Oh, does he? That's good to hear."

"We had three of them, but the coyotes got them. One by one. There was nothing you could do."

"Coyotes? Had your cats been declawed, by any chance?"

"I don't know. I don't remember."

"The vets insist on it don't they? Declaw them all—tear those evil little claws right out. That leaves them defenseless, though. Coyotes can kill them, bunny rabbits too, probably. There's the songbird angle, of course. A healthy housecat can kill three hundred a year, the bird fanatics say, but does that ever really happen? Cats like to laze around, I've noticed. My cat certainly does."

A wraith—the shadow of a shadow—hovered just beyond the edge of the front door. The woman glanced that way, then tried to hide it.

"Is that your son, ma'am? May I speak with him, please?"

"Blue jays get the food. They scare everything else away, the house wrens, the vireos, the finches. They're bullies, blue jays are. Big bullies."

"Yes, I agree. Are you a bird-watcher, Mrs. Bamberg?"

"No. I don't know anything about birds."

"My mother was. Had a considerable life-list, binoculars, the whole kit. Rarely got out of London, however. Saw a lot of starlings, crows, that sort of thing. One time, a tufted duck."

"Tufted duck?"

"Yes, in Regent's Park. But look here, neighbor, Bamberg lady. I have a small bone to pick with your son, a small mild bone. He sent me a note, a very strange note. I would like to have a word with him about it."

The woman appeared confused.

"'El Chueco.' That's what he called himself. I have no problem with sending notes, mind you, but the sentiments he expressed were, shall we say, nonstandard. But most important, he did not see what he thinks he saw. I did not do what he says to the dead girl."

The woman nodded. Nodded and nodded. Then she slammed the door.

When Landau showed Raboy the nonstandard note, the lawyer appeared interested, and his ponytailed investigator handled it with plastic tweezers, placing it in a cellophane sleeve. Before handing it on to the authorities Raboy's crew made photos of it—it was a hoax, no doubt, of no importance, but needful of documentation, even so.

Seventeen days later, on the twenty-fourth of January, he stood beside his lawyer in a wood-paneled courtroom in the austere Rene C. Davidson Superior Court Building, downtown Oakland, dressed in a good new suit. Everyone was wearing a new suit, prosecutor as well as defense attorney: Landau had bought his own at Nordstrom San Francisco, no longer forced to choose from the Big Man's rack, with its tentlike garments. He was as thin as he'd been in forty years, a forty-three long now, a bit haggard looking. Maybe I'll write a best seller of my own, he mused: *The Indictment Diet: Weight-Loss That Comes Whether You Want It To or Not. Very Rapid and Frightening.*

A packed courtroom, just like in the books by Grisham. It was only a bail hearing, but the marble lobby downstairs had bristled with camera crews, with a paparazzi-style energy. And oh, what a lift of hearts when Landau had entered by the Thirteenth Street doors, arm in arm with Masha Dimitriopoulous—you could feel the uptick of expectation, life about to get much more interesting. Katherine of KRON had been calling him the "Suave Monster" on Channel 4 of late—she'd hosted three updates just in the previous week, and this was really putting her over, she was becoming a big hit with this. Suave, never! Landau had yelled at the screen, and a monster only of scientific ambition, and that only for a few short seasons. But on the screen was his indisputable double, his electronic avatar, with his drawn-with-a-ruler wound minimally bandaged now, his intense gaze, and a grim new set to his mouth, the lower lip protruding. Masha had been with him at the arraignment, when the footage was shot—and maybe that wasn't a good idea, always to show him with a nubile young woman. People get ideas.

Raboy proved impressive in court. Something happened when he put on his own good suit—the long face, the tombstone teeth, the graveyard pallor became elements in a moral impersonation, as if some Russian *samizdat* poet of the eighties, survivor of the icy mines and of countless gulag beatings, had appeared amongst them, to declare to them the Truth. One thought of liars and sleazeballs when one thought of legal performers, but Raboy went in the teeth of that, seeming not to care how he looked, not to care about anything but the immense responsibility he had shouldered, the responsibility of defending an entirely innocent man. Yes, entirely innocent! In just the last few days Landau had been let in on the secret, that their strategy now was to seek full exoneration, with no more talk of "diminished capacity," of a diseased mind incapable of telling right from wrong. Landau liked this change, but he was unsettled by the wholesale turnabout: Had they merely been testing him before, seeing if he'd stick to his story? Had he somehow become a better bet now, with his dramatic cheek wound? The weight loss? What, was he more sympathetic now, therefore more likely innocent?

He'd escaped any more nights in police custody, at least—Raboy had secured that, by means of masterful maneuverings to which Landau had not been made privy. And now they awaited the appearance of the judge, Sherman Beane by name, by reputation a prosecutor's friend, a "liberal Scalia," as Carl Glebefelder had put it. The judge not appearing for minutes, Landau sat with his hands folded in his lap, admiring the high-ceilinged courtroom, the polished walnut wainscoting, and over on one wall, tall windows, which the bailiff ordered opened. He thought he heard voices down on the street—Oakland, like Metropolis in the Superman comics, was a stage-set of a city, with few pedestrians roaming among the high edifices, many of them handsome ones erected in the 1910s. He heard a single car horn tooting seven stories below—one single jaunty toot.

"Twenty bucks says I walk, counselor," he whispered to Masha, who was sitting by his side.

"Pardon?"

"Twenty bucks says he grants bail. I'm feeling hopeful, I don't know why."

"That would be nice. But it'll cost you more than twenty bucks I'm afraid, Doctor."

"Yes, I know."

She'd told him not to look around. But Landau found himself swiveling until he could see behind him, and there was Deena, with Harold sitting next to her, and Georges, and, surprise, a woman named Lenore Cruikshank, another of his San Francisco project managers, another lesbian if you had to know. When Landau caught her eye, Lenore smiled warmly—she who might as likely have made the sign of the devil. I appreciate your loyalty, Lenore, he said to her in his mind. Thanks for being here.

"Doctor, please. Eyes forward, don't gawk."

"I'm not gawking, I'm just rubbernecking a little."

"No, stop that."

Jad wasn't here, but Karin was, and Landau nodded to her. Jad had to work—his patients always came first. But wait—aren't I more important than they, just this one time? I'm the only father he has. I may be going from this chamber directly to Santa Rita, the county jail, to molder there till the trial proper starts. I may never be a free man again, walking the too-tling streets. You should support your father, Jad—support him in his need.

Some other supporters were here: three of his old postdocs, Linda Maturin, Heitor Burgos-Pereira, Emma Chin. Emma lived in Seattle, worked at the University of Washington now, the school of public health. Had she come down just for this? How good of her. And Heitor, good God, Heitor had some big job in Brazil, some public-health appointment, important politically, very onerous. No doubt there was some other reason for him to be in the States at this time, a conference or something, but that he had taken pains, was following his old professor's embarrassing troubles, that moved Landau. And Linda Maturin: a good egg, Landau had always been fond of her.

Now the judge entered. Landau's heart began pounding: something unpromising about the man, inimical, a man of about Landau's own age, bald, stooping, slight list to the right. Was that the Scalia reference? Smiling drily, pretending to be one of the guys, a friend to his courtroom clerks. Landau felt sweat under his arms, and he wished they could open those high windows wider—it was a warm day, the premature California spring ongoing. His lawyers were on their feet, but when Landau also tried to rise Masha pushed him back down.

A clerk made a formal statement, mentioning a case number. The judge now repeated that number, as he took his seat high above them.

"Counselor, I've read forty-four letters in support, have I missed any?"

"No, Your Honor, I don't think so."

The judge rolled his eyes. Forty-four letters: that was a bit much, no? Testaments to the defendant's character, wonderfulness, all-around harmlessness.

The judge looked over at Landau. "I honor you for your work, sir," he said unexpectedly, "your groundbreaking scientific work."

Silence in the court. Landau realized that he was supposed to respond. "Thank you, Your Honor. Thank you very much."

"Interesting stuff. You made sense of the AIDS epidemic when others were completely confused. Classic studies, eminently logical. Aristotle would've been proud. They teach those papers in the med schools now I understand."

"Thank you, but I was but one of many, sir."

"No, you came first. I read about it."

Astonishing. Astonishing. But that was the end of the direct address, and the judge got things rolling, calling on the prosecution to bring a witness.

Description of Elfridia Tojolobal's ravaged body. This much damage caused by mammalian dentition, this much by tormenting with a knife. As well try to convict one of the raccoons, Raboy had said—nothing tied Landau directly to either process. All right, all right, here was something, an IKEA-brand serrated kitchen knife, five-inch blade, straight cutting edge. Partial prints on handle and blade, belonging to the defendant. Suggestive but not dispositive, to use a word his lawyers liked to throw in. Dispositive evidence was what you hoped they didn't have.

The prosecution had purchased an identical knife and had conducted tests on a fresh female cadaver. Marks on bone-ends similar to those on victim. But anybody could have taken that knife out of Landau's kitchen drawer—his fingerprints were all over his knives, because he washed them by hand. Some cooking show had taught him that.

Judge growing impatient, it seemed—the point was not to argue the case, just decide, was defendant a flight risk? A threat to public safety? By subtle movements of his shoulders inside his suit, lawyer Raboy communicated similar impatience; there was a discrepancy in the forensics log, saying "December 21" on one page while on another it said that the knife had been found on the twenty-sixth. Knife found under the house, but the map of the dig showed other discrepancies, too, two locations for the supposed knife discovery, for instance.

Raboy now suggested that the whole excavation had been bungled, and there would be more to say on this at the trial. For now, can we not agree that defendant returned of his own free will from a foreign country, a country with complicated extradition arrangements with the U.S.? A country where he might have remained indefinitely? Furthermore, he had been cooperating mightily with the police, and the *radical and unreasoning disregard* in which he was held in certain quarters did not in itself argue for incarceration. A community distinguishes itself by the way it treats its pariahs, and just because someone is the object of a *dangerous and unreasoning hatred* does not mean that he should be denied his rights, etc.

Clumsily, endearingly almost, the prosecution now made its lame case. Defendant had a habit of vanishing abroad—twenty-three trips to Africa, scores more to Asia and Latin America, six to San Diego one single summer. If this man is not a flight risk, no one is. Raboy surged up out of his chair: he was outraged, and Landau could hardly understand what the matter was, why he was in such a high dudgeon. This was not a grand jury, Raboy explained, before which prosecutors might float any kind of bizarre theory; no, this was a simple bail hearing. Hard to tell what he was really up about, was it the mention of San Diego, where the other bodies had been found? Nothing had been said to Landau during the coaching about that—his lawyers liked to talk demeanor, what clothes to wear, that sort of thing, plus what he had revealed in his "incredibly stupid" meeting with the Berkeley detective recently. Raboy and team knew all about the lake meeting—maybe that was why they'd kept him in the dark so long, because they knew they were defending a fool.

An assistant DA, Wendy Waters, now tried to show that where Landau went, deaths to women occurred. But this was "circumstantial," and if they took this approach at trial, they were going to have a hard time. Raboy remained on his feet: like a venerable stage actor, he occupied space magisterially, his silence eloquent, unsettling. Landau could see that in a certain sense the state had no case, that in eight weeks they'd come up with nothing but a single steak knife—and the steak knife was too good to be true, too much of a smoking gun. A killer who left nothing behind, not a scintilla of DNA, as if he'd performed his monstrous resections clothed in a rubber bodysuit, had somehow dropped his principal tool. It made no sense.

"All right, all right," said the judge. "The question is, what good is served by detaining defendant pending trial, and what good if we go the other way. This is where I earn my salary, my impressively bounteous salary." Judge Beane's eyes sought out Landau's—it was an oddly personal look, half-amused, the look of someone you know at the gym, perhaps, some guy who holds the door to the sauna open for you. "You on your way in here, old-timer? Let's hope neither of us conks out. I haven't had my blood pressure checked lately."

Moments passed. That he was a traveler, continuously fleeing: well, how did you get around that? And women he knew *had* turned up dead, three. Someone coughed in the gallery. The judge examined a document. He really is trying to decide, Landau realized—I can see him laboring, in his mind and in his spirit. Landau's heart began pounding hard again, and he had a moment of excitement, almost a falling-in-love feeling. Followed by more common garden-variety dread, as the judge folded the page in half, mumbling to himself, now saying something a bit louder about having had to read *forty-four letters*, as if that were a new North American record. Defendant had brought along a whole generation of young health scientists, there was that to be said for him, and some had sent in heartfelt letters—here, he wanted to read one testimonial, from a woman student.

Maddeningly, the judge couldn't find the letter. He searched here and there, then turned to one of his clerks, who joined his search. Eventually she also threw up her hands.

Now he heard something about bail in the amount of, conditions thereof. Masha was sitting very still, Raboy even stiller—they were all still as statues. "That's two million," Masha whispered without leaning closer, "two million, Doctor. Not twenty, and not ten. *Two* million."

"Two million?"

"Right. And you only put up ten percent."

A victory, then; a glorious outcome. Nothing about electronic anklets, nothing like that, either. What was two million dollars to the likes of him, wealthy retired white-collar bastard living in the Berkeley Hills? Two million was nothing.

Raboy, as if from a great height—still cruising on his successful impersonation—whispered that they had witnessed an act of rare courage, the superior court judge pretty much putting an end to his career with this judgment. Try running on *that* ten months from now in Berkeley or anywhere. Especially if there were more killings.

Masha was glowing—Landau thought of a high school football quarterback after a big game. Clearly they were in disarray over in the DA's office, and what the heck was going on with them? Wendy Waters wasn't the brightest bulb, but she had never looked this weak before. Normally her plodding, little-steps manner put male judges on her side.

Deena came over, did not kiss him, only touched his hand. She looked shrunken—it occurred to Landau that she had been suffering on his account, worrying herself sick, losing weight herself. You forgot that you had that kind of friend. But you did.

Harold and Raboy were deep in conversation now, exchanging deep insider-lawyer *aperçus*. The courtroom did not quickly empty out; people seemed to want to gawk some more. The judge was gone, the prosecutors all gone, the last one now wheeling out a white document box on a dolly. So, the monster had gotten away with it! An old white judge lets another old white guy out on bail—some things never change.

Georges was with his earth scientist, waving from the back of the room. Heather Ming, that was her name, Landau now recalled. The crowd moving toward the door at last, Georges and she were borne in that direction, relentlessly away.

"Deena, you look like a scarecrow. You must be down to 105, darling."

"I'm all right. You eat, too, Landau, you look ill."

"Dad? It's a good thing, right, Dad?"

It was Karin, looking happy if anxious.

"Yes, I think so, dear. You know Deena, right? This is my very good friend Deena."

"Of course I know Deena. We've met on five Boxing Days."

"Oh, right."

Someone else was swimming up—it was Linda Maturin, old-school epidemiologist now, not one of Landau's sharpest postdocs ever, but solid, invincible. And she was pregnant again. Looked about six months gone.

"Linda! Let me embrace you."

"With pleasure, Professor."

After the embrace, "Professor, I wanted to say—as I said in my letter—I am a woman scientist today for one reason only, because I was lucky enough to study with Anthony Landau, who fought for me, who did not give up despite four years on a paper I should've written in one, miscarriages, traumas too numerous to mention, during which he stood by me. So don't say this is a man who harms women, no, that's *exactly* what he is not."

"Hear, hear," said Landau, feeling a little embarrassed.

"No, I'm serious. It just makes me so mad. You don't know how *rare* you are. How special and *rare*."

Landau felt emotional again. It was the goodness of hearing how good he was—sainthood, here we come.

And who is this handsome fellow sneaking up, agreeably nodding to everyone, not wanting to interpose himself—ever the gentleman, Heitor Burgos-Pereira, one of Landau's favorites, this one very bright, Heitor of Argentina. Heitor looked like some supple polo player, fresh from a hard-fought chukker at the La Tarde Club, Buenos Aires, pushing forty now, but ageless, suntanned, chipper. A treat to see him.

"Hello there, young man! What in the *world* are you doing in Oakland, Heitor? Did you get on the wrong plane?"

"Professor, I am so happy for you! This is the best result, right? To have some bail?"

"Yes, the best, although there's still a ways to go."

Heitor gave him the thumbs-up sign.

"Really, though, what gives? D'Iulio said you were in Brazil. Running Mato Grosso state by yourself."

"Oh, no. But I got some little thing at Stanford for a while, your good friends, Lucile and David, give it to me. Just some fooling around, bioinformatics, maybe they teach me how to use a computer, at last."

"Lucile and David? The Packards? If *only* they were my friends. So, you're around, then, Heitor. Let's have lunch."

Masha taking him by the arm now, move along there, enough celebrating. Three minutes later they were in an elevator, Raboy, Harold, Deena, Masha, Linda Maturin, and Landau. Linda suggested eating at one of the *pho* restaurants on Twelfth Street—Pho Ga 69 was her favorite, from when she used to live in Oakland. Raboy beckoned to Landau, whispering that he had made arrangements with a bail bondsman just in case, if things went their way today, that is. This guy was less of a crook than most, and they would go over to his office after they faced the cameras down in the lobby. Okay, you ready for that? Here we go.

The elevator doors opened, and hubbub ensued. Shouted questions, poked-forward mics, but Landau had been coached to say nothing, just to smile, and he did as coached for once. Then after the mad image-and-statement-stealing set-to they were out on the street, and here there was nobody, absolutely nobody. Eleven-thirty on a Wednesday morning, middle of the workweek, and not a single car was going by, not a single pedestrian. It was as if the neutron bomb had gone off. That was Oakland for you.

chapter 13

The next week an article appeared in the *New Yorker*, by science-minded Mark Wormser, which made only the most decorous mention of the criminal case. The focus was on Samantha Beevors—always at the right place at the right time, Samantha, a paragon of globetrotting epidemiological enterprise, a defining figure in the age of AIDS/TB/malaria. One of four principals on "Asymptotic stability of constant steady-states for a 4X4 reaction-diffusion system in malaria modeling," of 1994. One of two on "Optimizing the elgenvalue of the Laplacian in a sphere with interior traps," 2002. Sheer poetry, those titles, self-parodying titles—Samantha had always been good with naming.

Wormser had handed in his copy *before* the arraignment, Landau deduced: there was no mention of his being charged with a capital crime, although he was a central figure in the story, as a kind of dire *eminence grise*, a loomer, a Darth Vader figure. The account of his early modeling treatises correct, as far as it went. Some eat-your-spinach type math talk, Wormser establishing his own expert-hood, his bona fides. No mention of the *Entscheidungsproblem*, unfortunately, comparing Landau to the towering epochal figure of Alan Turing: Landau had enjoyed that, so he missed it now. But Samantha's contributions to the field were unthinkable without his own, Wormser proved, and the great mystery of twentieth century mathematical biology was why A. Landau, after three brilliant early papers, had made no theoretical contributions to speak of. Had subsided into a career rather ordinary, as if in retreat from his own inventiveness. The homeless studies, for instance. They were lovely, but many others could have done them, and they had broken no new ground.

Went home, cleaned his house top to bottom. Anti-mildew treatment for the shower. Washed the picture windows on the inside—get some young athlete to do the outside. He found dried blood under the lip of the downstairs sink, thought about calling the police, but no, it was his own, from the slashed cheek—no need to call in forensics.

Phoned Melody Fromm, to consult about his back. They forgot about his back and went swimming instead, at the new pool in El Cerrito. Landau and Georges loved this pool because the water was infused with sea salts, wasn't over-chlorinated, which made it almost like swimming in the sea. And afterward your skin didn't smell like Clorox.

A cold day, with rain-sprays. They hurried from the warm dressing rooms clad only in swim-togs, pulling on squeaky latex caps, and plunged directly into the water, because it was no fun with that rain hitting you. Ah. Ah. Landau nearly fell out of his outsized trunks—had to cinch them underwater. It was odd, he felt weaker without his vest of flab; before, he had bestrode the waves like a killer whale, making half the distance just by displacing volume, whereas now he moved by the flutterings of his feet and the pullings of his arms alone. No more manatee-miles for him—now he had to work for what he got.

Lunch afterwards. Melody had some patients coming at two, so couldn't linger.

"So good, so far?"

"You mean, the new office? Yes, I guess so," she said. "I had an office before. This is just a new partnership."

"How many patients?"

She named a modest number. All insurance referrals, paid at a low rate.

"That's good. Sounds like you're on your way," Landau encouraged.

"Maybe."

Here was what was occupying all her thoughts and feelings these days: not the new partnership but the divorce. It had come to that—a divorce. They had irreconcilable differences, Arthur and she. Arthur had started it all, carrying on with a finance senior analyst at the university, and now that that torrid fling was over, he thought things should go on as before, more or less.

"For me it's different. Something unforgivable has happened. I don't mean that what he did was so bad—it's only in the context of the marriage, which has been bad for years. I've given everything I had, and it's only gotten sadder and sadder. I can't do it anymore."

Landau nodded—divorce bad, sad marriage also bad. She had his sympathy.

"What I dislike more than anything is hurting another person. That sounds simpleminded, but that's me. Now he says that if I leave he'll be ruined, and he wants us to stay in the house. But I would go under. Like a swimmer under the waves."

She had a pretty complexion post-swim, Landau reflected, the skin a bit dry and stretched-looking, blanched, but growing rosy again. Though she was speaking of unhappiness and sadness she spoke slowly and quietly, taking small bites of her modest salad.

"Not wanting to hurt somebody else is limited as a guide to behavior. I recognize that. Maybe you're just trying to control that person by being so kind," she said. "Maybe that's why the marriage got so lackluster. Me being kind and good to the point where he wanted to tear my head off. He's had other women, not just the finance senior analyst. He's telling me all about them now. It just rolls off me."

It struck Landau that she was confident; most people would not have confessed so easily to being betrayed. She did not seem to be asking for sympathy, exactly. There was a disinterested tone, which interested him.

"What's funny is that I've been aware for some time of having turned myself into an unsexy good person, and I think that's how I struck back at him. I can be sexy and difficult, too, but I wasn't going to give him that. I'm sorry. This must appear so petty compared to the problems you're facing. I mean, you might go to jail for the rest of your life. And here I am telling you about Arthur. Boring Melody and Arthur."

He had a vision of her: her getting out of the pool half an hour ago. Not climbing out by the metal ladder but hoisting herself over the edge coping like an acrobat. Smooth shoulder, shapely leg. Blue tank suit. He had that before his eye, in his mind's eye.

"Petty, not at all. It's a relief not to think about that for a minute," he replied, "I mean, not exactly a relief, but a welcome change. All that madness."

Still, she was determined not to talk about the divorce. She had read about the bail hearing. And that woman on Channel 4 had something new to say almost every day. Next came the trial, was that right?

"Yes. In forty-four days I will appear in a court of law, with a jury and everything. Meanwhile it's just a waiting period, and I'm determined to take a lot of restorative swims. The lawyers want me to lie low, to recede. Become boring, actually."

"I hope it works for you."

After she left, Landau took a bus downtown, then another up into the hills. Elfridia Mattos had used to come to his house to clean on this same bus. Still raining out, colder now. Maybe winter wasn't over after all. Some people out on his lawn, a remnant-looking group, doing something in front of a wood structure with a rough pyramidal shape about seven feet tall. It's a shrine, he suddenly realized, to the innocent victims. Bits of paper attached, colored ribbons, homely drawings, and people were just standing there, silently communing—soon they would light votive candles, perhaps. Landau tensed as he walked by, one hand half-raised to protect his face, but they ignored him as if he had, indeed, receded from reality. A larger principle was in play, the issue of attacks against women, and he was but the ugly occasion. He himself was unimportant.

Calls from Georges, Jad, the *New Yorker* fellow. "Landau here, what's up, Wormser?"

"I thought you might not want to talk yet. Thanks for calling back."

"Yes, and so?"

Wormser wondered how he had liked the article. Landau made a noncommittal sound.

"It's only sixty percent what I wrote. They took out half the math," the writer explained. "There's a follow-up coming, and maybe one more after that, and we'll get more of the math in then."

"It's already too mathy, Wormser. Give your readers what they want, more of the dead girls, more slashing, bleeding. Think what Tina Brown would have had you focus on if she were still at the magazine. This isn't a brainy story, this is raw tabloid stuff. Take it and run with it."

"No, that's not how I want to go."

Next month there would be more about the Congo, too, Wormser assured him. He wanted to ask him a few questions about Samantha and their travels there together.

"We never did go there together. We went to South Africa, but that's different, isn't it? I remember that paper she wrote about Central Africa, modeling war effects, modeling the war as it was ongoing. She'd gone off the cliff by then, modeling her models of models."

"Why do you say that?"

"Look, they're all running up against the same problem, the modelers. Disappearing up their own behinds. I don't know much but at least I know there's a problem."

Wormser fell silent.

Landau, after several seconds: "You there?"

"Can I quote you on that, sir? I don't mean word for word, but can I repeat what you just told me?"

"No, why would you?"

"Are you working on mathematical limits again? Disproof of modeling? That's very close to your original work. Nonexistence of a certain class of solutions."

"No, I am not working on that. I have nothing more to say about that. I am a has-been, Wormser, you said so yourself. A second-rater."

Wormser was excited, though. The idea that Landau might be "working" again, that got his heart racing. Picking up the old treatise-writing pen.

"Could I email you a few questions, then?"

"What for?"

"Oh, I don't know. Look, I'm in New York today. I could be in Berkeley on Saturday. Let me buy you a croissant at Café Roma, on Bancroft, at 10:00 a.m. Saturday. Is it a date?"

"No, it's not. I'm off croissants. Anyway, my lawyers have imposed a strict press moratorium. Mum's the word."

"It would be off the record, if you prefer."

"Off the record, on the record. Stay where you are, Wormser, don't come. Don't buy that ticket."

Felt like an old tease afterward. An old pro, lipstick misprinted on her lips, but still able to get a rise from the young ones, with a bit of the old hoochy-coochy. Speaking the right dirty words.

Sat down at his computer. Wrote something half-coherent. Had an urge for a strong cup of coffee. Mentation, unfettered mentation. Once that had been his joy.

Three hours later, eight thirteen by the clock, some tapping at his front door. One of the votive-candle holders? Asking for a match? Outside it was full dark, rain pouring down now. A miserable cold day it had turned out to be, except that it had been fun to get in the pool with a female. He crept along his darkened front hall, peered out his foyer window, saw someone on his front stoop, someone shaped like a woman. Dorothea, perhaps? Come back for another slice at him?

"Yes, can I help you?" he asked, opening the door Mrs. Bamberg-style, only two inches.

"It's me again," said Melody.

Landau blinked. "Oh, right. Come in. You're all wet."

She had parked her car downhill, she said. Then taken a wrong turn walking up. She knew his neighborhood well, but still the paths and winding lanes sometimes fooled her.

"The streets rearrange themselves at night, mysteriously. Here, give me your coat. I'll hang it over the heater."

"I have a patient on your street," said the physical therapist. "Leora Bamberg? The MacArthur winner?"

"MacArthur winner? She won a MacArthur?"

Landau offered her tea or wine. Sensing an increase of social warmth indoors, Freddy appeared at the door to the deck, and Landau grudgingly let him in. They had cat talk for a while, Melody telling of a tabby cat she had owned once, named Luther, who had been a real character. Looked a lot like Freddy.

"Tabby cats are good," Landau opined, "although gray-strikes are also unpretentious."

"Unpretentious? Oh, I don't know. I'd say they're all damned cheeky fellows."

Nice to have a woman in his kitchen, an unexpected woman. He wanted to kiss her, just for appearing. He drank three glasses of wine too quickly, pushed the bottle away. She had put on a bit of blush, some lip gloss, a touch of mascara. Lovely, she was, made up or not. She was dressed in a longish dark skirt, long-sleeved charcoal sweater, complex shoes, vaguely fetishistic, with crossed straps. Otherwise she looked quite demure.

Remember, he told himself, she is anticipating divorcing. People who are divorcing are all mad, no matter how convincingly they dissemble being sane. Their worlds are on fire. They may need your assistance escaping the burning castle, but that's all.

In his bed later, both clothed except for their shoes, the bedside lamp casting mellow light, Landau asked if she would walk on his back. She declined to, saying that that wasn't really good for your spine. She arranged him on his left side instead, his topmost leg half-bent, and enveloped him in her arms while using her full body to press upon the bent leg. Then she rolled him onto his other side.

"Georges does that to me, too," said Landau. "It's an old chiropractor's move. I've never understood it."

"It helps loosen things up. Take a deep breath, and now let go."

You're the first woman to lie on top of me in over a year, he wanted to say. I've been deprived for quite some time, you see. Watch out.

"Something felt like it released that time."

"Yes, maybe," he said.

"It's never more than subtle when it works."

He wanted to compliment her on her bravery, coming to see him like this. Perhaps she was a crazed thrill-seeker herself, like the women who proposed marriage to murderers in prison. But no, he thought, probably not.

"Would it be okay if we just lay here? Lay here together for a while, with that lamp off?"

"Yes, sure," he said.

There—just lying here in the dark, together. She turned on her side with her back toward him. Landau put his arm around her. Then withdrew it.

"Don't you want to make love to me?"

A bit taken aback, he said, "Yes, I suppose. I haven't thought that far ahead."

"You can, but you have to do everything yourself," she explained. "I'm going to lie here perfectly still, like someone who's never been in bed with a man before. I'll do whatever you say but you have to direct me."

"Okay, fair enough."

"I don't even know how to take my clothes off. My leggings, for instance. I'd like to take them off, but I can't manage it."

Landau's hands didn't work properly. He felt like a bumbling youth himself, and for long moments he was unable to find the waist to her leggings. He pictured an elastic zone around her middle. What he found was much lower down, on her hips—these must be some new cut of tights, designed to perplex.

"I've taken down your tights now, young lady. Now turn over. I'm going to spank you."

She laughed. "Oh, please don't do that. Please—don't hurt me."

"Yes, but you've been a bad girl, a very bad girl. I can tell."

God, that's not a little girl's bottom, he reflected: that's a full luscious woman's derriere, warm beneath my hand, velvet smooth. He spanked it. Melody made a sound of alarmed surprise. She was a good play-actor—convincing.

"Keep your legs together," he commanded. "I insist that you be ladylike, no matter what."

Heavens, where does this come from? Why are we behaving in this nonsensical mode, instead of in one of a million others possible? He had an impertinent erection now—he was half embarrassed by it, half wanting to show her.

"Put your hand over here," he ordered.

"Why?"

"Just do it. I said so, and I am your commander."

"Oh, my. Oh, my. It's so big."

"Yes, and now get up on your hands and knees. I'm going to show you what to do with it."

Uncertain rustlings in the bed. She wasn't sure what he wanted, she was so inexperienced, you see. Landau tore back the covers impetuously, tossed his cushy blankets to the floor.

"Turn the other way," he ordered. "That's right—your face goes over here."

"Like this?"

He struggled to pull his pants down. "Yes, that's right. Now, be sure to hide your teeth. Put them behind your lips."

"Lhok thiffs?"

"Yes. Very good."

Good God. Good God. He could almost see her in the dark, the slurping sounds she made like echolocations. She was admirable in many ways, many.

"That good?"

"Did I tell you to stop? No, I didn't. Continue, or there will be further harsh spanking."

A lovely night. Lovely. The most fun in decades, it seemed to Landau. Couldn't sleep for a while, had to do it a second time, a second go, at his age! Then they both slept soundly, then awoke together at some dark hour of the night. Not much talk between them. But why had she said that fanciful thing, "You have to do everything yourself"? Had she divined something about him, the need to hear those words, exactly? Maybe she said that to every man she met—it was her patented icebreaker. Or maybe she had sensed something in his situation, his need to hear just that, just that.

Awoke at dawn, went to the bathroom. When he came back his bed was fragrant of sex. Oh, it's good to be a heterosexual sometimes! It is my way of choice! Fell into a fun dream as soon as his head hit the pillow, racing downhill in a powerful car, the Volvo longboat, eccentric vehicle from yesteryear. No view over the high dashboard. Barreling downhill faster and faster with no view at all, unconcerned about a smash.

"I had the most brilliant dream," he said as soon as he awoke. "Full of speed and thrilling danger."

"You like danger, do you?"

"No, I don't, actually. I'm kind of a timid soul. I'm so happy to see you here, though, on the neighboring pillow. So happy."

"Are you? You know, I've been quite shameless, and I want to apologize. You knew I had a thing about you, didn't you?"

"I—I couldn't believe it. I'm not an object of desire usually."

"You don't know. In a certain kind of woman's eyes you are—definitely you are."

"What gave me a hint was the lavender ink. Seductive, that."

"Yes, it always works."

Good God—and where did *this* come from? Normally, it took him hours to recover, days, the prostate no longer youthful, spendthrift, prolific.

"If you want to make love again," she said, "you'll have to lick my pussy. I'm a little sore."

"Okay, I can do that."

"I hope you don't mind me speaking so frankly. I thought with you, probably I could say whatever I want."

"Yes, that's true."

More fun. Great fun. They took a slow start on the day. He made them oatmeal for breakfast, then gave her an umbrella when she left, at eleven. It was raining again.

Now the swelling of the chest. The feeling of things not being so bad, after all, for a man of the world. Wasn't it Chekhov, in "Lady With Lapdog," who warns of the irrepressible male urge to preen, to light a cigar, following first sex? He had a sudden urge to work, sat at his computer again.

Wrote more of something. Printed out a paper he dimly remembered from the late seventies, by S. Boichenko, eccentric Ukrainian set theorist. All those years ago it had given him a special feeling.

Midafternoon, he set out on foot, by crooked streets and steep interconnecting paths down toward the university library. A police cruiser came into view, and it was in view again as he crossed Spruce Street. Absurd not to have a car, to be on foot at his age, in his situation. Was he inflicting on himself the deprivations of the maid, who had bused and BARTed everywhere, often schlepping cleaning tools? Why hadn't he bought her an old Corolla, say, as a friendly gesture? She would have loved that.

Walked the campus, did not stop at the library, after all. Squalling, spitting rain. People hurrying between buildings, raincoats flapping. Landau had his parka hood up, and in a reflecting windowpane he saw his wolfish silhouette. Was someone getting his image right now, "streaming" it on the Internet? Move along there, then.

On BART. At the MacArthur station, he transferred to the Fremont Line—his plan to go to his San Francisco office, to hunt up two other papers by Boichenko, unavailable online, yielding to a more obscure whim, to taste a new kind of Mexican food, called a *huarache*. He had been reading about huaraches everywhere—people were raving about them, food writers and common citizens alike. A culinary innovation, a flat corn oval like the sole of a sandal, bidding fair to replace the taco as the Mexican food-platform of choice. Got off at Fruitvale station. Signage in Spanish outside the building: International Boulevard reminded him of certain avenues in Ensenada, hand-painted signs, small shops, security bars, everything pitched at a low level of expectation, a high level of Mexicanness. Bar Azteca con Mesa de Pool. Supermercado Hudiberto. Carniceria Mi Pueblo. Mi Grullense, a van selling burritos. A brooding dispirit over all, possibly due to the rain. A quiet medium forlornness.

Cantina Chaqmal, a grim-looking place, squalid. Landau stuck his head inside and then slowly withdrew it. Serious drinkers in there, standing at a low bar. Several wearing baseball caps. One man was having a coughing fit that verged on gagging.

Here were two *huarache* restaurants, on a single block of rain-splashed International Boulevard. El Huarache Nayar was brightly lit and had gaudy Aztec warrior murals, bare-chested men in giant feather headdresses, at their feet half-naked women in sinuous postures of desire. The photos of combination platters in a window promised more than he could handle—better order à la carte. Down the block was a second restaurant, less gaudy, called simply Huaracheria, "the huarache-making place." Somehow it looked more promising, though it had but a single pair of customers at a table far in the back.

They were okay, the *huaraches*. Like oblong tostadas, beans and cheese and lettuce piled on, one of them called *huarache azteca*, pieces of fried cactus mixed with rib meat, and one called *huarache con huevo*, with an egg. He ordered one of each, although each was abnormally large. After eating he sat facing outdoors, underwhelmed by the experience, feeling the victim of a clever marketing campaign: he had been seeing that word everywhere, and it had predictably evoked in him the desire to taste this new thing, this *huarache*, as if that were something entirely new in the universe of food. But wouldn't you know it, the novelty had begun and ended with the shape of the tortilla. Fooled again.

An Oakland police car stopped out front. Landau observed it, the officers in the front seat bending forward, peering through their wet windshield—now one gestured at the window seat where Landau himself was reposing. Their dome light flashed twice.

"Professor? Is that you?"

What? Who?

Why, it was Heitor—Heitor Burgos-Pereira, right here by his elbow. "My God, what are *you* doing here, Heitor? I thought you were in Palo Alto."

"Professor. What are *you* doing here, may I ask?"

Landau gestured at his plates. "I'm eating *huaraches*. Like everybody else these days."

Heitor, the Brazilian health official. The gifted research biostatistician, former postdoc. He wore a dove-gray Gore-Tex duster, looked in a happy mood.

"This my 'hood, Professor, I stay around here sometimes. *Como te gustan los huaraches*, pretty great, hunh? First-rate?"

"Yes, each one was bigger than my head."

There was someone hiding just behind Heitor—a young woman, standing there patiently, unassumingly. Landau turned to see her better.

"Hello there," he said. "I'm Anthony."

"Hi."

Heitor made introductions: Graciela, she was a schoolteacher, she lived in the Fruitvale, just a couple of blocks away.

"What school do you work at?"

"Me? Oh, it's called Lakeshore Beginnings. It's been around for a while."

"Is that that fancy old Montessori school? Where the preschool costs a mere twenty grand a semester?"

"No, not that one, I know which one you mean. It's just a little independent school."

One of the policemen came indoors. He was a short-necked white man with an intimidating mustache, one that grew densely from his upper lip right up to the bottom of his nose. He seemed displeased about something.

"Heitor, I thought you had a Lucile Packard grant. Doesn't that come with an office at Stanford?"

"Yeah, but I been working up here, too. With your old friend Wally Winckelmann. He talks about you sometimes. You should come by."

"Maybe I will, sometime."

Heitor was Argentine, but he spoke fluent Portuguese as well as Spanish. And English, and French. Wait—his mother was Brazilian, Landau recalled, which pushed him further toward the Brazilian side. But he seemed de-Brazilified today—his accent less like Paul Henreid's in *Casablanca*, "Hi dair, my name iss Poul," more standard Mexican, border-states Mexican, "I bean stoodying thees bad Inglish for two yeerce, mano, an' I steal don' get eet, goddam."

"Winckelmann, Winckelmann. Didn't he retire years ago? What's with these old disease-counters, anyhow, they can't stay out of the game. Taking up the space that should go to you younger fellows."

"Yeah, but he's great, Wally is, he's just like you, Professor. The mind is a steel box, and you can't get anything past him. He's got everything up there in that box."

"I used to have something up there, too. Now I forget where I put my box."

Heitor and modest, pleasant Graciela walked out into the rain. The storm lessened, and the Oakland police cruiser, Landau noticed, was now parked at the curb. Several *huaraches* to go: he heard the policeman placing an order in the back of the room. Should I get a bag for this half *huarache con huevo*, he wondered, will they be offended if I leave it on my plate? No, I don't think it matters.

Not possible that the police had followed him here. Just not possible. Yet here was the patrol car, parked outside the window. The rain started falling again. Not buying a car to replace the BMW had been partly because of this, because he was sure to be followed everywhere, if he drove—he didn't want to make this experience a car-chase comedy, too. But they could follow you on foot as easily as in a car; pick you up when you came out of a metro, for instance. Ah, the bloody cell phone, that was it! He pulled his out, thought about smashing it. But no, I need it; I have to make a call right now, in fact.

Strangers called him just to rant these days. Yet he had refused to change his mobile number: it was *his* number, after all. He went to the WC. Toilet, bare sink, crank-style window over toilet. In some scenarios I would go out this way, he reflected, leaving my phone behind, to confuse them. But I like having the police know where I am, more or less. The Berkeley police are helpful, though I'm not sure about Oakland.

He made his call. He removed the window screen over the toilet, stood up on the toilet seat, and went clumsily out through the window, sideways.

There. Take that, you flatfeet, you. Hurried along in the misty rain, headed eastward. After a mile the rain was less, was no more. Suddenly the sky cleared—the overcast peeled away, like an opening eye.

"I am Anthony Landau," he said when the door opened on Fairfax Street, a small green house.

"Please, *señor*. With much pleasure."

He entered. Interview to be conducted in Spanish, apparently. Should be okay, if they didn't talk too fast.

"I need a housecleaner," he explained. "I want someone to come every two weeks, nothing fancy, no cooking or laundry, just the usual. Straight housecleaning."

"Where is your apartment, sir?"

"It's not an apartment, it's a house. A medium-big house."

"Fine, where is this medium-big house?"

Landau named his address.

"Berkeley, you say? Well, that's a problem, *señor*. We don't like to go that far," the woman said, "that can be hard for us."

"It's right on a bus line, the fifty-one."

"I will have to talk to them. It makes them difficulties, all that traveling."

The woman might have been Elfridia's older sister. The same height, but stockier, button-black-eyed—not Mayan-looking, very Indian-looking, however. Maybe fifteen years older.

"They tell me that they don't like to, that it's not good out there. With all that traveling. Anyway, I'll ask them."

"I would pay double."

"Double, you say? You'd go double?"

"Yes. Two hundred forty dollars a visit. Because of the travel."

Someone else now came into the living room. She might have been one of the cousins, but Landau didn't recognize her—couldn't see her that well.

"You're from Chiapas, aren't you?" he asked the first woman.

"Yes, I come from there, from around Comitán."

"Yes, it says so on your Craigslist post. I've been looking for you for a while," Landau said, "for some people to clean from Chiapas."

"Okay. Okay."

The young one in the corner switched on a lamp.

"I remembered that you all came from one town or place. I guess it was Comitán, I know I've heard that name."

"Yes, I come from Comitán."

Why was he sounding so insinuating all of a sudden, so threatful? He heard the tone of his own voice, but he had less than ideal control of himself in Spanish.

"Please. I just want to ask you one more question. Then, I'll go."

They were both standing very still now, both the women from Chiapas. The younger one in the back seemed poised for flight—just one more word in the wrong pitch, insinuating the wrong thing, and she was gone.

"Did your friend Elfridia have a boyfriend?"

"Did what?"

"Did she have a boyfriend. A lover. Anybody important to her like that. You know."

No response. Complete and utter bafflement, apparently.

"Because, that might explain things. I'm not a policeman, I promise you. I have nothing to do with the police, nothing at all. I am the man who was at the house, I'm Anthony Landau, it was my house where it happened, but I didn't do anything to Elfridia, I swear, and I feel just terrible about it, really terrible. Say someone came to visit her that day. A boyfriend, a *novio*, somebody she knew. They wanted a quiet place to be together, just for a few hours. I understand that, that's fine. But if that's not the way it happened, then I can't figure it out."

The possible cousin slipped out of the room.

"*Señor*, I don't know this person. Who is this, this Elfridia?"

"Elfridia. She was your sister. Or I don't know, your friend, your cousin. She got killed. Maybe she was your niece. You look very much like her. I know she was something to you."

He pulled some bills out of his wallet.

"Here are two hundred dollars, *señora*. I don't mean to insult you, but I want you to have this. I know your time is valuable." He laid the bills on a footstool nearby.

The woman watched him do this. She shook her head doubtfully.

"No, think about it, please. That's just for you."

The younger one came back in. Two other young women followed her.

Now a man came in as well, a stout, broad-chested fellow of about fifty, not much taller than five feet himself, wearing brown work boots. They were Red Wing boots—Landau could just tell. The man had the air of someone interrupted in the middle of dinner. All right, this better be important, what's up.

"There's two hundred dollars," Landau said. "And here's three hundred more. That's for all your trouble."

The man watched him. "Hey, don't put that there, amigo," he suddenly protested, in barely accented English. "Put that away."

"Sorry. I'm not very good at this. Excuse me if I did it wrong, I mean no offense."

"What's with you, man? Put it away."

"I want to know if Elfridia had a visitor. That's all. Tell me, and I'll go."

"A what?"

"A visitor. Someone who came to my house. Elfridia, your good friend. Maybe your sister, your neighbor back home. I don't know. Elfridia Mattos Tojolobal."

The man shook his head. He knew no such person, and even to be talking this way was all wrong, completely wrong.

"Nobody knows if she did?" Landau asked the assemblage. "If she had anybody she knew who came to see her at my house?"

The first young woman, possible cousin, dropped her head to her chest. Landau looked over at her.

"Did she?"

With a tormented look, this one looked back at Landau. She seemed to nod—anyway, it was something like a nod.

"Yes? Did you ever meet him?"

"No," she said.

"Did Elfridia tell you his name?"

"No, she didn't."

"But someone came, you think she had someone."

"She—had a hope."

"A hope, you say?"

"Yes. A hope that he might come."

The young woman dropped her head again. The short man quietly picked up the money, put it in his shirt pocket.

"Could you come over here, please?" Landau asked. "Talk to me for just a minute?" After a moment, the young woman came a bit closer.

"I just want to know—did she bring him to my house once, or were there a number of visits, was it a regular thing?"

"No. Maybe just once."

"Just once? And was that the day? The day she was hoping he would come?"

"Yes, maybe it was."

She didn't know, really. She looked stricken; it was a disaster, a terrible thing, and Landau felt bad for making her think of it again. Elfridia had been her friend: he saw that in her expression.

"I know this is hard for you. I'm sorry."

"It's okay."

"She was your cousin. Maybe your sister, even. Something."

"No, closer than that. Closer even than sisters."

"I understand. Was he from Comitán, this man?"

"I don't know. He was Mexican, from somewhere in the south. She said that he was worried all the time about the Immigration."

chapter 14

In the fullness of time Landau heard from son Jad. They talked about the lunch date they had missed because of the murder of Dolores Huerta—so what about this Tuesday, would that be okay? Meet at Kaiser again, in the windowless doctors' lounge, with the pastel furniture? The walls painted sherbet orange? On second thought, Landau preferred being somewhere else—how about that new *tapas* emporium, the one that was always bursting with revelers, on Piedmont?

"I hate that place," Jad said, "it's too hip for me. Too noisy, too."

"Okay. That whole neighborhood's full of restaurants, there has to be someplace."

They met at a Chinese restaurant, dependably obscure. Jad brought his own food, in any case: he was training for a marathon, feeding himself according to a strict regime.

"That looks like about five hundred calories, Jad. That's not enough to sustain a five-year-old. You should be eating like a bloody horse."

"It's over twelve hundred calories—leave me alone, please."

His son's lack of interest in his situation was curious, Landau thought. Maybe he had faith in Landau's innocence, plus faith in his lawyers; maybe he felt that there was nothing he could do, and things were sure to work out. Maybe it all seemed frivolous and empty, considering the suffering of Third World children.

"Things are okay with me," Landau volunteered, since he hadn't been asked. "The lawyers are handling things, and they've warned me to back off. In six weeks it'll all be over."

Jad blinked. Oh, *that* again. *That* sordid business.

"Sorry I missed the arraignment," he said. "Karin said it all worked out, anyway."

"Yes, it all worked out. It wasn't an arraignment, actually—it was a bail hearing."

Maybe it distressed him that his father was being tried for sex crimes. That could get to you, if you were a sensitive sort. Maybe he cared too much, too deeply—but no, just look at him, it wasn't the face of someone who was caring too much.

"Tell me about Samantha, Jad. I still don't understand what you were up to."

"What's to tell? We were friends, that's all. We stayed in touch."

"Did you ever have sex with that woman, Son?"

Silence. Sneering silence.

"Okay, don't tell me then. That's your business."

"I don't pry into *your* affairs. I leave *you* alone, don't I?"

My God—then he did. He actually did it, thought Landau.

"When did this begin, Jad?"

"When you brought her home."

"When I brought her home? You were fourteen. Thirteen, maybe."

"Yes, thirteen."

More silence. Jad ate carefully out of his lunchbox, his small backpacker's lunchbox.

"Jad, please tell me about it. I need to know."

"Look, she was fond of me, okay? She went out of her way for me. That's all. We became friends, despite different ages and everything. That's all that we were—close friends."

Flipping desperately through the memory file, Landau tried to recall the reality now lost to the years. All right, some unusual gifts, they were significant: the legendary drum set, for instance. But that was about it. He could picture nothing else. His explosive, more-than-a-handful girlfriend had often been tender toward his troubled son—it was a side of her that he'd liked a lot. Famous for rough stuff, for grudges and revenges, she had been sweetly indulgent around toddlers, shy schoolgirls, surly boy skateboarders. Had there been a sexual side to that? Unthinkable. Inconceivable.

"How did she come to it, Jad? How did it all start?"

"How did *what* start? It wasn't sex, not in the ordinary sense, if that's what you're worrying about. If that makes you feel better."

"Yes, it does make me feel better, as a matter of fact."

"Why would you even care, though? You were never all-in with her.

She was no more important to you than A or B or C, or X or Y or Z, for that matter. She was someone who *I* grew attached to, in an intimate sort of way."

Oh, this was too much. "No, I loved her, Jad. I loved her very much."

"You didn't. I don't accept that."

What? What did you just say to me, you impertinent pup?

"I loved her, Jad. I *loved* her. And she knew it. But that didn't mean a lot to her in the end. Still, she knew it."

"Consider what you did to her professionally, Dad. The cruelty of that. That was a deep blow. Ten years later, though, she's at your house, waiting for you in bed. Despite all that. All that had happened."

"She wasn't waiting for me, I don't know what she was doing. And she died, Jad. That's all that happened—she died."

"You have to explain why she was at your house. She came to see *you* that afternoon. She didn't come to *my* house."

Well, here's a simple explanation. She came to see me expecting me to welcome her back. In her demented belief in her own wonderfulness, she assumed that all would be forgiven; that I would welcome her with open arms. I'd seen her do that with others, larkily look them up after a savage break. She found the maid at home, came inside to wait. Then saw or heard something that disturbed her—maybe Elfridia's gentleman-caller surprised her. She gasped, put a hand to her chest.

"She was waiting for you. I don't think there's any mistaking what she had in mind," said Jad. "She often said she missed talking to you, fooling around with you. You used to make her good things to eat, eggs Benedict and things."

"Oh, eggs Benedict. I made eggs for her maybe twice. Extra butter and—here's the trick—Béarnaise sauce. Not Hollandaise."

"Maybe that's what killed her, the sauce Béarnaise."

Somehow, the frost was starting to melt. He seemed ready to smile, Jad—ready to share an understanding.

"It's flattering what you say, Jad. That she still carried a torch for me. It's just that it's completely wrong. She never carried torches—she marched on boldly, always, toward Armageddon."

"She spoke well of you, always. Kept up with me half because she got to talk about you, I think. I liked you two together very much. Those were the years when I actually thought my dad was a pretty happy guy."

Landau paused. Odd to be hearing about this now.

"I was the one she accused of sexual harassment, Jad. The one whose career she dropped a bomb on."

"I know, but she hoped you took that with a grain of salt. She didn't wreck your career, anyway—you know who wrecked it. Who gave up on it, grew tired of it. But that's another story."

The next day, Landau heard from his friend Detective Johnson, who wrote in reply to a recent email:

"I readily accept you into the club of hardworking criminal investigators, Professor. Congratulations on excellent work. Unfortunately, the people aren't on Craigslist anymore as of this morning. Are you sure they're the Mexicans we're after? We will be as sensitive as we can and nobody is getting into any visa trouble, but we need to talk to them ourselves, us police do. Please send me their address. Would be nice to see you again—maybe another walk?"

Landau was excited, very excited, because Melody was coming to see him that night. By midafternoon he was jumpy, feeling a quiet pulse down his arms, somatic proof of deep excitement. Oh, I'm on the sex-wavelength again, he thought joyfully, how wonderful. I feel so lucky.

Before she arrived, however, Byrum Johnson arrived with a grim face on, in a convoy of police cruisers, including a medical van and one Oakland patrol car. They said nothing and took Landau into custody. Thirty minutes later he was in a padded cell in the detention wing of the Berkeley Hall of Justice—regular cells were available, but they put him in a padded one just to be safe, in case he felt like banging his head against the wall.

He began to yell from inside, "Have I been arrested? If so, I would like to call my lawyer. There's something called the Bill of Rights in this country I've been told, please tell me if it's not in force anymore."

Another murder, another savage girl-murder. That was his guess. He began to talk more loudly and even to scream a bit—the idea came to him suddenly that one's ironic impersonation of full-blown insanity was tantamount to the real thing, and for a few moments he felt true panic, finding himself locked away in a padded box at the mercy of others, undependable others.

Then they were walking him down a cold linoleum hall, three Berkeley police officers, Officer Hashimoto among them. Carl Glebefelder was with them, too, and after some lawyer-speak Carl was walking him out onto the rainy sidewalk, no backward glances, no good-byes.

"What the hell was *that* about?"

"I don't know. The less said, the better. I think we're intended to feel the immensity of their wrath."

"Has someone been killed, Carl?"

"Yes. In the Oakland hills. Body found just this morning."

"Oh, Christ."

"You didn't have a raincoat?"

"No, they took me as I was."

Someone had called the law offices, eventually—some cooler head. Carl just wanted to take him home now, would that be okay?

"Fine, but can we go to the supermarket first? I have to get some milk."

"Okay. Whole Foods your sort of place, Professor?"

"Sometimes. But Andronico's would be better—it's closer."

Landau bought toilet paper and cat food, too. The attorney bought two six-packs of hearty winter ale plus a takeout clamshell pack of something Italian-looking.

"What is that, Carl, lasagna?"

"No, eggplant parmigiana. They make it pretty good here."

Unidentified Hispanic female. Found in Sibley Volcanic Park. One of the reports Carl had read said that the body had been buried under a log. Another said that it had been left on the leaves in a grove of trees—no burial attempt at all. Had Landau been to Sibley Park in the last couple of weeks?

"No, Carl. I haven't. That's not a place I go to. It's off my circuit."

"It's down Grizzly Peak Boulevard, isn't it, which runs pretty close to your house?"

"Yes. Look, I've been a good boy, Carl. I haven't slaughtered anybody, I swear."

"Okay."

"I can tell you where I've been every minute of every day, if I have to."

"Lots of cutting. The head was fully severed, they say."

"Oh, God. I don't want to hear about it."

"I'm sure there'll be photos online."

Carl was still studying his responses, Landau felt. Weighing what he said, his tone.

"You can tell Cleveland that I looked disgusted, Carl. That I almost threw up in your car."

"You just said you liked my lasagna."

"I didn't say that, exactly. I was just wondering what it was."

The whole mad circus again, all of it. Certain words and images are broadcast into the ether, and in response, 150 agitated people appeared on his lawn, surging, milling, threatening. Cars were parked up and down his woodsy block again. Landau recognized Katherine of KRON's pastel Prius, although you couldn't be sure it was hers—Berkeley was bursting with new Priuses these days. Press vans parked helter-skelter. Talk of a severed head awakens unusual interest, and wasn't that the title of an Iris Murdoch novel, one of her best? Does anyone read Iris anymore, the wittiest British novelist of the last half century? Overstuffed plots, professors and other over-educated types doing stupid, absurd things—what great material.

"What should I do now, do you just want to get out and go in, Professor?"

"Not really. But this is my house, Carl. The only one I own. I don't want to be scared away from it."

"I could take you to your son's place. And you have some friends around here, don't you?"

"Yes, I have any number of places to go. I'm just feeling sorry for myself."

What he was thinking was that Melody would soon be arriving. Maybe she was already walking up, having parked down below again. She would hear the commotion in the trees, see beams of LED light slanting through—was somebody throwing a street party, was that what it was? Oh, how nice.

"Okay, Carl, here I go. Wish me luck."

"Okay. Call us if you need us. There's an emergency option on the phone tree."

Once inside his house—not even spat upon, just spoken to impolitely—he phoned Melody to tell her not to come. But she wasn't picking up now. He hurried to his computer. There for his viewing was his current reality in a lurid feed, and he suspected that if he had switched the machine on a little faster, he would have seen himself actually coming in the door, phoning her, turning on the desktop. Wait, they were replaying his ascent of his front steps from just a minute and a half ago, the surging mob visible behind him. Head bent, shoulders rounded—his version of the Mexican crouch. Here was a closer view of his face, and he was smirking again, as if at some private joke. It was the expression his face took on when it knew not what else to do. If that isn't the expression of a serial killer, well, I don't know what is. Put that monster behind bars, please. City of Berkeley, can't you police your own streets? Protect your own women?

Deena called him at eight thirty. "Come over here, it's better," she said. "I'll come pick you up."

"Oh, Deena. No, it's gone too far for that. I don't know if I could get out of the house again, to be honest."

"I know, I can see on the TV."

Landau switched on his own TV. There he was—there his house was.

"There's only so much hyperreality I can take, Deena. Then my mind goes all wooshy."

"Have you eaten anything tonight?"

"No, but someone is coming over later. I bought a nice piece of halibut yesterday."

"She won't be coming with this happening."

"No, probably not. I hope not."

Deena said that they knew the victim—it was one of Georges' ex-girlfriends.

"Oh, no. Which one?"

"They showed her photo just a minute ago. Keep looking. You'll see it."

Landau watched the TV. Fearing what would be coming up on it.

"I'm going to call Georges. He must be going crazy with this. He must be out of his mind."

"Okay," she said, "call me back."

He did call Georges. Georges said, "No, she's fine, Heather's fine, she's sitting right beside me on the couch right now."

"Oh, thank God for that."

"Anthony—it was Angela. Angela Lindon. You remember Angela."

"Angela?"

"Yes, the musician. The one from the flower stand."

Landau thought, and soon he remembered. One of Georges' youngest, most appealing discoveries. A small-boned young Asian woman who played electric bass in a band. He'd accompanied Georges to hear her at a student bar on San Pablo one night. They'd stood in a crowd of sweaty young people, deafened by squawking anthemic rock for an hour and a half. Angela was of Filipino-Irish descent, worked at a flower stand during the day, the one on Shattuck close to Vine. Wrote all the band's terrible songs.

"Good God, Georges. I thought they didn't release the names of victims for twenty-four hours."

"They don't, but sometimes they do. They just get out."

"What must her family be going through, the poor, poor people."

Beautiful young woman, Angela. That was Landau's governing memory of her, not how talented or untalented she was, how she played the bass, but how extraordinarily beautiful she was. Georges had courted her with all his old lothario tricks, and they had kept company for a while. The affair had eventually collapsed amidst warm laughter on both sides.

"How sad, Georges, how truly sad. I don't know what to say. It's insane, it's horrible, I'm sick to death, sick."

"Why would anyone want to hurt Angela Lindon? That's like committing a crime against the world spirit. Against goodness and beauty and youth."

"*Is* there a world spirit, Georges?"

"Yes, there is, except when people murder it."

At nine thirty Melody called him. She was just then walking up toward his house.

"Melody, please don't come. My house is under siege. You don't need to get caught up in this."

"You're up there by yourself?"

"Yes, I am."

"All right."

Twenty minutes later, he heard her at the laundry room door, which he had agreed to unlock.

"How did you get over the fence?"

"I didn't have to climb the fence. I waited till nobody was looking, then I noticed that the latch was broken. I just walked through."

Now that she was here, what was he supposed to do with her? Should he kiss her? Press himself upon her? It seemed wrong under the circumstances.

"Can I get you a glass of wine, Melody? Maybe a whisky?"

"A whisky, I think, but later."

He was afraid someone would see her through a window. He lowered all the blinds. Pulled the drapes even in the hall, and dropped the shades in the kitchen.

"We should go upstairs, I think. They won't be able to see us as easily up there."

"Not unless they're in the trees," said Melody, seeming rather amused by it.

Her cheeks were full of color tonight. Her dark eyes flashing.

"Melody, bad things are happening all around me. I don't want anything to happen to you. I would hate that, bloody hate it. You really shouldn't be here."

"Let's not go up yet. You said you had a nice piece of fish. Do you want me to cook it?"

"I don't know. I'm not hungry, are you?"

"Yes, I am. I'm starving."

chapter 15

T he judge who had granted bail, Sherman Beane, was on medical leave, and at least for a while there was little chance of his grant of bail being revoked by some other judge, because the police had to investigate the new killing and then connect Landau to it. Then the DA had to decide whether to charge him with the new crime. He would be called in for questioning, Raboy warned, rough questioning, probably. Byrum Johnson had been taken off the case—had gone on medical leave himself.

"What! Are you serious?"

"That's what I'm hearing," said the lawyer.

"What's the matter with him?"

"I don't know. Nothing?"

"Nothing?"

"Look, he did an amazingly wrong thing. It was a political gesture as much as anything, showing that they could be pushed too far, even the squishy Berkeley types can. That you could make them angry."

"I don't get it."

"He shouldn't have put you in the cell. In the box. But someone told him he had to, and after that, he had to fall on his sword. He's probably on Prozac now."

Landau felt abandoned. In his fantasy he and his detective friend had been about to crack the case, by the judicious application of Occam's razor, among other things. Had been working up the San Diego murders, the mysterious Mexican man on videotape factor, the Chiapas group. Now, all for nothing.

"Get ready for some rude handling, Doctor. We're back with the Oakland PD, it's Oakland's case after the East Bay Regional police go over it," Raboy went on. "Officer Cheatham, Lieutenant Cheatham excuse me, wants another shot at you. Wants to take you down hard."

"Oh, fie on him."

"Have you put together that timeline I asked you for?"

"No, I'm working on it. The fact is there are stretches of time I can't recall at all. Usually they run between midnight and about 7:00 a.m. It's as if I black out or something."

"Funny. You still don't understand that you're playing for your life, do you?"

"No, I understand that very well."

"Not fun and games anymore, Professor. You're at liberty on only the thinnest of pretexts. The judge wants the charges consolidated, thank God. So you can't be denied bail in another court. Then he announces that he's having his gallbladder out. Think of that. Think what he's done for you."

Meaning what—that the judge was pulling a fast one on Landau's behalf? Was that possible?

"I want you to consider hiring a security service. And give me that timeline, please, hurry up," Raboy commanded. "I want to know who killed those women. You know who did, and it's time that I did, too."

"Do I know that? Well—that's a relief."

Raboy fell silent.

"That's the problem right *there*," the lawyer growled after a while. "*You're* the problem. *You're* not really trying."

"I bloody well am trying, counselor. I have no gift for playing detective, but that's not my fault, is it? You don't need to know who did it, anyway. You only need to know that I didn't."

"Don't tell me what I need to know."

Blustery, Englishy-weather. Egdon Heath-ish. Landau and two of his lawyers, Glebefelder and Dimitriopoulous, walked up a muddy path out of tall eucalyptus with a squad of Oakland police officers in attendance. What a strange spot for a park. It was a small dead volcano, Sibley was, with lava flows, but the rounded hilltops and upsy-downsy ridges did not add up to what Landau looked for in a park. Wasteland, that's what it was. An owner had given it over to the state, after tiring of paying taxes for generations.

Rain falling again. Landau put up the hood of his parka. Masha had a chartreuse slicker made by Sierra Designs—it said so on her breast—and Carl wore an old-fashioned belted raincoat and brown felt hat, made him look like a battered private eye, a young impersonation of one. Raboy was in Sacramento today, pursuing unrelated matters. Just listen to what Masha tells you, had been the order from the top—do whatever Masha tells you.

Hillsides with bright new grass. One slope ran up to a copse of small trees on a summit. Looked like the haircut on the actor in *Eraserhead.* Now Lieutenant Cheatham and another police detective, Nordwin, appeared beside Landau, the second detective also dressed Philip Marlowe–style, with an actual gray fedora. Lieutenant Cheatham smiled at Landau as if at an old friend.

"Good of you to come, sir. Your cooperation is appreciated, I mean that sincerely."

"Anything to help you, Detective."

"Not detective. Lieutenant. It's a little different."

"Okay, sorry."

Big, square-headed fellow, the lieutenant. Looked like an African-American Ernest Hemingway. Another thick, manly mustache: there must be a fad for them in the department.

"How you been doing, Doc, you hanging in there?"

"I guess so, what about you?"

"Oh, not so good. We can't stop these damned murders. Another one this morning. Yes, a whole other one. Over in the Fruitvale district. Pretty brown-skinned girl, all cut up, horrible."

"Wh-what?"

"That's right, number four or five, depending how you count. Mid-twenties, Mexican-looking, no ID. He basically vivisected her."

Landau, blinking, looked over his shoulder, wondering where his lawyers were.

"Are you fooling with me, Lieutenant?"

"No, I wouldn't do that. I don't fool around about murder. Murder's the real thing."

"I'm shocked. I don't know what else to say. Completely shocked."

"I hear you. He's shocked, Nordwin, did you get that? Completely shocked."

The other detective nodded.

They had taken him away from Masha and Carl, had walked him fast up the hill, to get a little separation. Now they were practically running together.

Just short of the top, the lieutenant stopped, panting, and said, "I can never figure out how to get inside here. You could climb over the rocks, or you could worm through the trees. Which is better, do you think, Professor?"

"I wouldn't know. I've never been here before."

Cheatham looked at Nordwin. "Yeah, but which approach would you take, anyhow? Would you just barge in, or would you maybe look for a little path?"

"Well, maybe some barging, some path-hunting, combine them."

"Okay, yeah. That'll do."

Here came Masha and Carl. Masha grabbed Landau by the coat sleeve— stop right there, say no more.

"Why don't you just push on through, then, Doc. Go on. I'll follow."

Masha let go of him, and Landau hefted himself over a boulder. Children must love to play up here: it was a sort of stockade of trees, with a secret space inside, a cozy hideaway. Two uniformed Oakland police officers were already in there, shivering. They said nothing.

"Okay, that works. What kind of trees are these, Professor, valley oaks?"

"I don't think so. They look like bay trees to me."

"Bay trees. Hmm. Okay, I see you know your trees."

Rocky ground, trees growing directly out of the rock. No one had told him anything, but this must be where Angela Lindon's body had been found. There were two flat spots. One was two yards higher than the other, and the lower one was where the patrolmen were standing.

"If you brought someone up here, you could hide stuff in the bushes so you'd have it when you got her up here, no, Professor?"

"Yes, Lieutenant, you could, if you wanted to do that."

"We found some duct tape over on that other hill. The gal this morning was bound with duct tape. Arms severed at the elbow. Hands bound at the wrist, kind of in a prayer position."

For some reason, Landau was thinking of the guards. The one who was shivering more was trying not to seem to be eavesdropping, but the other one was frankly listening to every word, staring bug-eyed at Landau meanwhile. What an opportunity for a simple patrolman. What a learning experience. Later he would tell his friends, "Yeah, I was there, when that smiley freak, the Berkeley Slasher, gave it up. Cheatham got him talking about the dead girls. There's two kinds of killers, see, binders and non-binders, and binders truss them up like a turkey, do painful things with rope or tape. Non-binders are different. He got him talking about all that, binding, and that broke him, the sick fuck."

"This poor, poor girl," the lieutenant was saying. "No tape on her. Her body was over here, head over there, six feet away. No signs of struggle. The dark stuff's all her blood."

Landau looked at the vast, sorrowful stain. He nodded.

"Appears she walked up the hill willingly. Killer took her shoes afterward because he didn't want any fibers found from his car. No slices through the nipples, so, that's different. Maybe he's losing that motivation."

"Losing what?"

"Losing impulse. Yeah, you see that sometimes. They stop carrying through on certain drives. Sort of let them fade out."

Masha now entered the ring of trees. Her parka had gotten wet and had a Day-Glo cast.

"Miz Dimitripolis. How tall're you, can I ask?"

"Five seven and three quarters, Lieutenant, why?"

"Well, would you lie down here for a second? To show us how a woman would fit?"

Astonished pause. "Are you crazy? *You* lie down, Lieutenant. *You* lie down in all that blood and rain and whatnot, *you* do it."

The lieutenant chuckled. "Okay, okay. Just kidding."

Now more serious: "Professor, this is a special place. It's in the guidebooks, a place where people come to on purpose, they call it the Faerie Ring. Out there is Mount Diablo, away across the valley, can you see it? Devil Mountain, in plain English. That's what 'diablo' means."

Landau tried but could not see Devil Mountain. Too much blowing mist today.

"This is an altar, an actual altar. In the spring they come up and have their ceremonies," the lieutenant went on. "The Volcanic Witch Project— you've heard of them, right? They cover it in the *Chronicle* every year."

"I'm uninformed about such things, Lieutenant. Local cults and so forth—not my area of expertise."

Landau looked more closely at the site. Some forest animals might sleep on the lower perch, when it wasn't dark with blood. Very little rain was filtering through the leaves overhead, because the branches were tightly woven. It was a private place, an uncanny place. An altar, yes, all right, he could see that.

He stepped back and sat upon a large rock. From here he had a good view of the lower spot, with no trees in the way.

"I think he sat up here, Lieutenant. Then, he watched her bleed out. He had an excellent view from up here."

"Yeah, think so?"

"Yes. You're like on a throne here. Your victim is displayed at your feet, near and yet not so close as to grab you. He would have liked that, degenerate that he is. Cruel maniacal bully."

The lieutenant nodded. Kept nodding.

"And since we're expressing every odd idea that comes into our heads," Masha said. She shook her head ruefully, then went on: "What was the weather like that day, Lieutenant, do you know? Was it fair, or was it like today?"

"Well, I'm not sure. I could look that up."

"What day was it, anyway?"

"Found her on the eighth. Lab says she was out three to four days. That makes February 4, February 4 or 5."

Landau happened to remember February 4. The fourth had been a Sunday. The weather had been blowy.

"You remember, Professor?"

"Well, I sort of do, in fact. The fourth was Sunday and it was cold and rainy. That was when the weather changed, around then, when it didn't seem like spring anymore."

What was this with the weather? They didn't know what else to talk about, he reflected, so they had to talk about the weather.

"Here's what I'm thinking," said Masha. "If it was a nice day, you come up here on a nice walk, it's not that hard to get into. But if the weather was like now, you'd have to be compelled. I don't know—maybe the guy had a gun at her head. Or maybe she wanted to come, because she liked the guy, he was attractive. Maybe there's something about him."

The lieutenant blinked twice—okay, maybe. But let's get back to something more important, what the *professor* can tell us, the professor himself.

"That's very smart, Masha. Because, it's a long way up from the car," said Landau.

"Yeah, and it's steep."

"I don't think you just amble up, not on February 4, in the rain."

"The blood puddles, though, Professor, what about the blood puddles?"

"The blood puddles?"

"Look, there should be two. Body here, head here. A head has a lot of blood in it. You can't believe how much. It's like a little barrel full of blood."

Landau thought about it. "If he were the same one who killed Dolores Huerta, maybe he did the same thing here, made expert incisions. Cut around her throat, then retreated up here for a ringside seat. I don't know how he subdued her to begin with. Half-suffocated her? Half-strangled? But he likes the bleeding, so while he's watching her, maybe he got excited. Have you checked around here for semen, Lieutenant? That would seem to be a possibility."

"Yeah, we checked, but we'll check again."

"Then, when she's fully exsanguinated—bled out—he cuts the head off. Puts it over there, six feet away. With no blood left in it."

"Over here, Professor?"

"Over wherever you said."

In the car afterward, the lawyers' car, Landau wondered what that had all been about.

"It's to be cooperative, sir. It's to carry through on that theme, you with nothing to hide, wanting to solve these crimes so, so much. More than anybody. But Mr. Raboy's always doing something else, two steps ahead of them. I don't know what, really. You were good today, though, Professor, very smart. You said good things."

"Did I, Masha? I wasn't indiscreet?"

"You were indiscreet, but in a good way."

chapter 16

The judge had his gallbladder out, and the district attorney delayed bringing charges in the murder of Angela Lindon. Wendy Waters was being taken off the case, the lawyers reported, and another assistant district attorney, Milka Resnick, was on. Resnick was four months pregnant. How would that play in court, what were the implications of that? No one could say, but the whole thing made Raboy nervous. Now less than a month till the trial started. Time to get organized.

Landau awoke the morning after the visit to the hilltop certain that Jad had done it, his son, Jad. Jad who had played with knives when a boy, who'd had an intense mumblety-peg period, aged about thirteen, out in the park throwing knives over and over in the dirt. Who'd taught him that game? Landau, Londoner, had not known the homely American pastime, and now he had the most amazing instant of recall: it was *Samantha* who had taught Jad, who had tomboyishly learned the game herself from her older brothers, Samantha who had given Landau's son his first real knife. With Landau's permission, of course.

My God, it was overwhelming, overwhelming. Think of the psycho-sexual implications. But—maybe not. His mind wiggled as fast as it could away from thoughts of his son as the killer, as the mad vivisector, to consideration of other attractive candidates, and why had Georges not been brought in for questioning, Georges, the former lover of the next-to-last dead woman? The police seemed not to be thinking about Georges at all.

He built a case in his mind quickly against friend Georges, Georges who had once had a key to Landau's house and might still have it, Georges who knew his comings and goings as well as Landau himself did. Georges had been out of the country when the maid disappeared and Samantha died, but that was a mere detail, his story of treating sore necks in Bali possibly a whole-cloth fabrication. Look at everyone, you foolish police! Landau wanted to say. Come on! Don't just focus on my son!

The fourth or fifth victim had worked as a nanny, for a family on Gravalt Drive, Claremont district. Just around the corner from Jad's house. In the early news and blog coverage, writers spoke of her as a preschool teacher, and Landau recalled the young woman whom Heitor had brought to the huarache joint, but that person wasn't named Marta Villacorta, she was called Graciela Something. Every Thursday and Sunday, Marta Villacorta had had the afternoon off from her family, the Stein-Pidgeons, and one Sunday she hadn't come home. Her body had been found in three dumpsters.

Heitor—Heitor as the killer. Heitor was a possibility, except that he was un-killer-like. Had arrived in the midst of all the action, from exotic Brazil. He knew Landau, was emotionally involved with him in a sort of way, as a former student. Had met Samantha Beevors once or twice. But Heitor liked women and always had friends among them, not just lovers but friends. His Argentine father was the only dark matter in his cosmos, a famous heart surgeon who had required that his three sons also become physicians, then had found each inadequate in his own way. Heitor occasionally told funny stories about the tyrant father, without real bitterness.

Just for fun, Landau tried out the Heitor hypothesis on Melody. They were in his bedroom on a Thursday night.

"I have this former researcher, Melody. He's in town now. He would have no trouble enticing a girl into a car—could probably get a girl to *buy* him a car if he wanted."

She nodded slowly.

"He has a fellowship in the area. He's taken leave from a sub-ministerial post in Mato Grosso state, Brazil, to do some more computerish thing. He's from down there, his mother's Brazilian and his father's Argentine. Went into public health and worked under a man I know, d'Iulio, to start out. AIDS was the thing when Heitor came up, but d'Iulio put him onto dengue fever, which is an almost eradicated disease down there. He decided he wanted to work on better problems. He came to work with me."

Interesting, but not exactly riveting, was what Melody seemed to be feeling. She crossed her athletic legs.

"Those shoes. You're wearing those shoes."

"You like them?"

"On you, very much."

"Go on, I'm listening."

"So, Heitor knew Samantha. Where Samantha was brash, world-conquering, he was self-effacing, bright but not wanting people to notice too much. Because he didn't want them to feel bad. I was surprised he took a governmental post, a political post. He was more private than that. Maybe it was because of some ongoing struggle with his father, proving himself. Lula, the president of Brazil now, is said to have brought him along. Lula is a smart, competent fellow, does not surround himself with corrupt cronies, or not only with cronies. I'm guessing that Heitor's mother had something to do with it, because she's from an important family, and they probably know people in the government."

Melody looked displeased. Landau asked her what was wrong.

"You know so many important people. I'm just a humble physical therapist. Why would you want to spend time with me?"

"I should think that's perfectly obvious."

"Come on, give me one good reason."

"I find you absolutely wonderful. I don't think of you as humble, the opposite, beautifully self-possessed. Not that anything's wrong with humble. As for knowing big people, I do know some big shots, because I've been on projects that billionaires and politicians take an interest in, but that doesn't mean I'm a big shot myself. Even in pissant Berkeley I'm not of the in-crowd, I'm not clubbable, I don't give off the right smell. I'm the guy at the dinner party who spills wine on his own shirt. Ask your husband, Arthur. He knows."

Melody seemed unmollified.

"I know, it's hateful to talk about high important people. I'm just trying to explain Heitor to you. Heitor has run a major institution already in his thirties. He's been near the center of power in a big country. The central state hospital in Cuiabá, if I'm not mistaken, was something he was responsible for. I'm thinking he burnt out and needed a rest, so he applied for a grant. He's a numbers person, a math-head. One of my most promising."

Landau was sitting on the edge of his bed. Melody now joined him, not getting too close, however.

"I don't think a person like you just described is the one," she said judiciously.

"No. But in the movies, that's what makes him interesting. I checked him on the South American sex-crime databases. I wanted to know if there's been a kill-spree down there, and it turns out there has. In the city of Cuiabá seventy-two young women dead in three years in the early nineties. That's before Heitor got there, of course. Mostly young prostitutes."

"Where is that, Cue-ee-abah?"

"Mato Grosso state. A city of about a half a million."

"Seventy-two seems like a lot, no?"

"Yes, it is. It's an outbreak."

All in a rush, Landau and Melody were in a hot embrace, stretched out on the large, engulfing bed. Landau had been thinking about her to an absurd degree lately. He was becoming besotted. And these kisses that they were sharing now: they were real kisses, kisses as they were meant to be. Thank God we humans can kiss, he thought—think of the state of things if we could not.

"I have to go to the bathroom for a sec," she said.

"Okay, hurry."

Landau rolled onto his back. He smiled at his half-timbered ceiling. Odd that this was happening now, in the shadow of the dead girls. Were the two developments somehow connected? Did such things happen often to people accused of dastardly crimes, was it a well-known phenomenon, the desperate-love-in-the-shadow-of-the-gallows effect? It was queer, the conjunction, definitely most inappropriate.

Had he met Melody a few months ago, he might have overlooked her entirely. I was awash in self-pity, he thought, grumping my way through life. Grumping about what? Oh, the usual complaints of the overly fortunate, that I wasn't rich and important enough, that the game was over and it hadn't turned out as I wanted. Jad said it well: You gave up on your own career, Dad. But it didn't feel as if I had. I simply ran out of steam, woke up one day and didn't want to work anymore. Didn't have to.

I still don't want to work, not really. I only want to kiss Melody's carmined lips. Find the murderer, too. Meanwhile, get out one more paper, perhaps, something on the theory side. And while I'm at it, why not cure cancer. Shouldn't be too difficult.

"This is so fun," she said, returning and immediately lying down beside him. "Kiss me, please. I'm ready."

*   *   *

He called Walter Winckelmann to talk about old times, but Winckelmann didn't answer, so Landau took the bus downtown on a blue-tinted chilly day, followed by a Berkeley police car. Winckelmann was in his late seventies now. Could often be found at his office in the grim Health Sciences building, pottering about. Had been emeritus for years, with no diminution of the desire to work. Still wrote a few dutiful papers a year. Was not a soft-money prof, like Landau, no, he had a regular appointment, with more institutional responsibilities. Had mentored an unconscionable number of accomplished epidemes, had built a whole empire, scattered over the globe. Nice man and something of a wise old dog.

The seven-story Health structure on Oxford Street looked like a stackable plastic box. The façade was a grid of giant Xs, suggesting cancellation. Why did people build ugly buildings, did they not recognize them as such? Any child could have told you that this one was a botch.

"Walter? Got a minute?"

The door was open to the famously disordered office.

"Oh, wow. Jesus, come in, Anthony. Anthony Landau, my God."

Quite stooped over now. More pallid, hair very thin. Still had the same broad bony shoulders that Landau remembered, the same raptor eyes—would probably live another thirty years, working right up to the end, riding to work each day on a young bicycle.

"You know, I was thinking of you just the other day. Not in connection with all this nonsense," Winckelmann said, "but about you and Samantha and that artemisinin affair, what was it called, the project in the eighties. 'Roll Back Malaria Now.' Roll back something, I can't quite remember exactly."

"It was Fight Back, I think, not Roll Back."

"Right, Fight Back Against Malaria. The big FBAM campaign."

"Ah, those palmy old FBAM days."

Winckelmann reached toward a listing pile of printed sheets. With gentle tugs he extracted a paper about a third of the way down.

"Page seven, third paragraph from the bottom."

"How do you remember such stuff, Wally?"

"I don't. Someone mentioned it recently, so I hunted it down."

Landau read the paragraph that Winckelmann had wanted him to look at. "Who are these people," he asked, "writing this wretched scientistic English? They should be punished."

"No, that's an important paragraph, Anthony. That's an extraordinary projection, and it has come to pass, like a veritable prophecy."

"I don't know about that."

The paragraph discussed chloroquine, a drug that had been highly effective against malaria for twenty years. Eventually, strains resistant to it had developed, rendering it useless. A new family of drugs, the arte-misinins, had been developed by Chinese scientists, but the artemisinins would themselves become useless in exactly twenty-four years, Landau and Beevors et al. had confidently projected, citing the usual factors promoting drug resistance, monotherapies, village self-medicators, poorly run inoculation schemes.

"It's a sort of Moore's Law in reverse," said Winckelmann.

Landau did not quite get the connection to Moore's Law.

"Call it Landau's Law, then. Landau's Postulate."

"It's not lawful in any proper sense, Wally, it was just a lucky guess."

"No, you showed your calculations. You arrived at it in a rigorous way. See the footnotes."

"Samantha wanted them in there, the figurings. She always liked footnotes."

It was the big new world-health worry: emerging resistance to the best combined therapies. Patients taking three to five days to clear their blood of parasites instead of the usual two. By mathematically precise steps you could arrive at millions more deaths in Africa and other hard-pressed places on the basis of one or two resistant villagers in, say, Myanmar, or backwoods Cambodia.

"Bad news," Landau said. "Terrible news. Why am I never right about the good things?"

"It's good to be right in any connection."

"Not sure about that."

"You noticed something, Anthony. Conceptualized it. You and Samantha."

"What's going on in Southeast Asia that it happens there, not in Africa?"

"Oh, I don't know. Harder times? Faster-collapsing economies? People go out into the forest when they're about to starve, to gather wild fruit, and they get fevers when they sleep outdoors. They give themselves counterfeit drugs and resistance appears. I've never been to Cambodia myself. I hear it's very primitive, but maybe its being less primitive than Africa is what condemns it."

"I was there in '04, on some brothel-hopping duty."

"Right, good for you."

"Wally, tell me something about Heitor, please. His government career has ended, apparently. Why?"

"Oh, I don't think it's ended. They want him back if he'll come. But he's a researcher at heart. He was bored and unhappy as an administrator."

"Why did he come here, of all places?"

"To work on your lucky guess? Estimate viral dynamic parameters? Something like that I think."

"That's just silly."

"Is it?"

"But why here, why not stay home in Brazil? He's got everything online."

"Have you ever been to Brazil? Not Rio but burnt-over rainforest Brazil, or a far-and-gone city like what's-it-called?"

"No."

"I was in Roraima for a year once. They hardly have towns out there, only crossroads with stores. Gold and bauxite mining. Yanomami Indians, Macuxis, lots of tribes. It's like the 1870s but with Internet mapping."

They talked on, Landau gathering that Winckelmann had no idea why Heitor had come to the U.S. A change of scenery: that seemed to be it.

"How's Maxine, by the way?"

"Oh, she's fine. She's been gardening a lot. Mothering Heitor when he'll let her. But you should come by, Anthony, she'd love to see you, she often asks about you. Come by for drinks."

"Yes, I will, please give her my best. "

Maxine Winckelmann: a laconic woman, verging on the hard-bitten. A retired econometrist trained at MIT. Professor at Wisconsin, Berkeley more recently. They were a childless pair, the Winckelmanns, by general consensus completely sexless, platonic partners of convenience; Maxine carried on with other men occasionally, one partner of hers having been Richard Flense of the History Department, who fancied himself a bit of a player. Wally himself favored graduate students from the tropics, dark males. In the nineties his office had been full of slender Sri Lankans with beautiful hands.

Landau had another bit of sleuthing to do this day. He took BART to El
Cerrito, hopped in a cab, rode for half an hour east, at the cost of fifty-two
dollars, then got on another random train. Took it for six stops. Rode the
wrong way for three more stops, then switched trains and rode the right
way to the end of the line, in the town of Martinez.

He had been to Martinez only once before, in all his years in Northern
California. A Berkeley person simply does not go to Martinez: the cultural gulf is too wide. Small town on an arm of the bay, oil refineries,
gun-owners, bayside foliage. Right there was a major affront to Berkeley
sensibilities, because you could see the refinery gantries through the low
trees, and Berkeley, though it had factories, did not do so crude a thing as
refine petroleum—no, it worked on solar technology, more like, on high-
end kitchenware.

As he entered the downtown Landau felt the impossibility of his position. He had emailed Samantha's husband, Bill Beevors, hoping to extract
information. Bill had been forthcoming—he was a sweetheart, Bill, and he
had told Landau all that he knew.

Yes, there was a child, a single female child. (Samantha had had a child!
Unbelievable!) Landau found himself walking along quiet residential
streets in modest weekday Martinez, trying to look inconspicuous, not
like a pedophile, nothing like that. It was the hour when schoolchildren
get out of school, when mothers hurry to pick them up, and he was most
concerned to look indifferently purposed, entirely harmless.

A school van passed, full of small offspring sitting mutely at the windows. Six- and seven-year-olds. He rounded a corner, and there was the
yellow van, disgorging its Juanas and Latoyas and Craig Jr.s, as he imagined they were called. Nice-looking kids. He wanted to see a child of about
eleven, though, not six or seven. Walked through the picking-up throng,
smiling upon everyone. Overcast day, a few drops just beginning to fall.

Martinez had an absence of tall trees. Maybe they did not grow well
near the bay, or maybe only intellectual compounds like Berkeley planted
gigantic trees that reached to the empyrean, as the minds of its scholars
were said to do. Different cars here, no gay Priuses, old pickups and dusty
clunkers instead. Humble buzz-bomb Civics, announcing their unmuffled
selves two blocks away. Here was the house he wanted, the number he'd
been told. He walked on past, did not allow himself even to peek, even so
he registered the low wood structure, askew picket fence, scruff of lawn.

No flowers or trimmed hedges, nothing pretty growing, nothing. How do you not grow flowers of some kind in California, where everything grows, even in sullen February? It was odd.

An hour later. From the end of the same block, he saw a ten-year-old sedan pull up at the house, and a girl get out and run inside, bearing an overloaded book bag. Skinny, long-legged, eyeglasses. Ringlety black hair. Putting on the most anodyne of expressions, Landau surged forward. At about thirty yards the driver's door of the sedan opened and a small woman, possibly of Asian extraction, emerged bearing grocery bags and a purse and a coat, something not quite right about her, a limp, a one-leg-shorter type limp. Japanese, maybe, and at twenty yards the schoolgirl burst back out of the house, without her book bag now, and ran to help the woman, imploring her not to haul those heavy packages. Half a head taller than the Asian person, pale skin, Landau-ish nose, noble nose. Oh, you just know these things, you register them in your heart. In the way she coddled the woman, who was no doubt her mother, taking things gently out of her arms, the woman beaming meanwhile, Landau thought he could read deep fondness between them, deep daughter-mother communion.

Walked on by. Did not allow himself a single look back. All right, just one, a look when they were at the door already, the mother just entering, the daughter holding the door open with a childish knee. Then she was gone, too. Landau walked on. Fought an urge to turn back, to knock at the door, to say something. It was raining steadily now, though lightly. His hair was soaked, so perhaps it had been raining for a while and he hadn't noticed. He walked on.

chapter 17

S ometimes the worst things happen. On the train ride home he was in conversation with himself, then with Samantha, then he reached a point of tenuous calm, an eye-of-the-hurricane place, because, what could you do? What in the world could you do? He needed to speak to Deena about this. Deena more than anyone, because Deena had no kids and had thought through the meaning of being with child as well as without, but he had left his cell phone at home, to foil pursuers, so could not call her. In case what he knew about cell phones from TV shows was true.

Melody was childless, as well. Or, maybe not. Crazy that he didn't know that about her. Arthur Fromm had a daughter, he knew that, he had heard her spoken of. Maybe the daughter was from an earlier marriage. Maybe Melody and the kid didn't get along.

His BART car was empty, and the elevated views of Concord and Pleasant Hill in the small rain lent his arguments with Samantha a certain *tristesse*, but it was good news, wasn't it, intriguing, compelling news? What one could surmise from the shape of a nose seen for about a second? Between Walnut Creek and Lafayette he was alone in the car, then an elderly Japanese man got on, who by virtue of appearing at this moment seemed a symbol—he wore an Oakland A's cap, like the unfound Mexican, he was Asian, as the diminutive limping mother was, and there was something grandfatherly about him, which caused Landau to reflect that he, too, was now a grandfather, or a second-time father. Good God! How was he supposed to feel about that, was there any feeling appropriate to such a case? He did not feel bad, only uncertain as to the way forward. Must talk to Deena, Deena will have some ideas.

"Deena, please call me back. Urgent matter."

As he was drying off after his shower she called. "Anthony? How are you?"

"Oh, fine. I'm putting on my robe now and walking downstairs. Going to go pour myself a stiff drink."

"Okay."

She walked downstairs with him. "Slivovitz, I think," he said. "Jewish firewater. You gave me the bottle, you and Harold. For Hanukkah one year."

"Yes, I remember."

Landau knocked back a glass. "Ai-yi-yi!" he screamed. "Ai-yi-yi!"

"What?"

"Ai-yi-yi!"

Some few seconds later he told her how he had spent the afternoon.

"Are you fooling with me, Anthony?" she asked.

"No, not about this I'm not."

"You need to speak to them then. To the mother and father. Announce yourself."

"I guess. But not now, with all this going on."

"Yes, maybe you're right."

"They'd be completely terrified. They'd take out a restraining order against me. I would do the same."

Deena asked for a record of all his seminal emissions with Samantha Beevors. Landau struggled to answer.

"She had a diaphragm," he recalled, "she believed in it. Would slip it in matter-of-factly, you hardly noticed. She was very anti-pill, because she went on it one time and had an acne episode when she went off. Were we on top of every drib and drab, exercising supreme caution? No, I can't say that. There was a certain devil-may-care-ness, especially when we were drinking all that good red wine in Argentina."

More silence.

Then he told her about the Jad connection. He heard Deena draw in her breath.

"Most unlikely," he hurried to add. "Jad says no, but some things you just don't tell your father, do you?"

"Did Jad go with you over there?"

"To Martinez? No. It would've offended him, to be part of that. He's anti-fatherhood."

"He is?"

"Yes, they don't quite see the point, Karin and Jad. Although their friends are breeding now, some of them. Maybe some day they might even have an accident and give me a grandchild."

"Some people are not made for it, Anthony. Maybe they know something about themselves."

"Yes, I'm assuming that's the case. But it seems selfish, even so."

He told her what Bill Beevors had told him about the adoption. That Samantha had wanted a family not that far away, willing to keep her informed about the child, and to permit some visiting. "The family name is Perry. I don't know the girl's name—she looks like an Ophelia to me, an Olympia, something starting with an O. The father may work for an oil company—a lot of Martinezans work for Shell. The mother looks like she was in a car wreck. I'm thinking Frida Kahlo and the streetcar, and afterwards, you know, she couldn't conceive, she was all messed up."

"Do not be cultural. You are imagining too much on the shape of a nose, please."

"I know that. But I had a feeling when I saw her—a feeling of joy, actually, wild joy."

"What do you want? Do you want to stick yourself in their private business? Maybe you should leave them alone."

"Didn't you just say I should announce myself?"

"Yes, but now I'm thinking again."

It was good to speak with her, even if she was as baffled as he. And how did I not have a child with *this* woman, he asked himself. Think of that, a Deena look-alike daughter or son, maybe even a couple of daughters or sons. Ungainly, secretive, good at math. Bizarrely good at languages. One goes to Cal and one Princeton, or maybe they hate all things of the mind, having had intellectual strivers for parents. Become drug-users, self-tattooers, rage-music listeners. You try to understand them, but they seethe with resentment against you even so—you spend your whole life trying to bring them around, but it doesn't work, it's a mess. Families are so often a mess.

"Deena, my inbox is too full, I can't think about this now. Maybe I'll write them a letter one day. I don't know."

"Yes, no hurry."

"She looks like Jad did at that age, when he got that storky neck. She's going to be a giraffe in that family—her mother's more pony, and I bet the father's also short, it's just a feeling I have."

*   *   *

Deena's office, in Durant Hall, was soon to be decommissioned, and a new Asian Studies Center, with massive library, was rearing up on a nearby hillside. She had told Landau she was glad about that—she'd have more space over there. Her old office, however, with its double-hung windows and high ceiling, plaster walls above mellow oaken wainscoting, pleased her. It was very Old Cal, redolent of the university in its heyday, when neoclassical structures built of marble had expressed the salient California idea. A public university to stand with the best in the world; an American Sorbonne. Her parents, who had mocked America, and as they aged had mocked everything Californian even more, had not mocked that, not much.

Weepy blue rain. She mounted her bike after work and set off gently downhill, the hood of her raincoat catching the wind, pulling back from her expressionless face. Messenger bag slung to strong, narrow back. At the northern edge of the campus she headed up Arch Street rather than Oxford, committing to a series of steep hills as she worked homeward, standing up in the pedals and going mildly sweaty within the first half block, because Arch Street was no joke, it was a lung-buster. The seat of her pants soaked through. The bike tire throwing rainwater against her, but she would be home soon, she would build a fire in the mead-hall hearth of her hillside house, it would be okay.

Mother still annoyingly alive. Lived in an assisted-living in South Berkeley, the mother did, noisily unhappy there, but she had always been unhappy everywhere. Life in its every quotidian manifestation displeased her. Harold had said no to her coming to live with them, which had led to the most savage battle of Deena's life with him, but she had been grateful to him in the end, had needed to be rescued from living with her imperious, unsatisfiable mother. Maybe Harold had understood that. Now she visited the mother two afternoons a week plus Sundays, was often queasy when she woke in the middle of the night, having failed to order Coumadin in her dream, or to renew her mother's subscription to *Sunset*, which had long provided delicious entertainment for its cataloguing of

172

California kitsch. The torment is to live out every trope of human decline, her mother had recently said, every page in the playbook, going from own house to internment cell to incontinent's bed, until you aren't even aware what a horror you've become. Then they can smother you with a pillow and you'll thank them for it. You'll really thank them.

On Eunice she stood up in the pedals for two blocks, and a local driver heading home, a friend of Harold Blodgett's from the gym, in fact, saw her from behind as he drove past, admired her damp derrière, was shocked when, passing, he saw who it was, Harold's wife, that glum-looking but fetching woman who had long played a role in his interior sexual dumb shows. Shapely ass, and you don't fool me with that Lotte Lenya deadpan: you're a very sensuous broad, and I bet you can't get enough of it. That night, after failing to read himself to sleep, he took himself in hand and while his own wife slumbered contentedly beside him, he thought of Deena Marjic in various poses, imagined her at one of her famous parties, leading him into the coatroom. Still wearing those damp trousers, and she puts his hand on her crotch. They fall onto the sofa covered with winter coats. Come on, hurry up, she says. Give it to me. I want you.

Harold's Lexus. But he wasn't supposed to be home yet—this was the second Wednesday of the month, when he and his law school buddies had their poker game. Wednesday nights instead of Fridays, because Fridays encouraged excess, too much alcohol; they were conscientious law school fellows, hardworking, and Wednesday games tended to end on time, which Friday games did not. And yet: Harold's car. The black Lexus.

Light on in the kitchen downstairs, another on upstairs. Harold's study was up there, on the second floor of their house on Keith, and something must have made him hurry home *before* the game, to check an important email on his home computer, perhaps, or to change something in a manuscript he'd been massively laboring over. He had three hundred law journal articles listed on his CV now—those were just the ones he bothered to list. Among constitutional law scholars of his era he was the most cited, because opponents on the right routinely used him as a straw man, while comrades on the left invoked him as a near-deity, the deepest wisdom-speaker of the age. His prominence had sneaked up on him, he liked to say; incapable of brilliant leaps, a classic plodder, he had built an intellectual structure brick by brick, its usefulness sure to be short-lived but for the moment, the laurels were raining down, the celebration was ongoing.

Deena put her bike in the shed. The house had discouraged her at first, being one of those modernist one-offs built in the sixties, with lots of deck and redwood siding going gray with age, not up to the high standard of Landau's vanilla villa, for instance, nor of her parents' snug Craftsman bungalow on Oxford close to Indian Rock. She was architecturally hypersensitive, like many veteran Berkeleyans connected to the university; you could tell you were at a Berkeley dinner party if the talk was all of equity loans for renovation, of master architects designing you a new pantry or bathroom, and Harold's house, which he had bought with his first wife, would never impress anyone.

They had been happy here, however. Lately she had come to feel in some ways profoundly satisfied, solidly married to a decent man, a kind and on most days a reasonable man. Small beer, but big to her. Children hadn't happened for her. A career like her parents' had never much attracted, not because they had convinced her that she was incapable of august professorhood but because rejecting that had been her way of settling accounts with them. Didn't want to hurt them, had always lived dutifully within beck and call, but if she was to be anything it would not be what they had been, peevish, resentful, disappointed academics. Disappointed Serb academics: a vast cultural inheritance of peeve.

"Darling? Are you up there already?"

Deena left her coat in the hall and went to the hearth. They hardly turned on the furnace anymore, regardless of weather; Harold had installed an advanced heating system designed in Sweden, one that passed water in sealed nickel tubes through custom-made andirons then along the baseboards, and it was almost as good as having the furnace on, in fact in some ways it was better. But as with the house itself it had taken her a while to get with the new program—when Harold wasn't home she turned the furnace on in secret, then built a fire in the hearth in the approved Swedish manner. She did this now, built a fire, getting a good one going. It wasn't like building a campfire—it had to be done the right way, the Swedish way.

"Darling, won't you come down? Should I make dinner or are you going out with your poker boys later?"

Ordinary happiness, that's what it was. He bought her novels in Min Nan and she got him books on paleoanthropology, his secret obsession. They had no dog or cat or tropical fish to take care of, no children—he had two grown daughters, one a legal star in her own right, the other a digital-design whiz—which gave them plenty of time for cozy mutual amusements, cups of tea brought in at night, love notes under the pillow. They were still alive to each other. Harold had been smitten from the start, and for her part she found him better looking as the years passed, even as his hairline receded and his face grew gaunt from all the exercising. The talk of him being Lincolnesque had done something to his jaw—well, he looked rugged, didn't he. Rugged but kind.

Landau had tried to get close to him, but Harold would as soon Landau did not exist: anyone who had ever slept with her was an affront. They joked about how jealous he was, that his "forbearing temperament" did not extend that far, not *that* far. Possibly for that reason, he persisted in the idea that Landau might have committed some of the murders. If he had dared to touch Deena, then, who knew what he was capable of? Samantha Beevors, for instance, still seemed suspicious to Harold, not a mere medical event, a heart attack. His friend Raboy had said that the forensics had been slipshod, a big gift to the defense; the prosecutors had followed standard procedure, but you had to assume that someone like Landau was capable of advanced medical trickery, and they hadn't gone the extra mile. Then, consider motive. The woman had set out to destroy him, root and branch. Harold had been around when Landau was going through the worst of it, winter of '95–'96, and he'd warned Deena that her friend seemed on a dangerous edge—seemed almost suicidal. He'd seen other big-time professors when their privileged worlds collapsed—a failed romance was as nothing to the loss of prestige, and Landau had had both from Samantha, heartbreak and scandal.

"All right, what's going on up there?" she now called out. "Are you looking at pornography again, your favorite 'Unshaven Girls' site? I'm coming to get you."

She started upstairs with her messenger bag, then returned it to the foyer. When they had parties, people often drifted upstairs looking for a bathroom, although there were two on the main floor; it was more just nosiness, something about the breadth and curve of the staircase invited exploration, and little objects sometimes went missing from her bedroom or bath. A pair of socks. A hairbrush. Landau had bought her a brush in Prague one time, with bristles that were kind to her fine, oily hair. Maybe Harold had destroyed it in a fit of jealous pique. But no, someone had snatched it, a man, probably—so Landau, amused to hear of the theft, had theorized. Landau, who'd often told her that she was an object of fascination. For all the good it had ever done her, yes, maybe she was; she had a shape or smell or look on her face that made fussy professors go too far. The first had been a colleague of her father's, a distinguished biographer of Kerensky. He had given her a quarter to take off her bathing suit top when she was seven.

What a long, absurd comedy, her embroilments with men! But here, look at this, they had eventuated in this marriage, of all things—in ordinary human contentment. Now the prospect of spending her sunset years with Harold Blodgett quietly pleased her. He was set to retire in another two years, and she would stop working a little later, and then they would travel together. First on his list were the caveman sites in southwest France. He wanted to see what the tourists were still allowed to see, the paintings of saber-toothed tigers and woolly rhinoceroses on curvy cave walls. The deep past called to her Lincolnesque husband—for some reason, he couldn't get enough of it.

"Harold, darling? What giffs? Hey, what's going on there?"

Here he was. Poised at his built-in desk, with the recessed lighting in the Bauhaus-style cabinet above. Some Web site on his computer throwing light on his face. Normally he was a huncher, forcing out the brilliant thoughts by postural contortion, but today he was sitting erect. All right, leave him then. Let no priceless idea be lost because I interrupted.

She took off her damp pants, then came to the doorway of his study again, when she failed to hear any keyboard chatter. The monitor had blinked off. She stood there holding her slacks upside down by the cuff, smoothing the creases. A raven honked out in the street. They were taking over the hills now, the ravens, chicken-sized birds that nested in the firs, in insolent glossy flocks. Drove out the blue jays, even—plus, all the little songbirds. Harold liked their vulgar toughness.

"Hear that, dear? Is one of your raven friends, calling to you. Making that sound in the nose. Saying to stop your work already."

Something about his perfect stillness. A paralytic stroke—maybe a seizure. She rushed to his side, letting her silky slacks fall in a puddle on the floor. He was as if cast in concrete, blood all down one side of his face. Blood filled one eye socket, as if the eye had been gouged out. Oh God, oh no, no. In his lap a glistening blanket of something unidentifiable, no, not a blanket, not that, innards, his viscera, piled up. Gleaming transparent integument connecting the blue-veined lengths. Oh, no—no, no, no. This cannot be.

"Harold!"

She shook him. Roughed him up by the shoulders. The shaking caused him to list in his chair, and she made a mewling sound and let go. Slunk away fast. One of her stockinged feet drew a brushstroke of blood from beneath his chair. She woke up suddenly. This wasn't happening, no, it was impossible, unallowable. She looked down upon it as if from a height, finding evidence of its unreality on every hand. This cannot count, I am not here, and he isn't, either, Harold is not here.

"Harold! Harold!"

An arm around her waist pulled her away, and when she turned against it something was already in her mouth, pushed all the way to the back of her throat. She screamed making no sound, and as she raged and thrashed she saw a face she knew, the forehead knotted in concentration, her captor taking care to accomplish this simple but important task, subduing her, hugging her still, quieting her. There, there, be calm. Now the hand went over her nose as well as her mouth. There, be quiet, I'm with you.

*   *   *

Landau had to go to the bathroom again: twice a night now, as regular as clockwork. Whether he drank little or a lot, he was up twice in the seven hours, the second time often with the sky going light out the window. Dawn patrol. Aim carefully now, come on, be a big boy. Do your business.

He returned to bed but could not fall sleep. Too many bumptious thoughts. Just what I need now, another child! A daughter, or a granddaughter! How do I make *that* right? It's not as if she's an infant, she's half-grown, with the imprint upon her of other people. Again I have been remiss, but maybe she's happy, maybe things are good enough as they are. To appear in her firmament now would not be a kindness, but an imposition. Better to remain in the shadows.

But no—I have to make myself known. I have to because that's who I am—I'm Landau, the one who goes too far. Not some stoical other, some distant benefactor out of a Dickens novel, pulling strings till the last chapter. What's the fun in that, I ask? Where's the contact, the warmth, the hurly-burly?

He slept then, then a pounding at the door and a simultaneous ringing of his bedside phone awoke him. More police. Blank stares, icy ones. Byrum was back on the case, apparently, because here he was: he suggested that Landau come downtown with him, "downtown Berkeley" suddenly seeming as ominous as the Tombs, in Manhattan. From the useless literary memory bin came another scrap of prose, from Dickens' ill-tempered book on America in the 1840s: "What is this dismal fronted pile of bastard Egyptian?" the great Londoner had inquired, upon being shown the Tombs, a risible bit of typical American vulgarity. Nothing about America pleased him, Dickens—it had all been done wrong.

Byrum said that they weren't arresting him, but that he might want to call his lawyer anyway. "What is it this time, Byrum, have I killed another young woman? Or two?"

"Come along and I'll tell you. I'll make you an espresso in my office."

"I don't remember an espresso machine. Your office barely had a chair and a cabinet, as I recall."

"You're right, it's down the hall. It's not a good one, but it makes passable espresso."

Another trip in a patrol car. Did not bother to call Raboy or the subsidiaries, just didn't feel like it. A patrolman was driving, Byrum beside him in the front seat. They were silent. Didn't even turn around to look at him.

"All right, I give up, Byrum. What's happening?"

"I'll tell you when we get there."

"Don't throw me in the padded cell again. That gave me uneasy dreams."

Something big afoot, very big. It was the same excitement he'd sensed at the courthouse that day, when all the newsmen had seemed on the qui vive, loaded for bear. Not as many camera crews as then, but here was Katherine of KRON, looking very lovely, and here were several others camped out on Martin Luther King Jr. Way, their video equipment on. All right, another dead girl, he could read the signs. Another enormity.

Byrum walked him indoors, Katherine of KRON calling out above the others as they passed, "Jad, what about Jad, Professor? Did you teach him how to do it?"

"What was that? What did she say?"

"Never you mind. We go in here," said Byrum, and he took Landau toward an unexpected door.

They really did have a machine. Landau couldn't see it, but he could smell the coffee—it perfumed the halls. Here was Masha Dimitriopoulous, Carl Glebefelder also, but who had summoned them, since he hadn't? Oh, life in a legal action is very different from TV: he had learned that much. There was a lot of unofficial give and take, the police and prosecutors and lawyers bleeding into each other, assisting or pretending to assist each other, and was that just because it was Berkeley, California? That notorious dingbat town?

"Harold Blodgett," Masha was saying.

"What?"

"Harold Blodgett is dead, sir. I'm sorry to have to tell you. He's been murdered at home."

Landau stared at her. Byrum returned now to the small conference room with his trusty laptop—they were going to have a little chat, that was all, get this whole thing sorted out.

"What did you just say, Masha?"

"I said, Harold Blodgett has been murdered, sir. He was attacked at their place on Keeler Street."

"Keith Street," Carl corrected softly, touching her elbow.

"Keith, thank you, Carl. It happened last night. I'm very sorry to have to tell you that."

Byrum sat down at the plastic-topped table—fooling around with his laptop.

"Please," Landau urged in an odd voice. "Please, don't say that. I have to call Deena. Can I use your cell phone, please? I left mine at home."

Masha made no response. It was as if she weren't understanding him.

"Masha, please, may I—"

"All right, okay, here we are," Byrum declared, having at last gotten his computer sorted out. He turned to Landau with a hopeful look.

"Early this morning, sir. A neighbor saw some lights on in the Blodgett house. Too early, he thought, a half hour before dawn. He knows them, has lived on Keith for eighteen years. There was also a light on in the professor's car. Someone had opened the door and left it open a crack."

Landau began to feel sick. He needed to sit down.

"The neighbor, Perlwasser, went over there. He had a key but the front door was already open. No one answered his call, so he called us, which is the right thing to do, of course."

"Thank you, Detective," said Masha, in a tone of I'll-take-it-from-here.

Carl Glebefelder broke in: "Professor, Deena Marjic was also attacked. She's in a coma. I know she's a friend of yours. I'm real, real sorry."

Landau grabbed the back of a chair. "Oh, fuck. Don't say that."

"I know."

"No, that's not right," Landau insisted, and he sat down heavily in the chair.

After a few moments he went on: "All right. Now tell me what happened."

The detective: "Suspect waited in the house, seems like. When Professor Blodgett came home he killed him. Then Mrs. Blodgett came home. He used a sharp instrument on her as with these others. There was a profound loss of blood, the doctors are worried. She, I'm sorry to say, she may not make it, sir. She was probably bleeding for a half hour. Then something scared him away—maybe the neighbor coming over."

For an instant, Landau saw Deena's vulnerable, amused nakedness, under the tyranny of a madman's glittering blade. Saw it with shocked clarity, then shut off that vision, definitively. Would never entertain it again. He blubbered as he had in the kitchen that night, sounding like a walrus with bronchitis. Could not stop.

"All right," he said after a while, the others waiting patiently before him.

The good news was that she wasn't dead. She had been deprived of oxygen for a while, and brains do not thrive without oxygen. But, she was still here.

"Motherfucker. *Bastard*," said Landau, wiping the tears from his cheeks. "The vile, degenerate coward. *Motherfucker.*"

Here was some better news, sort of better. Landau was not a suspect. The police knew where he had been last night, they had followed him, and he had come home at five and had not left the house again. He had made two phone calls, the last just after eleven. The officers had made a report.

"She said about Jared, though, the KRON lady was saying about Jared, my son Jared," Landau protested.

"Oh, right. Yes, they arrested him, sir," said Masha. "They took him in this morning."

"Why?"

"He was on Keith, sir. They asked him what he was up to and he didn't have a convincing answer, so they took him in."

"On Keith Street, you say?"

"A couple hundred yards away from the house," the detective put in. "From the crime-scene house."

"No, not Keith. Corner of Shasta and *Keeler*, not Keith," Carl Glebefelder corrected. "That's close, but about a third of a mile away."

"Was he dressed in short pants? Wearing funny, springy rubber shoes?" Landau wondered.

All three looked at him.

"Breathing heavily? Sweating? Because, he's a runner, you know. He runs all over these hills. He's training for a marathon, running some absurd number of miles a week, sixty or seventy. He's a road racer, I mean a foot racer, and he's always training."

The detective pursed his lips. Shook his head.

"He runs from Oakland to Richmond and back sometimes. Over the mountains to Orinda and then up. Then, he goes to work. A normal human being would go home and lie down for forty-eight hours. He's on a tight schedule, with the only time to train in the morning, before he goes to work."

A doctor, you see: my son is a doctor. He is an honorable, people-helping doctor, not a killer, Landau was trying to say. Masha gave him a distressed look. Don't defend him too warmly, she seemed to be signaling; that's not what we want you to do.

"What is it, Masha, what are you winking about?"

"I'm not winking, sir."

"Yes you are. You're practically waving at me behind Byrum's head."

Deena. Deena is dying. The idea hit him anew as he left the police station, accompanied by the lawyers, and he had to sit down again, on a concrete bench. Masha patted him on the back. He needed to go see Deena, attend this most awful thing, but he also needed to see Jad. Could Cleveland and Co. represent Jad, too? But no, probably not—separation of attorneys, that was an important principle.

Masha thought that Jad might be released in two days. Then, depending on what evidence they gathered meantime, he might be rearrested.

"But that's not fair. They should just leave him alone," said Landau petulantly.

"I know. But they consider him a suspect now. Maybe the leading suspect."

"He is *not* the leading suspect—don't say that. That's completely wrong."

"We'll talk about this later, sir."

"No, we'll talk about it now. You will *not* build a case on the idea that my son is a deranged psycho killer. You want to create reasonable doubt and lay the charges off me, but I won't have it, I tell you, I won't allow it. Not with my son you don't."

"All right, all right."

She was patting the back of his head now. "And please, stop patting. I am not a poodle."

"Sorry."

Go see Deena first. You need to see Deena more. Without a car, he walked the nine city blocks to Alta Bates Hospital, but got nowhere—she wasn't at Alta Bates, she had been taken to an allied facility in Oakland, where critical care cases went. Oh, Deena, not critical care, not for you! All wrong, dear! Hooked up to a ventilator, she probably was, with food arriving via feeding pump. He could foresee a discussion that might transpire in a few weeks' time, the grave ICU physician and the conscientious hospitalist saying, "In the absence of an advanced directive, Professor, we have to make certain hard choices." Landau being only a friend, but in the absence of a living husband, any children, any brothers or sisters, a friend would be all they would have. All right—she still had the half-batty mother, the old Mitteleuropean narcissist in extended care. Mrs. Marjic would tell them to pull the plug, of course. Would offer to do it with her own bony hands.

"Karin, this is your father-in-law speaking. I can cash some CDs if necessary," he said into a remnant pay phone, which miraculously still worked, "and I have the name of a good lawyer for Jad, someone who was recommended to me some time ago. I'll do whatever I can to help, just let me know. Leave me a message any time."

Back to the Department of Health Sciences. To Wally Winckelmann's large office.

"Wally, do you live here more than you do at home? That's what certain people are saying. That's how it is with some of you venerated disease-fighters, I've heard, and I respect you for it."

"Anthony, what's the matter—you're all red in the face. You look stricken. Sit down, please, sit down."

Landau peered around the office. Surveyed the nearby work spaces—looking for a special someone.

"Wally, is Heitor in today?"

"I don't think so. I haven't seen him."

"If he comes in, would you please have him call me? It's a matter of some importance."

"Okay. Sit down, Anthony, you're gasping. You're sweaty."

"That's because I just ran all the way here from Alta Bates. It must be over a mile."

"Closer to two, I think."

"I think I ran, but maybe I walked. I'm not sure."

chapter 18

Two days later he found his way to the Summit Medical Center, down-town Oakland. Melody drove him, then waited in the car while he ventured up to the fourth floor, to try to talk his way in to see Deena. What if he were the killer, coming to finish her off? Cut her throat in her hospital bed, in case there were a few brain cells left? But the staff wasn't worried about that: they let him right in, happy to have a visitor. Flowers were not allowed in rooms, but balloons were okay, and somebody had left a bunch around her bed. Deena, get up, sweetheart, come on! Pull out these tubes and tear off that foolish mask, and come away with me, we'll go dancing. You're still alive, that's what counts, and where there's life, there's hope. I can see you're alive.

"Nurse, what's that whistling sound?"

"That's the next generation infusion pump. Don't touch it, please. It's working properly."

He wanted to speak to her neurologist. But the neurologist wouldn't be in for some time. Here came the pulmonologist, and Landau had a tête-à-tête with him, asking many astute pulmonological questions. The pasty-faced young doc was forthcoming, but then he turned stern and didn't want to talk anymore.

"Doctor, where are you going?"

"I have to go upstairs now. I have an appointment."

"Wait, can't you give me a few seconds more?"

"No—I have to go."

He's made me, Landau thought. Recognized me from some Webcast, some TV bit. Doesn't he know that the whole case is falling apart? Why, it said so in today's *Chron*, on page one above the fold: "Attack on Berkeley Woman Not a Copycat Crime, Prosecutors Say." The attack resembled the attack on Dolores Huerta in many ways, and the same instrument was used this time, too, probably. But if it was not a copycat crime, perpetrated by some wannabe monster, and if Landau had been elsewhere, then he was not the killer, right? Wasn't that logical?

He had been home in bed—had not slashed his best friend with a box cutter, eviscerated her husband. In a chat room he sometimes visited, an idea was being floated that he was the ringleader of a demonic cult, committing this or that murder while sending followers out to do others. Some self-described forensic psychologist had been speculating along these lines for some time, and certain dim-witted enthusiasts were persuaded, angrily persuaded.

"Nurse, who brought those red balloons?"

"I don't know—her son?"

"Her son? Mrs. Blodgett doesn't have a son, not that I'm aware of."

"Nice young man. He was in yesterday for twenty minutes."

"Has she had many visitors?"

"I don't know. You could check with the desk."

No log of visitors was being kept. But was that possible, in this day and age? When a patient is the victim of a criminal attack? Deena's room contained eleven half-deflated red balloons, but the desk nurse couldn't remember who had brought them—maybe a relative, maybe some staffer, bringing them in from another room, to cheer things up.

That night *ferdy77*, a chat room stalwart, launched out on more Landau-cult speculations, and it was only with difficulty that he refrained from entering the lists with him. Damn those lawyers, anyway: hadn't they said that they were trying to "shape the discourse," move it this way not that? The point was that Landau must not seem to be doing any of the moving—anything he wrote could be used against him.

Melody drove them home. The delayed reckoning with what they were doing and in what circumstances was now upon them; if they had had separate bedrooms, they would have retreated to them now, to lie awake through the night, sighing. It was rude to be happy having fun sex. But they did not have separate bedrooms, so Melody slept beside him, and Landau awoke with an indiscreet erection at two thirty-two, his standard time for a first bathroom visit. When he returned the arousal was still there, an ungovernable registering of her presence. Ignoble condition, subside! Get thee away!

"Are you all right?"

"Yes, I'm okay," he said, "sorry to disturb."

"Would you hold me, please? I haven't slept a wink."

In the morning he hurried to his email. Sent Byrum a message about the hospital, that someone masquerading as Deena Marjic's son had brought her balloons. If this had been caught on a tape: oh, if only.

Byrum responded in the old genial vein. He brought up the San Diego cases, for some reason. Nine women had died in the time period 1992 to '97, then no one after that. Unless you counted the five hundred to seven hundred women killed in borderland Mexico, not far from San Diego after all, since about January of '96. That was the Mujeres Contra la Violencia count of unsolved murders of women, not disputed by the Mexican federal police or most other authorities. The Mexican attorney general, the one who had recently been appointed to replace the one who had recently gone into hiding, had made a connection in a recent speech between San Diego and the unsolved *maquiladora* murders, so maybe Landau and his lawyers hadn't been so far off, all those weeks ago, to bring up the San Diego cases.

The man on the tape in the church basement: they were on it, still investigating. Thank you again for your suggestion, Professor. This being a Sunday, the hospital tapes wouldn't be available today, but when they arrived tomorrow they'd inform him if they learned anything. Should they be looking for someone in particular? Did he have a name for them?

He began to type in "Heitor Burgos-Pereira," then paused. Typed in "Georges Vienna," then erased that, too. He wasn't quite ready yet to launch a full-scale witch hunt, a witch hunt aimed at any of his friends. He had been so pushed around the bend because of Deena that he had seized on Heitor, then Georges, and now he was thinking of Jad, Jad as the killer. But was any of them more suspicious now than three days ago? Was there evidence?

Jad spent one night in jail, then was sent home. No call from him nor from Karin—well, they were grown-ups, they were on their own, obeying their own impulses. It was Masha who told him about the release.

Out of nowhere, he felt the urge to write. Put in two intense hours, Melody making him coffee then quietly leaving, losing himself in a mental space of excitement and fear—the fear being that the mood would lift too soon, that he would fail to transcribe this diktat from some inner space, this fragment of inspiration. *Did* get something down. The set-theory paper of his hero, Boichenko, in the desk drawer by his right knee. Did not need to read it, just to feel it there, sending forth illumination. Some day I will go to western Ukraine and locate his grave, pay him proper homage, Landau promised. For all I know I have roots myself in the Ukraine—half the Jews in the world have those roots.

Blinking, exhausted, he stumbled into his kitchen. Freddy had been fed. There was a flat, bluish light in the room—it was a light he recognized, what he thought of as the light of things as they are, his *Ding an sich* light. He had seen this light seven, eight times in his life. The light, and the automatic outpourings from his brain that sometimes accompanied it, were the core of what he was. Good to be reminded. The answering machine was flashing but making no noise: Melody had turned off the ringer. Now, why hadn't he thought of that? Some genius.

The bluish light with aura-like vaporings persisted, like a subtle chord at the end of a solo piano piece. When at last it began to fade he found himself thinking of Deena. Deena, are you contacting me, is that what this is? Is your spirit leaving us, venturing into the beyond, at this instant? But I won't let that happen—I forbid it. I will give up all math intensities, all light shows in my head, if only you'll stay around. I need you, my friend. You are my dear friend.

From Richard Flense came a message about a funeral. It was to be held Monday, the normally rapid Jewish interment delayed by the Sabbath and a police necropsy. Harold Blodgett had been Jewish, despite his resemblance to Ralph Waldo Emerson. Landau had known he was, but still it was a shock to be reminded.

He took a taxi, not wanting to drag Melody into everything. Was Blodgett a Jewish name? It had been Brustein, before, he now recalled—Brustein or Blodgettstein, something ethnic. Raised in Davenport, Iowa, the son of a scrap dealer. BA Iowa State. He was the least Jewish-seeming man Landau knew, but here at the end, at the interment end, yes, he was Jewish.

Many people milling uncertainly on the gentle hillside. It was like one of their famous parties, only outside. University people predominating. Many had thought to bring umbrellas.

Hard to say whether it was raining or not. Landau's face got wet just from being outdoors, but the sky was part blue, with stringy clouds. Here was Katherine Emerald of KRON, not wearing a headset today but rather a dark hat, dark clothes, no jewelry, no makeup. Madly beautiful, what an extraordinary face. Had she known Harold personally? Been one of his law students? Anything was possible.

Everyone left Landau alone, as if by prior agreement. You cad, you monster: so he imagined them all thinking. But a few cast semi-benign looks his way, remembering, possibly, the article in the *Chron*, or something they'd heard on TV. Wait, he *didn't* do it, isn't that right? Isn't that what the authorities are thinking now? In that case, just avoid him. He might still be the Cragmont Ripper, and anyway there's something unseemly about him.

There it was, the grave, the immemorial grave. Two overalled men with mud on their knees stood nearby, on either side of a backhoe. They were Mexican. At another funeral he had attended some years ago, two arrant Irishmen had been the gravediggers, and Landau could still recall their smirking eyes, their slicked-back biker hair, although not who it was who was being buried. The Mexicans had laid down outdoor carpet. They weren't smirking, no, their expressions were respectful, and both had assumed the classic stance, the Mexican handworker stance. It was a reasonable way to stand, after all, at the edge of a deep hole. Eyes downcast to avoid tripping in.

Now began a slow, reluctant-seeming movement toward the grave. The university would be staging an elaborate memorial service in a few days, so this was just the planting, the basic act. My God, but this is all wrong, Harold, I can't believe this, thought Landau. *You* have been murdered, you, Professor Blodgett? I thought you'd live forever. You were quietly enduring, like the Washington Monument. Like the Constitution.

An apparatus hung over the grave, it's purpose to lower the coffin in a controlled way. It looked like a bed frame made of galvanized pipe, which put Landau in mind of plumbers, flooded basements. Six men brought forth the coffin, made of stark unvarnished wood, one of the six, remarkably, the right-wing law professor who had been at the soiree some weeks ago, the reputed Bush White House torture-memo writer. He was a broad-backed fellow, tall for a Chinese, well able to bear his part of the load.

Rain definitely falling now. This winter has played us a clever game, Landau thought, starting out mild, fooling us, lulling us. A rabbi began to intone in Hebrew, and he turned his gaze in that direction. The rabbi was standing under a tarp the Mexicans had erected. In front of him were two tall, impressive-looking young women, Harold's daughters, Landau knew, and there was Richard Flense, not a special friend of the deceased but at the forefront whenever someone was passing over—he was writing his Big Book on Death, you know. Landau began to notice other people he knew, professors and their white-haired spouses, departmental secretaries, deans, admins, a vice provost—look, over there was a contingent from the East Asian Institute, Deena's little office. He noted a tranche of liberal law scholars, Harold's "poker boys," as she had called them, and the Chinese man was now quietly, unashamedly weeping—that was not mere rain on his face, no, the man was moved.

Georges' head of gray curls loomed up ahead, darker than usual because of the rain. He was five yards closer to the grave, with his friend Heather by his side. Landau wondered if the murders had brought them closer. Either they were strong in their effect, a rash of local murders, or they were part of the background noise, the general world awfulness, something that you endured—cruelty's toll. Hard to believe that you, yourself, would be taken, you amongst all these people. The Angel of Death had passed over you so many times before, therefore, probably it would again.

He listened to the Hebrew. He liked to hear it, the mellifluousness, the ancient-sounding-ness. Maybe prayers were better in a language that you couldn't understand. You could imagine an immense, profoundly satisfying eloquence being perpetrated, words achieving magical force. An umbrella opened over his head. He turned to find Graciela, Heitor's young friend, the preschool teacher, close by his side. She looked not shy today so much as southern Italian, in an Empire-waisted black dress, black net stockings, black gloves, and medium heels despite the soggy going underfoot. She smiled with her beautiful chocolate eyes.

"Hello, Professor."

"Hello there, Graciela. Thank you. I was about to steal that lady's umbrella, and that wouldn't have been nice."

Heitor was on her other side. Bareheaded, bespectacled. He looked like a thoughtful young public-health researcher, which was what he was. Had he known Harold personally? Landau couldn't put that together. All of Berkeley knew all of Berkeley, somehow, somewhere.

"Professor, hello," he said softly.

"Glad to see you, Heitor. Though not glad about the occasion."

Graciela kept trying to include Heitor in the umbrella coverage. But he stood apart, unconcerned for the wet.

"Did you know him well, Heitor?"

"No. I knew her better."

"You knew Deena? How?"

"You introduced us. Boxing Day, 1992. You told me that she was your best friend ever. I remembered that."

"Hmm."

Later, a procession. People lined up and threw dirt upon the lowered casket, everyone who wished to did. Landau took the shovel and tossed down a sodden clod. Never thought it would come to this, Harold. Surely a mistake has been made. Many others had dropped down shovelfuls before his, so Landau's made hardly a sound. One of the daughters stood before him, staring at him in a seeming cold fury. She met the eyes of each mourner as he or she approached, signaling recognition, appreciation, but the look she gave Landau was not gracious, was not appreciative at all. He understood how immensely presumptuous it was for him to be here today, acting like any mourner, just another clod-thrower. I know I'm innocent, but can these people be expected to think that? No, they bloody well can't.

Later, outside the cemetery gates. He looked around for a taxi. Heitor and Graciela pulled up in a little car. They wanted to drive him home, get him in out of the wet.

Heitor drove, Graciela beside him up front. The backseat contained a folded blanket that exuded a strong floral scent, as if from a recent dry-cleaning.

"Professor, how is Mrs. Blodgett, will she recover? The paper said that it was very bad," said Heitor.

"Yes, I'm afraid it is, Heitor. I think she'll survive, but there may be brain damage. Have you been to see her?"

He said nothing. Maybe he hadn't heard.

"Heitor," Landau continued. "What happened in Brazil? I was surprised to hear you weren't working down there anymore."

He inclined his handsome head. "It's all a political thing, Professor, you know that. Me, I'm more of a private guy. I just want to go to the lab and play the numbers. I did that job but I didn't like it."

"Big jobs are big opportunities. You don't want to be like me, Heitor, riding a theory horse into irrelevance."

"Irrelevance, Professor? No, I don't think so. Not you."

One of the more attractive things about him: that he admires me, unreasonably esteems me. I must once have spoken to him in the right tone of voice, Landau reflected, given him "space" in which to grow as a junior colleague. Therefore, I now have credit with him. It's the mysterious mentor-disciple dynamic, and by happy happenstance I never had to step on him professionally. Why don't I have the same credit with my own son, though, where it really matters? I spoke to him in the same tones, I was careful not to step on his abnormally big feet, yet he and I are always under the Indian sign. Completely bolloxed.

"Wally said that you were onto something, Heitor, with the mosquitoes."

"Oh, I don't know. Working out your old paper, I guess. Trying to."

"*My* old paper? But that was just a spoof. Surely you know that."

"Okay—if you say so."

Graciela turned around. "Are you cold, Professor? Please, use the blanket."

"No, I'm fine, thank you. How's the teaching going? You still at Bright Beginnings, Lakeshore Bright Beginnings, whatever they call it?"

"Yes, but I'm quitting. I'm getting a degree in library science."

"You are? Well—how smart of you. The modern world is all about library searches, isn't it? Digital ones especially. Have you ever had to engage with the Dewey decimal system? It's an old curiosity from back in the Stone Age, from my time."

She laughed: "Yes, I know what that is, but that's only for local libraries now. On the university level, it's more the Library of Congress system. Epidemiology, that's in the RA643s, RA649s. I looked you up already."

"Thank you. I'm honored."

Jad's house was nearby. We could stop, Landau thought, I could say hello. But I can't just drop in on him, and besides, I need to get him and his wife over to *my* place, have them on *my* turf for a change. Remind them of the patriarchal splendor. Maybe have a party. But Deena wouldn't be there to help me with it, and my celebrations in the past were always about doing something with Deena, like Judy Garland and Mickey Rooney putting on a show. Without her I will have no social existence to speak of, I will be but a rough, dark brute, shunned by the family of man. A Heathcliff, a Grendel.

"Professor, I got something I want to show you. If you would look at it sometime."

"Sure, Heitor, what?"

"Just a little something. Bunch of notes. Maybe you'd take a look at it."

"Of course. Whatever you want to show me, I'm always happy to look, Heitor. Your stuff's always intriguing."

"Okay. That's good."

Could barely keep his eyes open. Suddenly wrung out, exhausted. He tried to think of Harold, Harold in the cold, cold ground—his mind veered away from that, was unwilling to undertake the labor of parsing the meaning of that, if any. Thought of lunch instead. Mentally went through his refrigerator, constructing a plausible sandwich. A plate of hors d'oeuvres to go with. Some honey ham in the refrigerator if he wasn't mistaken. Deli-bought ham.

He invited the young people inside, to be polite. Heitor gnawed a cold chicken leg. Graciela bit daintily at a gherkin.

"Wait a minute—wait. I'm remembering something," Landau said. "'The waitress was a vampire named Perkins. Was extremely fond of small gherkins. While she served the tea, she ate forty-three. Which pickled her internal workin's.'"

Not sure what she'd heard, Graciela smiled shyly. Heitor made no response, stood up from his chair, went over to the deck door, where the cat Freddy often showed himself.

"Don't let him in, please. He goes absolutely mad for ham," Landau warned.

Heitor looked right and left. "No, nobody is here, Professor. I don't see anybody."

"My cat. Actually, you could let him in if you want. He doesn't eat all that much."

Heitor slid the door open. "Professor, this door was unlocked. The latch was completely open."

"Oh?"

"Somebody could come in here, like that woman. The crazy one that sliced your face."

"Probably I failed to lock it myself. I'm not a very locking-up sort of person. I'm easily breached."

On a whim, he joined the young man at the door.

"If you were last here some years ago, probably you've never had the full-on deck tour, have you, Heitor. I'm most excessively proud of my deck, anyone who knows me will tell you that. Come on. Let's look around."

Landau led him outside. The rain was still dripping.

"This whole backyard, this was as nothing in the old days. A scrub jungle, an eyesore. Tall weeds and trash trees and things like that. I grew up on the hard streets of London, so to come in possession of a patch of authentic California hillside in its native state was for me a thrill. I was too in awe to touch it, almost. I rejoiced in the savage animals that came to visit, deer, skunks, wood rats, squirrels. By the mid-nineties my back-to-the-land phase was over, though, and I began to think of improvements."

He took Heitor by the arm. "First thing, we tore out the brush. Put in a flagstone walk and a terrace, but beware what you start haphazardly—the stones called out for more than just a rickety back stoop. This lovely deck was the result, a standard California white-wine deck you might say, but it has individuality, a real architect designed it. Let's go down beneath it, shall we? I want to show you something."

Here came Freddy the cat. He came hopping out from underneath, stepping sprightly in the rain.

"Freddy, I've told you a thousand times not to go down there, haven't I? Yet you disobey me. You are a bad animal." His pet eluded Landau's grasp, Heitor's also. Squirted off into the yard.

"As I was saying. The planking is redwood from Mendocino County, second-growth, kiln-dried. Every two years I treat it with polymerized tung oil, which requires hours of hand-rubbing according to a recondite protocol handed down by the Cistercian fathers, I believe. I have a Mexican crew come do it, since it's far beyond me physically. Tung oil, as you probably know, is a marine product, used on oceangoing yachts. People debate tung versus urethane, but for me it's the best of the UV-resistant stains by far, and a potent fungicide-mildewcide to boot. Gives you that breathable yet water-repellant surface. Circa 1850 Exterior Varnish is the best brand, and once you've taken the high road, you can never go back, regardless of the expense. You've done the best possible for your deck, and you feel fulfilled."

Some mad energy was upon him. He kept hold of Heitor's upper arm when he tried to turn away.

"The maid was down here, Heitor, the maid Elfridia. Some people have speculated that she was being butchered in the kitchen when Samantha Beevors arrived, but Samantha was already upstairs, I think, having a nap. She heard something, came downstairs to investigate. Then ran back up with the killer at her heels. Coronary event. Heart attack. The killer may have stood above her watching her die, we can't be sure. Some heart attacks are lightning fast, like a light being turned off, but others take a while. The pain is said to be horrific."

Here came Freddy again. He rubbed up against Landau's leg, then Heitor's, afterward circling them both twice.

"Here's where it gets a little tricky, though. He goes back downstairs. The maid is bleeding to death on a tarp, and I say that because they didn't find her blood on the kitchen floor or anywhere, so either he mopped it up extremely well or it was spilled on a removable surface. He took her away with him because he didn't like to leave her here, and he didn't like being in the house himself, either, because Samantha had spooked him. A few days later, he brings the body *back*, though, which was dangerous to do, because the police were watching. It must have answered some deep need in him, to run that risk."

Perfectly immobile, Heitor waited for him to finish. The professor needed to say these things, to work these sad possibilities out in his mind; the least he could do was to listen.

"A deep need, a compulsion, I say. He'd already sliced her, so the fun part was over. Psychopaths are very particular about the remains—TV teaches us that. Some care more for them than for the living body. They must be treated properly else the whole exercise is a failure, a catastrophe. Freddy, leave me be, I tell you, just stop that," and Landau half-kicked at his cat, sending it scooting out into the yard again.

He could see Heitor's face better now. It was dark beneath the deck, but his eyes had been adjusting to the light. Heitor looked morose; he had heard the professor's words, and there was wisdom in them, he was ready to admit that, although, the whole topic was unfortunate.

"And then, he tried to blame you. Put this on you," said Heitor commiserately. "But it isn't because of you that this happened, Professor—the crazy man, he just wants someone to hide behind."

Landau nodded. "If only I could prove that, Heitor. To everyone's satisfaction."

"Yes. Unless—maybe he knows Samantha, too. Maybe he's like me, someone who knows you, works in the lab sometimes, I don't know, maybe many years ago. To find her in your house, that doesn't seem right. That upsets him. Still in bed with you, after everything! She was always in bed with people, even with d'Iulio, who was a hundred years old. And her work was never any good—we know that, it was shoddy. You old guys, you steel boxes, you knew it, but you let her go on anyway. You didn't put up fences, keep her from making messes. Because, I don't know, she's a woman? A woman with a big mouth? Who can make trouble?"

Landau's heart started beating hard—it was to hear such a thing spoken, plainly spoken.

"So, another scientist, you're saying."

"Yes, possibly. *I* didn't kill her," Heitor laughed. "But I wanted to sometimes! People who knew your work, who respected it above everything—many would like her to just shut up. So, maybe this bad one, this one with a screw loose, who slices them up, he met your maid, and maybe he didn't even know she was your maid. Look where she meets him! Whose house it is! Then, Samantha's here too. *Que engendro*, too freaky. So he brings the maid back because that shows you something, I don't know, it hurts you too, because you disappoint him, a lot. You let her get in again. Crazy Samantha."

Landau was silent for a while. "Too complicated, Heitor. And her work wasn't ever shoddy—it was perfect in its way, odd but perfect. Just a little bit off in final direction. She needed colleagues who could get into it with her, get her to laugh at herself, save her from herself. But she scared off all the good colleagues eventually. Me included."

"No, no, she was never that good. Never a serious person."

Two minutes later they walked up from beneath the deck. Here was Freddy waiting for them: Landau smiled at him, blinking in the mist—he couldn't see for a moment, drizzle was in his eyes, and there was steam on the glass sliding door. Then he saw inside, saw Graciela, just now popping a morsel into her mouth. She caught sight of them, too, and waved. Landau put his hand on the door and pushed.

chapter 19

The surveillance tape from the hospital showed a young man with a prominent Adam's apple walking along fluorescent-lit hospital corridors, then riding an elevator, then signing in at a reception desk—so there was a sign-in regime in place, sometimes—a young man whom Landau eventually recognized as his neighbor's teenaged son, Dylan Bamberg, Bob Dylan Bamberg, to give him his full appellation. Byrum had captured six frames with a computer program and sent them over. Any comments, Professor? You know this lad?

Instead of emailing back, Landau phoned. "Yes, he lives on my street, Detective. His mother goes to a physical therapist who's a friend of mine. I think he's just a curious kid who's stirred up by all this weird stuff going on, weird violent sexual stuff. Maybe they want to keep an eye on that, the parents. But I don't think he's a killer. I think that's far beyond him."

Byrum grunted. "Yeah, okay, maybe."

"His mother won a MacArthur. She's a distinguished social psychologist researcher-type. You know any MacArthur winners, Byrum? Any close personal contacts among them?"

"Actually, I think I know who she is. She's the one who does the old experiments over, trying to get at what they're about. Changes the parameters. Strips away the veils. The one where they had students giving electric shocks, and they turned into sadists, supposedly. She showed that that was full of logical flaws. She's a big debunker, a major-league skeptic-debunker. She *deserves* a MacArthur."

"Okay. You're a very well-informed person, Byrum. I think I've told you that before."

"Yes, I think so, not that it's true."

"All right, you asked me if I had a name to give you. Here's a name," and he spelled out, with raging internal personal resistance, the name *Heitor Burgos-Pereira*.

The detective fell silent. Then said, "I think I know him. He's on some of your papers."

"Right, he used to work for me. He's from South America, half Brazilian, half Argentine. So he's mostly down there, but lately he's been up here on a fellowship."

"Just off the top of my head—he was in San Diego for a while, too. That raised a small flag for us."

"He was?"

"Why are you telling me about him now, Professor?"

"Oh, just process of elimination. He's the only one who might have been at some of the right places. He's not a killer or a bully or anything like that, as far as my poor brain can determine things. If he is, then I know nothing about my own species. I hope this doesn't get him in a lot of trouble. I'm giving you his name only because while I was lying in bed last night unable to sleep I thought that *not* to give it would be wrong. A dereliction."

"Too bad he's in Brazil. Might be hard to get hold of."

"That's what I'm saying—he's here. He's been at Stanford for a couple months. He sleeps in Oakland."

Byrum betrayed no special interest. He brought up the San Diego murders again. All nine women had been attacked within sight of a body of water, pond or bay or river. All on or around the full moon. It was a kind of cluster, as these things went.

"And Heitor was there, you say, sometimes."

"But the murders up here are different," the detective added. "No bodies of water, different periodicity. It could be someone wants to be taken for the one who did those crimes, but isn't managing it, quite, is stumbling over himself."

"You're losing me. I remember how much respect you had for Occam's razor, detective."

"Why don't you describe the Bay Area cluster, Professor. Just put it in your own words."

Oh, no—the infernal invitation to put things into his own words.

"Ain't we pals no more, Byrum? You seem to want me to say something wrong. Something I shouldn't."

197

"No, no, I'm just curious."

"I don't think so."

The policeman called back twenty minutes later. What they had on Heitor was that he was director-general of medical services administration in a city in Brazil that Byrum had never heard of before, and two weeks ago he'd been quoted in a newspaper there on a planning issue. Was Landau sure he'd seen him here? According to the federal databases the detective could access, he wasn't in the U.S.—those databases were often in error, of course, showed foreign nationals on work visas years after they'd gone home, or failed to show them at all if they'd entered the country in some non-standard way. He'd know more in a couple of hours.

"Byrum, he drove me home from Harold Blodgett's funeral. He was in my house on Monday."

"Okay. It would help if you had his cell number. I called Walter Winckelmann's lab like you said but no one answered."

"I'll go over there. Winckelmann's always there. He might be eating lunch."

Byrum was sending him a document now, another thing that came up when you Googled "Burgos-Pereira."

"Is Portuguese one of your languages, Professor?"

"No."

"Nor mine, either, but I figured it out, sort of. Officer Hashimoto's former live-in girlfriend was a capoeira instructor, and she helped. Want to know what she said?"

"Sure."

"It's about an epidemic. A kind of pretend scientific paper about an epidemic. A parody, I guess."

"A parody?"

"Yes, she says it was pretty funny in parts."

"Epidemic of what?"

"I don't know, epidemic of death? Something like that."

"What?"

"An epidemic of death. That's what the words in Portuguese mean. Women killed by guns, by knives, by chainsaws. By rat poison, by cars driven over their heads. I don't know half what she's telling me, but she kept on laughing, though it didn't seem all that funny."

The email arrived a few seconds later.

"Okay, got it. Where's Heitor's name on this? Whoa—Wally Winckelmann! Winckelmann's name's all over it!"

It looked like a paper published in an American journal. An actual research paper, with hyperlinks that worked, and the publication, *Revista Brasileira de Saúde Materno Infantil*, was named at the top of every other page, as was customary. Fifty-three pages, seven pages of notes.

"Can I call the samba instructor, Byrum? To ask more about it?"

"Capoeira, not samba. I'll have her call you instead."

"Okay."

But she did not call him that day, the instructor. Landau used a ten-page Portuguese supplement in the back of his Spanish dictionary to puzzle out the text. It was about fatal violence against women. Treating fatal violence as a subject in population medicine. Incidence rates compared for different countries and times, prevalence rates analyzed to explain why the epidemic was chronic yet prevalence approached zero. Well, because all the subjects were dead—was that the joke part?

Many studies were out there like this, there was a vogue for them now. Landau read them on review committees. It was the epidemiological equivalent of studying the Holocaust: to read and think and write about this was to disappear down a black hole of misery. Somebody had to do it, but if you were the one who undertook it you consigned yourself to a lifetime of bitter gloom.

Heitor hadn't written before on anti-women violence. His name appeared nowhere on the paper, yet when you searched "Burgos-Pereira" it was the fourth item that appeared on your screen, over and over.

He had a sudden urge to call his son, to hear his voice, just for the hell of it. Then, a similar urge to call Georges—suddenly missed him. It was a moment of loneliness, of feeling cut off from his main males, maybe because he was in the process of betraying one of them. The moment passed.

The point of the paper seemed to be that there was much morbidity among young Latin women, that rates were shockingly on the increase. Here followed a discussion of trends in four Central American countries, all of which were seeing sharp increases in gang violence. Existence of gangs implied violence against women, because warring gangs considered women simple property, like trucks or houses. It was fun to rape the other guy's woman, then when you were done cut off her head. Learned investigators said that the organized gangs accounted for just a fraction of the carnage; sexism within families and cultures, endemic sex oppression over the *longue durée*—it wasn't just the gangsters doing it, no, of course not.

He wanted to talk to Winckelmann now, but he forced himself to sit and read on. Consider Mexico. And the tone of the prose changed—the prose he was reading with the help of his dictionary. Consider Mexico as a "cohort study." If you took the border region and looked at the population of females aged ten to twenty-five who within a five-year period had ended up dead following sexual assault, against an equal number not assaulted or murdered, what did you find? What were the confounding variables, accounted for by stratification, or by regression analysis, and which really mattered?

Crazier now. Psycho weirdness coming on. Some risk factors self-evident, such as early onset of sexual behavior, or, consider the girls who touched themselves. Girls whose nipples were preternaturally dark or protuberant. (Wait a minute, does that word mean "protuberant"? He checked his dictionary again. Seemed to.) The look of them performing fellatio with a gun to the head. Razor wounds, how they had begged and sobbed as they were ritually cut. What had happened on the eleventh through fourteenth of February 2002, in the village of La Isla, fifty miles southeast of Ciudad Juarez. In a social hall with the windows mostly broken out, six girls from Nuevo Casas Grandes, another tiny village, all fourteen-year-olds, kidnapped from a school playground and kept for four days by a group associated with the Zeta gang. They killed one by putting a chain used to pull engine blocks out of trucks around her bare chest and between her legs. Landau stopped reading. He was thinking of the capoeira instructor, that she had found this funny. He pushed on: the girls all ended up in a field within sight of the Rio Grande, buried in a sandy wash with one hand of one of them showing through, as a marker. Twenty-four men had participated in the "study."

He had read enough. No, he made himself read a little more: Ximena R., the "prettiest" girl it said, had been raped a specific number of times and cut with a surgical instrument in a way that made Landau gag. He put the printout down. Why was Walter Winckelmann's name on this? How had *that* happened?

A Berkeley police cruiser followed him as he descended Euclid Avenue. At a stop sign the policeman asked if he wanted a lift.

"No, but thanks, Officer."

"Wherever you go, I go, you know."

"I know. It makes me feel all warm."

The cruiser pulled through the intersection and kept just ahead of him for two blocks. Then, shot off for a while.

A few weeks before, Raboy had sent him an email containing a quote, from Kafka's *The Trial*, that went: "If you want to help you must give it all your energies, you can no longer do anything else." The point was that he could expect to be consumed by his trial; it would take him over completely. Counter to that prediction, Landau had been unbothered now for more than two weeks, and with the start of the trial just eight days away, the phone wasn't ringing off the hook, they weren't copying him on documents, indeed, he felt ignored. The state's case was falling apart. That was good news, although it did not fill him with joy. He had Deena to thank for that. He had had to lose Deena and Harold in order to skate, not to face prison time or the gas. To go free.

He would visit her later, Deena. Bring her more balloons.

Winckelmann wasn't there. Landau ran into a young public-health type coming back from the men's room. He said that Professor Winckelmann hadn't been in today.

"Isn't he always here? Sleeping on the floor?"

"He might be in later, you could check."

Landau introduced himself. "I'm an old friend. If he's not here, what about Heitor Burgos-Pereira, then, can I see him?"

"Who?"

"Heitor Burgos-Pereira. Guy in his early forties, infectious diseases specialist, from South America."

The public-health man took a moment. "I know him, I think, but we don't work together."

Landau had been calling the wrong number, it turned out. There was a new office number, and Heitor was probably one of the extensions; Landau could leave a message if he wanted.

"You don't happen to know his cell number, do you?"

"No. Like I say, we're not together."

Worried about Winckelmann now. Winckelmann not coming to the office was troubling, if you were already in a troubled frame of mind. He walked out of the building with the giant Xs on the facade and headed up Oxford Street, trying to remember where Wally Winckelmann lived—he could picture the house but not recall the name of the street. Waved futilely at a taxi going past. Settled in for a stiff trudge uphill, deep into the Berkeley professorial ghetto. Everybody connected to the university lived in the hills, it had always been this way, from time immemorial.

Would harm come to Winckelmann, was he in jeopardy? But why? Because whoever had killed Harold might now have a taste for senior professors, males. What was it Heitor had said: "You didn't put up fences, you steel boxes, you." Winckelmann and he had failed to police the discipline carefully, to protect it from the likes of Samantha Beevors, maker of messes. Some young episeme somewhere had been driven to madness by that.

He might be looking to kill me, too, Landau considered. Whether it's Heitor or Emory Musselwhite of Oklahoma or someone else I can't recall at all, his deep respect has curdled into the old kill-thrill, the savage hunger, because, in the end, it's always Daddy's fault, isn't it? Something like that. Now on his mind's screen he saw the name of Winckelmann's street. He tried the new office number and chose Heitor's branch on the tree: "Landau here, I'm trying to track you down, Heitor. Maybe you're in Palo Alto today, your other office. Nobody down there seems to know your information though. I'm on my way up to Wally's. It occurs to me I haven't been able to phone you because you have some kind of throwaway. I myself am using a throwaway phone—I'm fond of the ones that look like hard candies, in candy-apple red or green. An unbelievable number of minutes."

What to say, what did he really want to say?

"Heitor, I've read your paper. The one you didn't sign, the outbreak-of-death one. There's facetious intent, I see, which if one is a native Lusophone may be more entertaining than I was able to find it. I want to talk to you about it. You write as if you've been conducting a study with hundreds of these lost girls. We're going to have to have a refresher on what constitutes a cohort, but forget that—I'm more concerned that you're putting yourself at risk, consorting with these Zeta people. That's not for real, is it? Yet, there was a flavor of the actual. You brought poor Ximena R. into the room as they say a good writer must do. 'What he wrote on her nipple with the scalpel was the same inscription as on her lips.' That's just so eloquent, Heitor. My translation only approximate, of course."

He hung up. Now made another call: "Jad, this is your father speaking. Please, pick up. It's important."

When Jad did not pick up: "I'm on Keeler Street, just above the pocket park. We used to call it Ray Milland Park, because the real name is Remillard, remember? You climbed the big high rock at age seven. I was so proud of you, you had such gumption. On the street above it is Wally Winckelmann's house. Winckelmann, the public-health man. It's not on Grizzly Peak, it's the street just below that. You know the one."

There, now I've called in my location, he reflected. Why don't I just call Byrum and get some squad cars up here? For that matter, why not call Melody, bring her into it as well? Well, it's because I have a date with her tomorrow, and I don't want her thinking I'm a big baby. A wuss.

Finally, the house. Impossible that anything bad could happen inside such a substantial-looking edifice. Shake-sided, complex rooflets, maybe Bernard Maybeck had designed it, Maybeck the historical genius of Berkeley residential architecture. The redwood siding looked nearly new, and Landau estimated the cost of such a shingling job at five figures, over twenty grand for sure. Think of it! You didn't own such a house, it owned you. You were its sugar daddy.

He made another call: "Melody, I'm thinking of you at this moment. I'm looking forward to tomorrow very much. We'll have a good time, I know we will."

He waited, considering what else to say. Thirty yards down the block he saw something that rang a bell—it was Graciela's car, parked under a flowering plum. Fey white petals scattered upon its hood.

"Melody, you remember the Brazilian Hypothesis? Well, I'm about to test it. I wish I had a gun. I guess I'm more American than British after all. Tomorrow I shall cook us something special, scallops in a red wine reduction, perhaps, or some local cod. Are you a mad shellfish fan, as I am? We're compatible in so many ways, so many."

What's the matter with me? Am I about to wet my pants? He shut his phone and knocked boldly on the door. Knocked again. It came open a groaning inch; uh-oh, another citizen who doesn't lock up.

"Wally? Anthony Landau here, I'm at your front door. I wanted a word with you, but it can wait. I can come back later."

The Winckelmanns owned two collies. One was lying on a sofa just beyond the entrance hall—bred into stupidity, collies were, their long noses associated with diminishing braincase volumes. The Winckelmanns' dogs were always getting into neurotic mischief, and Wally himself spoke of them in a way that seemed to pose the question, why have these animals not been put down? Removed from life's makeshift stage? Landau waited for the one on the couch to challenge him, come sniff him out, but it was too tired, apparently.

"Wally, what's your old dog's name?" he called out. "Veronica, Victoria, something like that? If this is the female? I hope she's not a biter."

The dog looked dead. Well, it was dead. The neck was askew, and blood had pooled in a corner of the sofa. The sofa was dark leather, the color of half-dried blood.

"Wally—something's happened to Veronica. She's not moving."

He had walked halfway down the hall now. He paused.

"You know what? I think I *will* come back later, Wally. Or, better, I'll come to your office tomorrow. See you there. We'll talk."

He hurried out the front door. Breathing heavily. Paused on the portico.

Could that *not* be her car, Graciela's? Ten- or twelve-year-old Honda, dented grill, faded, unwashed: it was the official car of Berkeley, almost, even more than the Prius was. Berkeley being a town of *luftmenschen* and *luftfrauen*, of impecunious writers and perpetual grad students who subsisted well below the strata of important university personages, a refuge of financially stressed outcasts who needed to keep the old wreck running. It could be anybody's.

No, come on, it was *her* car—he had just been in it. Then, they are around. Must be inside. What I should do now is call 911, because something odd has happened, and I need my police escort, my backup.

He heard female sobbing nearby. It seemed to be coming from an upper floor. Into his phone he said, "I would like to report a home invasion, robbery, murder, mayhem, I don't know what. My name is Landau. That's L-A-N-D-A-U, and I'm at"—looking to either side of the portico—"two blocks north of Ray Milland Park, and here's the house number, seventy-one. It's the big tall redwood-shingled house."

There came a scream from within, strangled hysterical scream. Landau rushed back inside. No, what are you doing—don't be a bloody fool, he told himself. The second-floor landing offered six doors, four shut and two open. The scream was coming from up higher, though, from floor number three or four. These houses had countless floors, they had been built for large families at the turn of the twentieth century, rich Californians with servants.

On the third-floor landing was the other collie, its head cut off. The head was turned to face the body, in an alas-poor-Yorick arrangement. Screams from behind *this* door, paroxysmal female screams. Landau felt a sudden loosening in his bowels.

When he went in, Heitor took a lazy playful swipe at him—narrow blade, silvery, long. He backed away now, Heitor, making funny conciliatory gestures, his face full of cringing mirth.

"Heitor! Heitor! What have you done!"

"I know, Professor. It's just what happens. That's all."

"Put down that knife! Do it now!"

Heitor seemed about to laugh. But he tossed the bloody straightedge onto a throw rug.

"Step back now! I say, step back!"

Heitor stepped back.

Small room. A woman's foot showed around the corner of a bed. Anklet sock, running shoe, looked brand-new.

"Is that Maxine, Heitor?"

"No, I don't know who she is. She was just here. Another maid."

Landau stepped that way for a look.

"She's dead, is she?"

"Yeah, now she is."

This is happening, Landau told himself. Do not let the top of your head blow off. Remain within this scene. Remain in it.

"What have you done to Wally, Heitor? Did you kill him, too?"

"No, he went to his bedroom. The old people, they wanted to lie down, that's all. They were tired."

"Show me."

"Okay. But we don't have much time, Professor. She gonna be dead if we don't go soon. She's bleeding bad, somebody cut her up, and—no, don't do that," he said, when Landau pulled out his phone. "She gonna die if you do that."

"Who is?"

"You know." And he pretended to put something in his mouth—a pickle, perhaps.

Landau thought for a moment. "Where is she, Graciela?"

"Come on, Professor. I show you."

"I'm not going anywhere with you, Heitor. That's not happening." He picked the barber's blade up off the rug. Folded it in his pocket.

Heitor drove, and Landau, a few mental steps behind him, sat behind him in the backseat, twisting with discomfort. He was not in this car. No, he *was* in it, he had gotten in it voluntarily. Gotten in a car with a madman, to follow a madman's plan. Oh, a grave mistake, idiotic, he told himself. But here he was.

They passed his policeman a short distance downhill, hurrying up in his cruiser. Landau did not cry out to him, did not fling himself from the car door: he wanted to, but he could not make himself feel that that was right.

"She's already dead, Heitor. I know that," he said from the backseat. "Why did you kill her, that lovely girl?"

"Maybe she's dead, maybe not, Professor, who knows?"

"What went wrong? Why are you a homicidal monster?"

The driver threw a winning smile into the rearview. "Funny!" he said. "Funny! You always posed the good questions. Never simple ones, no, and that's why you are the top rate."

"All right, and now tell me."

A few blocks later the driver said casually, "There is a someone inside the someone inside me. They keep hatching. I want to see what comes from it in the end, that's all."

"Amusing," Landau replied. "Very suggestive. But that removes you from agency, and that's not right. As if some outside process were slitting the girls' throats. *You* are the process, Heitor. You, you're the mind of it."

"The mind, the mind, I think I got a problem with my mind."

"We can get help for you, Heitor, I'm sure we can. There are medicines, operations, chemical neutering—I'll find out about it."

"No, the only medicine for me is the one that they inject with the governor waiting on the phone. There, that will give me the cure I need."

Landau said nothing to that. He looked away.

Soon they took the old freeway south. Did not exit at Fruitvale Avenue, went inland of that. Once upon lesser streets Heitor declared, "You look at my paper, first. Then, you can help her. You can have her if you want."

"What paper? I've already read your crazy paper."

"No, the one that no one has read yet."

"Oh. What's so special about it?"

"What is *your* new paper about, Professor, why don't you tell me?"

"*My* new paper? But I don't have a new paper."

"Yes you do. I know it. It's in the air, in the sky. I can feel it that you are writing, that you're thinking, because me, yes, I'm thinking too."

Landau began to say something. Again, he could not. He sat quietly the rest of the way.

A house on a steep street, a block of charmless stucco bungalows, *echt* Californian. Twisty camphor and other off-brand trees, trees not seen in high-end Berkeley, too scrubby for that. The street was steep like a ski jump. Landau had never been here before, so he looked around.

And here it was, the madman's house of horrors. Anonymous little house, ecru in color. "He was hiding here among us," he could imagine a neighbor telling a reporter, "third house on the left up there. I'd say hello when I walked my dog. Clean-cut young man. No question how he got the girls, looked like Antonio Banderas in *Tie Me Up! Tie Me Down!* He always petted my dog, Sugarbaby."

"Have you killed many women here, Heitor?"

"No, I live here, that's all. You'll see."

Landau was betting on a Japanese landlord. The shrubbery had a bonsai look, and there was an area of clean beige sand, with black rocks arranged within it.

"What's this set you back a month, Heitor, about three grand?"

"Almost. But I won't stay here much longer, so it doesn't matter."

He left the door to the house open behind him. Landau did not have to go in, and for a puzzled minute he stood outside arguing with himself. Again, could not find a pretext upon which not to go ahead. Deeply gloomy inside, drapes and blinds all closed. A lamp came on in another room. Tatami mats, shoji screens, plus rental-house furniture from the eighties. A trace of a Mexican-food smell: Heitor had been eating takeout, Landau guessed. Maybe from that *huarache* place.

"I have to check her out before I do any reading of papers," he announced to the empty living room.

"Okay, that's fair," came a voice from farther within.

Graciela was in a bedroom with taped-over windows. She was dressed in a flannel nightgown, her hands tied to the bed frame. Her eyes had been taped shut. Something was at her throat, a collar or bandage made of old towels, bloody, soiled.

"Graciela," Landau said from the doorway. "Graciela, I'm here." Heitor held him back with a hand against his sternum. Her ears were taped over, too. She shifted minutely in the child-sized bed.

I need to awaken from this. This cannot be happening, Landau thought, this tired episode of sordid captivity-theater, it cannot have her in it, and me, too, it feels all wrong. Heitor pulled him roughly out into the hallway. In the kitchen he asked for Landau's cell phone. When Landau would not produce it, he searched his pockets till he found it. Crushed it under his shoe.

"That won't help you, they're on their way, Heitor. They're going to find you very soon. Have you been giving her fluids? She looks weak. She looks half-dead."

"She has an infection, that's all. I give her some pills."

"What kind of pills?"

Landau suddenly rushed the kitchen doorway. Heitor got in front of him, they wrestled briefly, and Landau ended up on the floor, panting.

"I don't read anything till we tend to her," he declared from his position, flat on his back.

"Don't read it, then. I don't care."

After a few moments, Landau got to his feet. Smoothed his sport coat. Dusted his knees.

Not a research paper, more like a book. Three hundred manuscript pages, neatly stacked on a desk in another back room. "Madmen are not necessarily explosive, chaotic, unstructured," some voice in Landau's head calmly explained, "some are highly orderly, yet that doesn't make them more predictable." Six sharpened pencils in a plastic tray, a *Physicians' Desk Reference* on a nearby shelf. A statistical compilation in Portuguese.

"You know what would help me, Heitor? A cup of coffee. Will you get me that?"

"No, no coffee, nothing."

"No?"

"No, get started."

Sometimes you could tell about a paper. You only had to put your hands on it, if you knew the author and what he was about, what his tendencies were. Landau had always sampled Samantha's work this way, first by a mumbo-jumbo laying-on of hands, a kind of low-level feeling of emanations. Then he read every word carefully, of course. He had once known Heitor well, too; had known him as well as any student. There was energy coming from the stack. Landau felt it, even without putting a hand on it. He nodded.

It read terribly, parts of it not readable at all. A mistake to have composed it in English: Heitor spoke English passably well, and once he had written well scientifically in three languages, but that skill did not stay with you, you had to practice, practice. He could make rough sense of the mathematical symbols that Heitor was using, but what was this here, drawn freehand on the twelfth page? It looked like a Rubik's Cube of sections of spheres. Something like a Venn diagram in three dimensions—that was all he could tell.

"I see four or five intersecting spheres, Heitor. That's sixteen intersections for four, and I don't know how many for five. If I remember my four-dimensional geometry, it's something like a tesseract, and I remember we talked about those way back in the eighties. Sixteen intersections corresponding to sixteen vertices. Good show, fellow. I'm eager to see where you go with this."

Heitor turned away, fighting a mad grin of pleasure.

Why not read some more. Nothing to lose. Garbled madman's drivel, depressing brain-misfirings, mostly. Occasional glimmers of straight thought. He read then skimmed then slowed down to read some sections microscopically. Surprising outbreaks of clarity. They didn't add up, but they were there. The mind is flawed, the monstrousness has leaked everywhere, like a bad battery. On balance, horribly, terribly mad.

An hour later Heitor came back in with a cup of tea.

"Thank you. Tea for the old Englishman. Sometimes the old ways are best, I guess."

"Bloody right, old sport."

He left, locking the door behind him.

It was like reading a printout of the genome. Scores of pages of indecipherable junk, then, a coherent passage, a gene, as it were. Five or six of these, obliquely deriving one from another, the coherent passages all bearing on topics in set theory, bringing to mind S. Boichenko, actually, Landau's lodestar, his current mathematical soul-brother. Good God, Heitor had come close to reinventing him. Had glimpsed the few radiant ideas.

He wanted to ask how this had come about. He felt sadness, catching glimpses of a ruined mind, then he recalled that Heitor was the razorer, the girl-dissector, the crusher of lives. Graciela was in another room at this moment. He lurched to his feet, toppling the cup of tea. The fluid stained the page of genius: ah, how sad.

He called out. Grabbed the locked doorknob and throttled it, then threw himself against the door over and over. Calling out all the while.

Half-past three a.m. He awoke with a jolt in the desk chair. In his left hand he held a thick wad of manuscript pages, and instead of putting them back in the pile he stuffed them inside his sport coat. That way, he could pull them out to argue some fine point, if necessary. What did you mean when you spoke of the square of the set of null sets, Heitor? Very suggestive, that. Explain yourself.

Again, the study door. Instead of throwing himself against it he stood on the wobbly roller chair and put his foot directly on the knob, forcing it to crack, to shear off. Ah, most gratifying. That was progress.

Heitor was just coming out of the captivity room as Landau turned a corner in the dark hall. A second's worth of illumination from the opening and closing door revealed an increase in Heitor's bulk, and Landau heard an odd crinkling, making him think of Christmas presents, of torn wrappings. Like the wolf on the fold, he rushed forth and leapt upon the younger man in the dark, riding him to the floor. Heitor was dressed in a shower curtain, it felt like.

The youngster struggled to stand up. Landau would not let go of his leg, however, and Heitor stabbed him twice in the chest, twice in the thigh, efficient downward thrusts.

"Ow! Ow!" Landau roared, twisting away.

The femoral artery is in the thigh: he thought of that, and if that were nicked, well, one could bleed out quickly. Maybe I'm going to die. But he did not feel badly nicked; didn't seem to be bleeding much. Ow, though. Ow, that hurt.

A light came on. Heitor was wearing a plasticized lab coat flecked with blood. He disappeared briefly and returned with a kitchen towel and a can of cold diet soda. He put the can on the floor by Landau's legs.

"Your manuscript, Heitor. It protected me. It guarded my chest."

"Okay." Heitor said something else in Portuguese.

"I want to talk to you about it, Heitor. It needs work, but it's a fantastic start, in parts. I advise you to rewrite it in your own language, in Portuguese, *then* put it in English. I'll give it to some people I know. They'll be thrilled to see it."

"No, don't lie to me. You fell asleep when you were reading."

"Means nothing. I fall asleep often when I do anything these days. I'm getting old. What's important is that this is a bold, original piece of work. Where did you hear about Boichenko? I never told you about him, I don't think—I hadn't thought about him myself until recently."

"Boy-who?"

"Boichenko. S. Boichenko. He's Ukrainian. I rely on him deeply, but I see I've been doing it all wrong. Your paper showed me that. You're channeling the greatest set theorist of the twentieth century. You're reincarnating him, almost."

"I have only read your papers. The three real ones you ever wrote."

With all the strength that he could summon, Landau grabbed the killer's legs at the knee, like a jilted lover refusing to be abandoned in a Victorian novel. He sawed frantically at the back of the right knee, and when Heitor felt the bite of the straightedge he struck downward against the top of Landau's large head, over and over with his scalpel. A knee tendon gave way. Heitor toppled over, onto Landau, the plastic coat crunching between them. Manuscript pages slithered out as Landau, somehow getting on top, eyes now splashed with blood, brought the razor up toward Heitor's face. He slashed this way and that, seeking the throat but unable to quite find it. His grip grew uncertain for all the blood on his hands, seeps and spurts of it, like a plumbing job gone wrong.

Blow after blow against his own head, his own neck. At last he had to push away, pumping with his legs. Heitor made an *arrrwwargh* sound, a sound of indignant animal fury. Landau could recognize him no longer, his face was all wounds, nothing but wounds, blood from eyes to chin.

Heitor rolled onto his knees. His right lower leg lay sideways to the floor. With powerful blind strokes he crawled forward, the blade in his fist describing energetic half circles. Landau retreated as best he could, found himself on his feet, stumbled into the torture room. A wan light revealed Graciela on her back, the nightgown hoisted above her waist, ankles tied apart, courses of moist and drying blood along the insides of her legs. He turned as Heitor on one knee shuffled unstoppably forward, and he fell upon him from above, judging the moment to catch Heitor's arm at its weakest point, when just about to hit a backhand. Heitor *arrrwwargh-ing* like a demented pirate, through much blood in his mouth. Landau struggled to keep the blade-arm pinned, and their faces came together, their bleeding faces came together.

They tumbled again. Landau now roaring too, Heitor's blade finding its way into his chest over and over. He sought the throat one last time, Heitor protecting it by a tightly tucked chin, Landau prizing with his left hand, forcing the chin up a quarter inch, a half, then there was a wholesale giving way, and with the razor in his slippery fingers Landau sliced this way and that, roaring with all the intention that remained in him, with as much of purpose and will as he had ever summoned in his life.

chapter 20

J ust as dawn came Mrs. Roger Plenicott, who lived three doors down from 4257 Avigdor Avenue, Oakland, in a gray-painted stucco house with a double-slab driveway occupying most of the front yard, saw a man in a sport coat at her front gate.

He looked drunk. Too blotto to take another step, his shoulders slack, head hanging to one side. All right, move along there, mister, bye-bye, be gone. Why my house, why am I always the lucky one? she asked herself. We need a dog or a higher fence, but she had set herself up for this, by turning her lights on so early in the morning. That attracted the loonies.

Her gate came open, and the stranger staggered forward. Fell ten feet short of the front door. Rolled over onto his back, then just lay there, face to the heavens.

"Roger. Roger. Would you come down here, please?"

Her husband was not to be roused, however—he was in the bedroom upstairs, whose door she had shut when she descended, unable to sleep.

"Roger, a man is lying in our front yard. He has collapsed and is lying flat on his back, not moving." The stranger's lips were moving, though; then, that stopped too.

The sky lightened fractionally. He was filthy dirty, the bum, a real mess. In winter she sometimes volunteered at the shelter on East Fourteenth Street, and she was reminded of the old Mexicans she sometimes saw there, men of forty or fifty, used-up men with nowhere else to go. They worked for twenty or thirty years sending money home, then the family ties frayed, the wives found someone else or didn't want the old vaga-bond back. Meanwhile Juan Valdez has developed liver disease. If they can't work they have nothing, really nothing. She saw old woolly white bums, too, men who had known the benefits of American citizenship but had gotten nowhere, life's casualties, authentic losers. Dressed in clothes from Napoleon's retreat from Moscow. This one had wads of paper spilling out of his sport coat, an old hobo's trick to keep from freezing when they slept out.

Now she saw him differently, the light changing a bit more. It wasn't filth or oil on his face, it was dried blood. Gaping wounds on his neck and head. "Roger, we have an injured man here! He's been in a car accident, I think!" she shouted much louder than before. "Would you come down here, please? I need you."

She wrapped her housecoat tight around her and went cautiously outdoors.

"Hello there—can you hear me, sir? Are you still alive?"

The old man opened his eyes.

"Are you okay? Do you know what day of the week it is, by any chance?"

Landau did not move or speak. All the telegraph lines were down.

"Try to wriggle a foot for me," Mrs. Plenicott said. "The right one, say."

Landau wriggled a foot.

"Okay, that's good. That's the left one, but okay. I'm going to call the dispatcher now. We don't bother with 911 around here, we're too close to the hospital, no need. The hospital's over there on thirty-first."

Landau said nothing.

Three days later, five days before his trial was to begin, on the fourth of March, 2007, Landau underwent a procedure at Kaiser Oakland, where he had been transferred from Highland Hospital. Jad dancing attendance as a good medical-doctor son should. Jad had intervened to prevent his father from coming under the care of one Aramis Vazkanoush, an elderly former chief of surgery board-certified in abdominal and vascular but in the last year or two erratic, according to an OR tech who logged road-miles with Jad in the hills. Jad nominated for the surgery instead a young woman trained at Stanford and UCSF, a personal friend who did Pilates with Karin two days a week. The problem, as it became clear to them all, was bowel spillage not picked up on the initial peritoneal lavage, when they had been more worried about blood loss and the scary scalp and neck stabs—"Your father has an unusually robust skull," one of the neurosurgeons had reassured him, "almost as massive as Richard Nixon's"—thus it was not till after the neck and head men had worked him over and he had been transfused with autologous blood deposited at Kaiser four years before, upon Jad's suggestion, that careful attention was paid to his abdomen, where numerous nasty occult wounds were found.

The neck stabs could have done him in. They had nicked the vertebral artery but missed the carotid. What a truly lucky day it had been, just immensely lucky, you know! When Jad and Dr. Toomey told him that, how lucky he had been, Landau felt the opposite, but he did not speak. Melody came to visit him the day before the surgery. He could barely hold his head up, and though he mumbled this or that to her, he wished she wasn't there. After the surgery, which took eleven hours, with drains now coming out of him everywhere and a normal bowel movement very far in his future, he felt hardly better at all, but the sight of her affected him differently.

"Is there something I can do for you, dear? Is the pain too much?" she asked him.

"No. They. Have. Me. On. Wonderful. Drip. Pure. Heroin. I think," he said, panting with each word.

Melody smiled. "Use it all you can. Don't stint. We'll get you through withdrawal later."

"It's just, it's just," he tried to say, but then was too full of feeling to go on.

"I know. It's all right."

He asked her to go visit Deena. Take her some new balloons. Melody said she would, and she gave him some news about Deena, too, that Deena had awakened one evening and looked around her, while several friends of hers from the Asian Languages Department were standing around the foot of her bed, patting the blankets and crying. Though she still wasn't saying or moving much, Deena might be able to go home soon, the doctors thought.

"Oh, that's wonderful, just bloody wonderful," Landau said, and he began to blubber.

Melody also cried for a while. "Just rest, darling. Things are going to be okay, you'll see."

"No, they aren't. Not for that girl they aren't. I could have saved her if I'd been a little bolder. Should never have let her leave my kitchen that afternoon. When the ambulance got me, I couldn't talk. Had lost too much blood I guess. When you lose blood you're useless, you don't care about anything, even living, you're at a loss."

"It's all right—they found her, they got into the house."

"No, they didn't. She died. She died."

"She didn't die. Who told you that?"

Landau had heard it from several sources. A cowboy, a nurse with an evil grin, a little birdie who flew through the room. Many voices in his head.

"She's all right, sweetheart, she really is. She's going to be okay, she's fine, Gabriela."

"Not Gabriela. Graciela."

"Graciela, sorry. The young nanny. The really pretty one."

"Not nanny, preschool teacher. Soon to be a distinguished librarian."

"Okay. The point is she's okay."

Landau *had* told the EMTs that morning. He had roared and raged as he was being put on a gurney, insisting that they go up the hilly street, go into that off-white house up there, save the girl who was bleeding.

"No, I didn't roar or do anything like that," he insisted. "I tried to but I couldn't make words come out. I was useless."

"That's just how you remember it. It says different in the papers. You *did* speak."

"Oh, the papers, the papers. They'll print anything."

Byrum came to check in on him. He had brought Landau the new biography of Glenn Seaborg, the plutonium discoverer, and Landau thanked him for it.

"Why don't you read it first, though, Byrum? It's more your line. He's one of your special guys, after all."

"Thanks, I already have my own copy. And here's something else for you. More reading materials."

It was a small package, tightly wrapped in anonymous brown paper. Inside were three volumes of impeccable antique pornography. Somehow they had ended up in a recycling bin at the police station on Addison Street, Berkeley, just the other day. Byrum had happened on them as he was throwing out some stuff of his own.

"My, my," said Landau, fondling them. "Isn't that amazing? I thought I'd never see them again."

Masha Dimitriopoulous also came to visit. Again she warned him not to be indiscreet, not to say things to the police that he shouldn't, for instance. He wasn't out of the woods yet legally—he could still be charged with a capital crime.

"Please, Masha, I'm a sick man. Don't annoy me."

"You killed a man, Professor. You could be charged with first-degree murder."

"I killed a mad killer. The razor-slayer of seven people. And that was just his latest score."

Masha had her laptop with her. They Googled Heitor Burgos-Pereira for the heck of it. Landau told her to open the fourth link down, but it wasn't the same, it wasn't what had been there before.

"Strange!" he said. "Look around some more, will you? I want you to read it. It's a kind of paper he wrote."

Masha still could not find it, even after more searching.

"It was a fake scientific paper," he explained. "The detective says that when they write accounts like that, anything looking like a summary account, the end is near for them, the orgy of evil is burning out in them. He might have faded into a sort of normalcy if allowed to, to emerge twenty years hence with new savagery, perhaps. It was mixed up with this other orgy, this mental-math orgy, and as he felt it all coming together he kind of imploded. Somehow I was the seed of that. He needed to be near me, to have reference to me, to find consummation. Well, I understand that, sort of. I need to be near significant others when I do my work, I keep totems nearby. That I touch in the dark of night."

"You and the *killer*, Professor. You and the friendly *detective*. You're always teaming up, aren't you, forming little partnerships. You need to rely on us, instead, your lawyers. We're here to *help* you."

"Yes, I know. But I have always been a collaborationist, Masha. I believe in teamwork. Working alone is less fun and more lonely."

Four weeks passed, Landau recuperating at home. He arranged for Graciela Sanchez-Murillo to be seen by a tissue-regeneration specialist at UCSF, a highly touted doc who happened to be the first American to have replaced a thumb with a big toe. The doctor examined her and declared that she had received top-notch care at Highland Hospital. A hand surgeon named Gupta was the wizard there; he had happened to be on call the day she was brought in. Hand surgeons were top of the line; anybody could fix ruined faces, but hands were really hard.

Deena, sent home six days after Landau, identified Heitor Burgos-Pereira as the person who had attacked her after first disemboweling her husband. She typed rather than spoke her statement on an augmentative communication device that made her sound like Stephen Hawking. In contravention of several rules of prosecutorial procedure, Byrum, who had taken her statement, emailed Landau her responses. Later that afternoon Deena also emailed him, mentioning the detective and saying that she was getting a load together to go to the dry cleaner's.

There occurred an earthshaking transfer of wealth from Landau's retirement account into the account of Raboy Steck LLC. Landau tried not to think about it.

A second *New Yorker* article appeared, full of math talk. Whether because of production lags at the New York-based magazine, or because of a lingering anti-California bias, the interesting parts of the story, the throat-slitting, the naked girl tied by her ankles, everything that had happened after March 2, 2007, did not see print, although anyone who was interested had been feasting on such details online for weeks. Still with more he wanted to say about the estimable Landau and Beevors, Mark Wormser again begged for an interview, and Landau said that he was too weak to see anyone right now, but that he might feel better in six months. Try him then.

He was in a time of consuming no fibrous roughage, no spicy or greasy food, of not letting the Steri-Strips over his incisions get wet. Now off the magical drip but consuming Combunox at the maximum rate, he felt supremely confident some days; one morning, he opened his computer and searched for what he had written a while ago, and when he found it he could barely understand it. The whole idea of generating research during a slasher episode, a time of dead women and men and sexual mutilations, caused his delicate stomach to turn. Am I similar to Heitor, after all? he asked himself. Am I a slavering ghoul without a soul? But no, I am not like Heitor, not in the most important way. I killed no helpless women nor am I inclined to write the epidemiology of my own crimes. I just want to do some math. This thing of limits to computer modeling, the experts say it's trivial, but I say not so fast. I say that hasn't been fully demonstrated. I want to have a go at it when I have the strength.

On April 15, a Sunday, he rode with Jad to Martinez. They stopped at a mailbox in front of a post office and Landau put in his tax forms—he had filled them out himself this year, he had plenty of time.

Father and son said little. Landau was still upset with his son. They had talked things through, had no secrets about Samantha anymore, and to know all is to forgive, people say—but no, not quite. Sometimes to know all is to be appalled.

"I'm thinking now it's a mistake to bring them a bottle of brandy, Jad. What do you think?"

"Why a mistake?"

"We don't know them at all. The father might be a recovering alcoholic. They might dislike liquor for religious reasons. Brandy might mean frou-frou Berkeley, snooty France and all that—a sixer of Bud might be better."

"Everybody likes a bottle of good brandy. It's okay, Dad."

Byrum had interviewed Jad twice. He had reported the results to Landau. Jad's presence on Keeler Avenue on the morning when Deena Marjic and her dead husband were found had been coincidental, although you had to wonder about the playfulness of fate, to have put him there right then. At a second interview, Jad told Byrum a significantly different story. Not different about why he was there that morning but different about other things.

"I started by asking him about Doctor Beevors again. He said that she was a special person, deeply intuitive, and that she'd encouraged him when he was in a dark time in his life. Told him he wasn't stupid, which he'd always thought he was. Maybe this rings a bell with you. He's always compared himself to you."

"Actually, it rings no bells, Detective. I didn't tell him he was stupid, why would I do that? He's my son."

"Okay. All right. He got the message from somewhere, anyhow. When he was fourteen and a half they went to bed the first time. The wild thing just happened, to the complete surprise of both of them. I like your son, Professor, he's odd but he says what's real. It was the most beautiful thing he ever dreamed of, he told me. Nobody will ever understand, but if you look back in history, young men used to be brought along by kindly older women, and I don't know if that's true, myself, but that's what he told me. So beautiful, so personal it was. It never seemed like she was poaching or doing something wicked or perverted, the opposite of that. The opposite. It set him up for good changes in his life."

Oh, Christ, thought Landau. I'll set *him* up, the little sneak. The sly fornicator.

"And you think this really happened?"

"Well, why would he say it if it didn't?"

"I don't know. It's just beyond my experience in life, is all," said Landau. "It doesn't comport with my sense of things, of reality's stolidness. She was a wild one, Samantha, ungovernable in many ways, but she wasn't *self*-ungovernable. And she had a kind of delicacy, especially with young people."

"It's an outlier kind of behavior, definitely, I grant you that. I've been reading about her in the *New Yorker*, by the way. Fabulous article. I can't get enough of that math stuff, not when someone explains it clearly. What a powerful mind she had—powerful, idiosyncratic rational mind."

"She went far beyond the rational, Byrum—how wonderful, how endearing of her."

Jad had needed to tell him, tell the detective, to prepare for telling Landau. He was deeply ashamed, this thing had shadowed his whole life, the detective thought. His big fear for years had been that his father would find out and never have anything to do with him again.

"Now, why would he be worried about that? I'm not a cutting-off sort of person, Byrum. Look at me, I'm an absurd softy, I take in everyone, I even took in Heitor."

Yes, yes, but Jad had been afraid, even so. This was primitive stuff, this mixing of parents and sex; it was Greek tragedy stuff. The murder investigation and the approaching trial hadn't made Jad able to come out and confess it, that's how powerful it was—only after the killer had been found was he ready.

Landau shook his head. "I still don't understand, I'm afraid. Was he prepared to let his father take the fall? Be charged with Samantha's death, too? That doesn't suggest wrestling with guilt, only not giving a fuck."

Perhaps it would help to try to say what had happened at Landau's house. Could the detective make a stab at that? he asked politely. All right, here goes:

"First of all, Jad was there, he now says. He found her, dead in your bed. They'd had some arrangement, she told him to meet her at your house and he still doesn't know why. She doesn't know the maid comes on Wednesdays, and probably she just comes in and goes straight upstairs. Lies down in your bed for a nap. Then, she hears voices downstairs—I'm speculating, but she goes down, thinking maybe Jad's arrived, is coming in by the back deck, but it's Elfridia, bloody on a tarp. Tied up with torture knots, breasts mutilated, throat half-cut, I don't know what all. Heitor's there. Confronts her with the box cutter. Doesn't slash her, because she isn't one of his sample, his brown girls. She's someone he knows, and that throws him off.

"Runs upstairs. Has a fatal heart attack. Heitor puts on rubber gloves to deal with her, because the blood of one shall never touch the other, that would violate some principle with him. Doesn't cut her up, either, but does the thing with the vibrator up the behind, as a desecration I guess. Finding her there made him angry with her but with you, too, his idol. The two halves of his mind were coming together—that was exciting, it was overwhelming."

"What about Jad, though?" Landau asked. "Where was he this whole time?"

"Jad arrives later. Had worked a half day at Kaiser then had meetings. I don't know that he was going up there to have sex with her, maybe just to talk. Finds her in your bed. No sign of the maid because Heitor had carried her away in her car, Samantha's car. Jad doesn't stay around. His first thought is you'd killed her, because you'd found out and flipped. He didn't know what to do—didn't want to call the cops, that would make big trouble for you, so, he just left."

Landau wasn't sure. It was possible but too antic, too Keystone Kops. He could imagine Samantha running up and down his staircase, though, pursued by a maniac, that image popped readily into his mind. Naked, breasts flinging, long thighs flashing. Beautiful thick hair all disarranged. Staircases and murders, staircases and kitchen knives, what was that from? Oh, *Psycho*, of course. The film that inaugurated modern times, released 1960. But who was the stuffed mother in this remake, the mummy down in the basement? *He* was, he was the dummy not the mummy, the stuffed shirt that all the other strands had come together around. Was there something about him that induced such madness, that drove colleagues like Samantha into dereliction and young men like Jad and Heitor Burgos-Pereira over a dangerous edge? Probably. Probably. Probably it was all his fault.

"Byrum, thanks for putting this together. I've talked it over with Jad and we're not yelling at each other anymore, which is good. The idea of him getting in bed with my all-time most important lover doesn't hurt so much—maybe because she's dead, I don't know. And he is my son, after all. I'm glad he had her, in a way. She was, with all the unbearable things she ever did, a truly fabulous piece of ass."

*   *   *

Martinez. Clear day, semi-cold. Spring in California doesn't mean much, nor does autumn, it's a digital climate, the rain is either on or off, the thrilling cloudless blue is up or not. Jad was at the wheel of his new Honda Insight, driving with ironical attention—he often looked lost in thought, yet still performed well. Maybe he was reflecting on the odd purpose of this journey, or on the Honda Insight itself, a most unflashy car for a former skateboarder. He wasn't shredding but merely saving the planet now. And where had his furious edge gone? Did it matter?

In a fast way of understanding his son that had to, therefore, be wrong, Landau imagined that Jad had packed all his rebelliousness into having sex a few times with his father's lover, and after that he had never much wanted to go off the straight and narrow. Had become stodgy. But he was a good person, seemed happy, and maybe the developmental journey wasn't over yet. There might be more odd steps along the way. Swerves to come.

"I'm really afraid, Dad," Jad said softly. "I'm all in a sweat."

"Why?"

"Well, what am I supposed to do here? I feel completely at sea. Completely stupid."

"We're both stupid, don't worry about that. Do what seems least offensive. It's all a colossal fuckup, a mass blunder for the ages. But now we have a chance to make it a little better. Start out by saying hello."

"Am I her father or her brother?"

"I don't know. But when you lay eyes on her, you'll know you're not nothing to her."

Since his imagination was carrying him away, Landau had come up with a new theory of Samantha at his house. She had wanted to talk to both of them that afternoon, to both Landau and his son. Knew that Landau would be home eventually, intended to wait for him as long as it took, wanted to have a little sit-down with her two special fellows. Knew that she was dying, had been having heart events, syncopes, who knows— a person knows, though, a medical person does. All right, now I've got something I have to say to you, fellows. Sit down and listen carefully.

"At least, she worked it out with these people in advance," he said. "Arranged it so she could come out occasionally and get to know the girl, and the girl could know who she was, and that gives us a little room to maneuver."

"Great. That should make it a piece of cake."

"You're excited, Jad, that's all. Excitement comes out in funny ways. My best hope for it all is that I end up a granddad. What's yours?"

"I don't have any best hopes. I have nothing."

"Come on. Don't be a sourpuss. How's Karin doing with this, by the way? Is she upset?"

"Oh, God. I'll be lucky if she doesn't divorce me. She's incredibly, incredibly upset."

Some late plum trees were still flowering, and wisteria was breaking out—every other house in the neighborhood was bedecked. They got briefly off-route because Martinez had both a John Muir Drive and a John Muir Avenue, and Landau couldn't read the poorly printed MapQuest page without his reading glasses, which he had left at home. Then they were in the grid of streets of modest wooden dwellings, and here was the picket fence he remembered and the flowerless yard. He thought of the Nipponesque landscaping of the house where Heitor had imprisoned Graciela, and he remembered the Asian adoptive mother with a limp and the Japanese man on BART. Mere coincidence? Reality threw these resonances up at you all the time, as if a distracted author were tossing whatever came to hand into the mix.

They parked the car. Landau waited for his son to catch up with him at the gate, so that they could walk through together. They were exactly on time, and he imagined the family watching them anxiously from indoors, even more on pins and needles than they were, if that was possible. Maybe the father would refuse to shake Landau's hand. Maybe the brandy had been a mistake, should have been left behind, was likely to establish the wrong tone, an offensively celebratory tone. He imagined the eleven-year-old girl refusing to come out of her room, sobbing in there all afternoon. This was too much for an eleven-year-old to handle, she already had a father and a mother and all the family she needed.

They walked through, and the front door came open. The young girl, not wearing her spectacles today, dressed in a pretty knee-length frock of dark blue, her hair done up fancy, paused for a second atop the stoop. Then she was hurrying down toward them, already holding out both hands to them, wanting to see them up close, wanting to know them.

Acknowledgments

The author wishes to thank these advisers for their thoughtful and expert responses to his inquiries about criminal procedure, while absolving them of any responsibility for exaggerations or mistakings of their elegantly rendered advice: Michael Vitiello, Distinguished Professor and Scholar, Pacific McGeorge School of Law; Joseph Taylor, Professor of Law, Pacific McGeorge School of Law, and former Prosecuting Attorney in the Sacramento and Ventura County District Attorneys' Offices; Dr. Elizabeth Albers, Forensic Pathologist, Sacramento County Coroner's Office; and Venus Johnson, Deputy District Attorney, Alameda County District Attorney's Office.

About the Author

Robert Roper is the award-winning author of *Now the Drum of War: Walt Whitman and His Brothers in the Civil War* (2008) as well as of *Fatal Mountaineer* (2002), a biography of the Himalayan climber Willi Unsoeld. His books of fiction include *Royo County Tales*, *The Trespassers*, *Mexico Days*, *On Spider Creek*, and *Cuervo Tales*. Many of his cultural essays appeared at Obit-mag.com and he has also written for the *New York Times*, the *Los Angeles Times*, *National Geographic*, *Outside*, *The American Scholar*, and other Web and print-based publications. In 2002 he was awarded the Boardman Tasker Prize, the principal world prize in mountaineering literature, given by the Royal Geographical Society of London and the British Alpine Club. *Nabokov in America*, a study of the Russian writer's U.S. years, will appear from Bloomsbury in 2015. He lives in California and Maryland and teaches at Johns Hopkins.

CPSIA information can be obtained at www.ICGtesting.com
Printed in the USA
LVOW11s0006280915

455965LV00001BA/39/P